M000197151

Praise for ~~...~~ JadeAnne Stone Mexico Adventures

The Hydra Effect

Jan M. Flynn, award-winning author of Corpse Pose: and Other Tales

JadeAnne heads to Mexico City for a break from her partner, and now ex-boyfriend. But her sharp intelligence, curiosity, and inability to stay in her own lane, land her in a snarl of trouble. In short order, she's evading drug cartel thugs, uncovering a human trafficking network, and confronting high-level Mexican politicos with questionable connections, all in a lushly realized setting one can just about smell. *And* taste – JadeAnne might be in the middle of a gunfight, but she's never immune to the temptation of a good plate of tacos *al pastor*. She and her loyal dog Pepper are a team you can't help but cheer for.

Set Up

Heather Haven, multi-award-winning author of the Alvarez Family Murder Mysteries

This is a blowout of a story. It starts on the backroads of Mexico in the middle of the night—just a woman, a dog, and Mexican Banditos—and escalates from there. If you are looking for a fast-paced, action-filled thriller about the adventures of a young PI and her lethal but well-trained dog, this will be your cup of tea. Or should I say margarita? Jack Reacher step aside. You have met your match in JadeAnne Stone.

JC Miller, author of the bestseller, *Vacation*
A routine investigation takes a mysterious, chilling turn when JadeAnne is abducted at gunpoint then deposited in an opulent, albeit creepy manor. Moment-by-moment, her story unfolds in real time as she experiences the sights, sounds, and myriad flavors of Mexico, the underworld of political corruption and high-stakes criminal activity roiling beneath the surface. When nothing is as it appears, and no one can be trusted, Jade's adrenaline surges—her mettle is tested. Told with humor and humility, grit and beauty, this page turner delivers.

CT Markee, author of the Otherworld Tales, Irish/Abaddon Series
...a fast moving tale of crime and danger in Mexico.
JadeAnne Stone and her dog, Pepper, get in a custom camper van and drive straight into trouble in the first chapter: a missing person, a kidnapping, a drug cartel, and a suspected murder. The plotline is devious and surprising. There are plenty of twists and turns in the story to keep you engaged. This is a complicated well-crafted story...I absolutely love the descriptions. It's a good read that I highly recommend.

Kirkus Reviews
"With a likable duo and a vivid, appealing setting, this adventure series is off to a promising start."

Second Edition
First Printing, 2019

Book design and format by Lisa Orban
Cover by Villa Design

This is a work of fiction. Names, characters, places, and incidents
are either the product of the author's imagination or are use
fictionally, and any resemblance to actual persons, living or dead,
business establishments, events or locales is entirely coincidental.

ISBNs
978-1-64456-460-8 [Paperback]
978-1-64456-461-5 [Mobi]
978-1-64456-462-2 [ePub]
978-1-64456-463-9 [Audiobook]

Library of Congress Control Number: 2022936042

INDIES UNITED PUBLISHING HOUSE, LLC
P.O. BOX 3071
QUINCY, IL 62305-3071
indiesunited.net

DEDICATION

To

Marty Smith

You opened the door to Mexico for me.

and

Lucia Rangel

Muchas gracias, mi maestra de español.

Other Books by Ana Manwaring

Set Up (2022)

COMING IN 2022

August 17
Nothing Comes After Z

November 16
Coyote

THE HYDRA EFFECT

Revelations and Betrayal in Mexico City

A JadeAnne Stone Mexico Adventure

ANA MANWARING

INDIES UNITED PUBLISHING HOUSE, LLC

CHAPTER ONE

Lura's Funeral

Wednesday, August 8, 2007

Heat seared across my back; someone had me in their sights. I scanned the wide plaza bordered by the church and a low, ornate, red-painted building, but I couldn't see anything that looked out of place for Coyoacan. No *malos hombres* behind the well-pruned park trees or black phantoms in my peripheral vision sighting sniper rifles from the rooftops along Calle Felipe Carrillo. As if I'd actually see my assassin. I hurried across Plaza Hidalgo toward La Iglesia de San Juan Bautista.

I couldn't shake Senator Polo Aguirre's hateful outburst after my friend's death last week, "I hold JadeAnne Stone responsible for the death of my cousin." And Aguirre was a dangerous man, —a criminal involved with marijuana and heroin cartels—hell, he headed up a drug cartel, didn't he? Wealthy and powerful, he had the backing of Mexico's ruling class. I had my dog and a prayer.

But *no importa la culpa*, if the senator wanted to retaliate against me because his kingpin rival in Ixtapa, Arturo Rodriguez, blew up his cousin Lura on the pier in

1

Zihuatanejo, then he had the means to do it.

I hurried on.

Parking in the Coyoacán district of Mexico City was a joke on a good day, and I was afraid I'd be late to Lura's funeral. I'd driven the *cuota*, toll road, Mexico 95, from Acapulco that morning after a lousy night's sleep in a rent-by-the hour motel recommended by the waiter at my resort hotel in Papanoa. Located near the highway on the pimply backside of the posh Acapulco hotel district, the motel was filthy with trash, both on the ground and on two legs. But it was late and I was too exhausted to search for something better.

Revelers appeared to be coming or going from the disco next door, which had cranked up the volume of the music so loud that the shock of the bass almost felt like the bomb blast I'd survived in Zihua—the one that killed my friend Lura. I'd peeked out my door a couple of times when the thumping and screaming particularly obnoxious and was reminded that most hookers don't look like Julia Roberts in *Pretty Woman*. God, what an ugly lot—and they're screamers. "*Ay Papi! Cójeme Papito, eres mi rey*." Well, if I ever needed to "do it" in Spanish, I'd know how.

The plaza was filled with vendors. I noticed a couple of kids selling hippie paraphernalia—Mayan braided wristlets, peace sign earrings and pendants, Balinese batik shifts, tie-dye headbands, Rasta-colored t-shirts—the usual stuff found on any street vendor's table in Berkeley. The pollution that afternoon stank and hung yellow and gritty around the vendors and their customers. I could barely breathe, and scurrying across the plaza had me gasping so heavily that I slowed down, forced to catch my breath. A clown proffered me a bouquet of helium balloons while a white-clad man pushed an ice cream cart by, his bell jangling. I salivated. A scoop of coconut ice cream would have been a balm for my smog-irritated throat, but I swallowed hard and hurried on.

THE HYDRA EFFECT

"Lay-dee, señora. Tengo tu futuro."

I glanced toward the throaty voice. A gypsy-like *bruja* sat at a folding table and laid out Tarot cards on a black velvet cloth. Seeing my interest, she pulled a card from the deck in her palm and displayed the Knight of Swords. I slowed down.

"Venga, lay-dee. Así es el futuro." She swept the displayed layout to the side and placed the card in the middle of her cloth. "A *príncipe* looks for you, señorita." She paused and extracted the King of Hearts from within her deck and placed it over the first card with a meaningful look. I started to move on, but she flicked a third card out of the pack and crossed it over the King. A man lay dead with a forest of swords sticking out of his back.

"¡Ay! ¡Dios mío!" The witch crossed herself and gathered up the cards, her wrinkled, bony hands moving like the wings of a hummingbird.

My heart dropped into my gut and shivers ran up my spine. Someone walking on my grave. I hurried the last couple hundred feet to the church. Well-heeled mourners in small groups filed between the massive, scarred wooden doors leading into the dim interior. Most of the women appeared to have stepped from the pages of *Vogue* magazine, and I could see a lot of important jewelry sparkling on fingers and ears and around necks and wrists. I stood back to calm down, admiring the lovely relief sculpture on the façade, and checking out the attendees as they arrived, hoping to see someone I knew. Like Anibal.

I glanced at my watch. Last minute mourners in limousines and chauffeur-driven SUVs drew up to the curb opposite the main doors. Uniformed drivers helped rich urbanites, *chilangos*, out of the vehicles and onto the sidewalk. It was obvious by the unusual lumps under jackets that some of these drivers were really bodyguards. Drug mafia, I supposed. I mean, do senators need bodyguards? I

3

wouldn't know. I realized, too, that there were way more armed police in the area than should be normal for the funeral of an American. Again, my skin rippled with the thought of being sighted in somebody's crosshairs. I shuddered and pushed through the crowd into the church.

After the bright haze in the plaza, it took my eyes several seconds to see in the shadowy interior. I could hear the sounds of clothes rustling and jewelry jingling, coughing, the thump as someone's butt landed too hard on the pew, and what may have been muted sobs floating in the pious atmosphere. It struck me that there was no music, no conversation, no babies crying; there lacked life at this celebration of death.

Lura would be pissed off. She'd have wanted a wild Irish wake. "Let's all get drunk and dance and tell funny stories," she'd have said. Maybe that would come later. The phone message I'd received from Lura's cousin Anibal two days before only said where and when the funeral would take place.

I made my way up the center aisle toward the altar, looking for a place to sit and made out the Aguirre family in the front pew: Senator Polo Aguirre sitting ramrod straight, eyes forward, and absolutely still; a thin, bent woman perched to his right, swaddled in black—black dress, floppy-brimmed hat draped in a black veil, black gloves. The Matriarch.

To his left, a grey-haired man and a small woman with short blonde hair leaned into each other. The woman appeared bird-like, her movements quick and restless. She reminded me of Lura in a way. Next to the blonde sat another woman whose hair shone dark and glossy. She leaned in to speak to the man next to her and I could see she was wearing dark glasses. I'd noticed other people wearing dark glasses inside and thought it must be a disguise for the drug people. The woman had to be Lura's sister Alejandra, or

Alex, as Lura had called her, and I bet she wore them to hide swollen eyes. I assumed the man next to her was her husband, Jason.

And then I saw him. Anibal. He was straining around in his seat to view the crowd. Looking for someone?

Our eyes locked for a heart-stopping moment then he started out of his pew. I wanted to see him, and I wanted to run away and hide. What if he blamed me, like his half-brother, the senator, did? My stomach clenched and my skin prickled. I backed up the aisle and fled into a rear pew. The hard looks of a pair of burly, neck-less gorillas with suspicious bulges discouraged me and I stumbled back into the aisle.

Anibal had made it halfway up the aisle, a hint of a smile on his lips. Butterflies danced in my heart—no mistaking it. I'd flirted with him before the explosion. A smothering blackness drifted down from the nave's ribbed vault and settled around me. My muscles went weak, and I staggered forward, jostled by the crowd now rushing for seats.

Oh, God, I can't! I can't. It was too soon. Lura was dead, my client was dead, drug cartel people were mad at me, my boyfriend had dumped me, and the Aguirre family blamed me for everything. How could I get involved with one of them? I simply needed to pay my respects and head out of Dodge.

I felt as exposed here in the church as I had outside, and my neck hairs were damp again. I needed to sit down and blend in. Ahead of me in the aisle, I saw a pew with only three mourners. One sported a familiar square head. It couldn't be. Zocer was dead, wasn't he? Didn't I see him killed trying to save Lura in the blast?

Elated, I rushed toward him and collided with Anibal.

"JadeAnne! Where've you been? Why haven't you answered my messages? I've—we've—been so worried about you—Polo too. And the whole family. We've got a seat for you. C'mon."

He took my hand and pulled me toward the family pew. This was certainly a change from the hateful outburst a week earlier. To give the guy credit, though, he did stand up for me against Aguirre when that maniac tried to scapegoat me.

"Ani, no. No! I can't sit with your family. That's reserved for the…well, the family."

"We're expecting you, Jade. Besides, what about that night at the Krystal? I thought—"

Anibal went silent. We'd reached the family's pew and all Aguirre eyes turned on us. The men stood up and waited until I sat. I packed in next to Jason and sat down as Lura's coffin was lugged in by several gorilla-guys and placed on the waiting stand. The priest in purple robes appeared with his incense and smudged the high altar. I guess he was afraid this crowd would bring in some bad juju. Judging from what I'd seen of the Aguirre family, the padre was right-on.

When the incense disbursed, the prayers began. I hadn't been raised in the Catholic Church and had only experienced Mass a few times in childhood after a Saturday night sleepover with a Catholic girlfriend. Most of the congregation knew the words, when to stand, when to kneel, and when to sit back down. I followed Anibal's lead and, thirty minutes later, found myself kneeling at the communion railing with my mouth wide to receive a small wafer and a slurp of some pretty awful tasting wine from the same chalice as everyone else.

We took communion in the first group since we were sitting in the first row. I dreaded the hours it was going to take to move what I estimated to be three or four hundred mourners through communion. But I was wrong, it took all of fifteen minutes. That priest knew how to manage a crowd.

After Christ's body and blood fortified the congregation, the rest of the family, sans Anibal, clustered at the closed coffin. I squeezed my eyes shut against the memory of

Lura's burned body suspended in the doorway of Ristorante Mare e Pece's exploding kitchen.

"Is she going to be buried here?" I whispered to Anibal, hoping to switch my thought train.

"No, Uncle Beto is taking her home to L.A.," he whispered in reply. "They'll have a memorial there and a burial service. My aunt and uncle are pretty broken up."

"Those are Lura's parents?" I asked, gesturing to the grey-haired man and his tiny blonde wife.

"Yeah, and that's Alex, my cousin, and her husband." He gestured with his chin, eyes red and full.

The group stood at Lura's coffin, holding hands, crying.

"Who's the lady in black?"

He sniffed, and blew his nose into a pressed white handkerchief that had materialized out of nowhere. "Aunt Lidia, Polo's mother. She arranged the service—all these people are her friends, Polo's colleagues, and government VIPs."

"Lidia has some dangerous-looking friends. Do you know many of them?"

"No. I was never part of this group. Aunt Lidia doesn't completely embrace me as family—just like Polo."

"That reminds me, I thought I saw Zocer back there." I swiveled around toward the pew with the square-headed man, but he was no longer there.

"Impossible. He's dead. His funeral was yesterday."

"You went?"

"No, private family funeral."

I lapsed into silence as the family filed back into our pew. No testimonials to Lura?

The organist began to play something from Beethoven. Mourners streamed up to the coffin- and left flowers, mementos, candles, stuffed animals, and dolls on the lid. Or they just touched it. Some knelt and prayed. The bodyguards escorted their charges and stood back, scowling at the

7

congregation while the mourners said their "goodbyes." The procession went on and on and on.

The music changed from *Amazing Grace* and *The King of Love Mine Shepherd Is* to out and out dirges. I recognized Verdi's Dies irae from the Requiem Mass, and some Bach. I felt the low notes more than heard them and was moved to tears. It wasn't that Lura and I were so close—we'd been acquainted for less than two weeks, but I felt uncomfortably responsible. If I hadn't accepted the case from her banker husband, Daniel Worthington, would he have killed her? No, this was naïve thinking. He had known where she was and intended to kill her from the start. I'd been set up to flush her from the protection of her cousin, Senator Aguirre, before she connected Worthington to a major money laundering scheme.

I'd been chewing it over to the point of obsession for days. That is, in between mourning my recent breakup and looking over my shoulder for Rodriguez's goons. I hadn't come to feel any more comfortable with the conclusions I'd drawn about what really was happening than before I'd drawn them, and as far as Worthington was concerned, his intentions had been lost the moment Anibal put a bullet through his head to save me from being murdered. It was all too bizarre, and now I was sitting in a pew in a colonial church in Mexico City mourning someone I barely knew as though I were one of the family—holding hands with her sister's husband and leaning on her cousin, her best friend—crying. Am I a hypocrite? I just wished it would end and I could go hug my dog and go home. But home would be so empty without Dex.

"Where's Pepper?" Anibal asked me sotto voce.

"In the *combi*. Is Coyoacán a safe *colonia*?" I replied under my breath.

"Depends where it's parked. This is a pretty wealthy district, but you're not safe anywhere in Mexico. That's why all these *ricos* have bodyguards." He laughed softly.

"It's on Xicoténcatl," I stumbled over the indigenous name, "just off Centenario. Pepper's guarding—he'll tear any carjacker's arm off and beat him with it," I said with more confidence than I felt. He didn't tear any arms off when Aguirre's thugs hijacked me off Ruta 200.

"Don't think about it, Jade, it'll just bring you down," he whispered, giving my hand a little squeeze.

How did he know?

"We're going to Aunt Lidia's after. You're coming, aren't you?"

"I don't think so, Ani. I need to get going. Find a place to sleep. I didn't have a very restful night."

"You'll stay with me. I've got a house in La Condesa. There's a great coffee house nearby, La Selva. We'll go read international newspapers and drink espresso in the morning."

Anibal's warm smile and gorgeous coal eyes looked inviting. I was tempted.

"Uh-uh, no way, Jose." I drew my hand back into my lap and shifted toward the aisle to focus on the mourners coming forward. Was he crazy? With what his family thought of me? Anibal slumped away, his jaw tight.

Two men in dark glasses, trailed by their burly boys, headed the column of people approaching the casket. They glanced side to side as if looking for someone. Anibal stiffened, and I studied him from under my too-long bangs, hoping he wouldn't notice I was watching him. As the men came even with our pew, Anibal turned abruptly toward me and sank his head into my chest, making sobbing sounds, and I found myself staring into my own eyes mirrored back at me from the closer man's sunglasses. He had a sneering little mouth under a scraggly mustache and beard, and I felt the hatred he projected toward me. Or was it toward Anibal? The look chilled me to the bone.

The men passed on, tapped the coffin, and moved off

toward an exit. I watched until the door closed and whispered, "Okay, Anibal. What was that about?"

He sat up, stopped his phony sobbing, and shifted away from me.

"I mean it, Anibal. What's going on?"

"I miss Lura so much," he said, voice catching on her name. He gave me a sad sack smile.

"So do I, but why don't I believe that's the whole story here?"

He turned back to me with an angelic expression. "I don't know."

"Yes you do; you knew those men. You didn't want them to see you," I accused. As if anyone in the church hadn't seen us up here on display in the front pew.

"Who are they, Anibal Aguirre?"

"Shhh. I'll tell you after—on the way to Aunt Lidia's," he mouthed, rolling his eyes in a feeble attempt to indicate he didn't want the others to know this big secret.

I sat back and shut up. How much longer would this go on? I couldn't see any way to get around it—I was going to be properly introduced to Lura's family soon. The heavy atmosphere weighed on me like water. I didn't want to meet the Aguirre-Laylors, that was for sure. Not if Aguirre had told them what he thought about my involvement in their daughter's death. It wasn't true, but I felt so conflicted. Did I give myself too much credit? Aguirre probably wouldn't speak my name. And he'd never say anything to his brother, Lura's father. Neither would Ani speak to Aguirre. And the events leading up to her death came so fast and furious, Lura wouldn't have had time to talk to her sister. I rationalized and let my tense shoulders slip from around my ears. These folks didn't have a clue who I was, and I'd keep it like that.

I slid closer to Anibal and perched on the edge of the pew. "I've gotta go, Ani. I wish I could visit with your family, but I just don't think now's the time."

"You can't go, JadeAnne. We're expecting you," he replied a bit too loud.

"I'm sorry, really. Please pass my condolences on to everyone, especially your aunt and uncle, but Pepper has been in the bus too long and it's warm. I've got to take care of him." I started to collect my purse and get up.

"Jah-dey, please," he whined. "You can't leave now."

"Leopoldo, control that ill-mannered boy," a reedy voice quavered.

Startled, I looked down the row. Aguirre faced his mother. "Yes Mother, I'll take care of it presently." He turned toward me with a look that could kill. I shrank back into my place and pretended to concentrate on the priest who had reappeared into view now that the mourners had said goodbye. Good, we're getting out of here.

"Anibal, you are disturbing your aunt's peace. Please be quiet," Aguirre whispered in his ridiculous formality. "Oh, and Miss Stone, my mother wishes to have your company at our gathering. I hope you won't disappoint her."

I smiled weakly and shook my head. Beyond him, I could see the old crow nodding, one bony hand clutching at her Leopoldo.

The padre led the remaining congregation in the Lord's Prayer. *"Padre nuestro, que estás en el cielo. Santificado sea tu nombre. Venga tu reino. Hágase tu voluntad en la tierra como en el cielo. . ."*

Few remained in the cavernous church. Mostly old ladies in black mantillas, Lidia's friends, no doubt. Squirming around, I couldn't see any men in sunglasses and it came to me that I didn't feel like I was being watched anymore.

"Perdona nuestras ofensas, como también nosotros perdonamos a los que nos ofenden. . ."

Maybe that's what I was supposed to do—forgive. God

was telling me right there at Lura's funeral, I had to forgive. But whom? The list was long.

"And deliver us from evil for thine is the kingdom and the power and the glory, forever and ever."

Okay, I'd forgive myself. And then I'd let the Aguirre family forgive me, too. Amen.

CHAPTER TWO

Tía Lidia

Squinting against the still bright afternoon, I pasted a smile on my lips and shook hands with Anibal's family, greeting each member with murmured condolences as Anibal introduced me.

"Uncle Beto, Aunt Molly, this is JadeAnne. Jade—my cousins Alex and Jason Radcliff. You know Polo, and this is Aunt Lidia."

The old woman offered a gloved hand and snatched it back the moment I shook it. I frowned at Polo and noticed his cheeks streaked with tears and his eyes puffed with dark circles. He looked a wreck—old, tired, defeated.

"Mother, behave yourself," he admonished, frowning.

Lura had been his anchor since his wife and children died. Was he going to hold up? The big Senate battle in September and the future of PEMEX and Mexico's oil industry weighed heavily on the horizon—as if he didn't have enough worries.

"Senator, you have my deepest condolences. I know how hard this is for you, losing Lura."

"Thank you, Ms. Stone. Your kind words are comforting. We shall see you, then, at Mother's?"

I didn't hear malice in his voice, but the idea of spending time with the Aguirre clan still put me off. "Thank you, but I don't think I can come, Senator. I, uh, I need to take care of Pepper."

"The dog will be welcome, Ms. Stone, as long as he does not disturb the guests or Mother's dogs. Anibal, escort Ms. Stone to her vehicle then direct her to the house."

"Gladly," Ani replied and took my elbow to steer me toward the street. "See you all at Aunt Lidia's," he called over his shoulder.

So much for ditching out to find a hotel. Maybe it was better to spend time with people, but the Aguirre family? Anibal's grip on my arm was nothing compared to the vise clamping my guts. Should I make a run for it?

"Where's the *combi*?"

"I told you, a few blocks up on Xicoténcatl, or something like that," I again tried to pronounce the strange Aztec name. "But, Ani, you don't really need to come with me. I'm fine. Just give me the address and I'll drop by later, after I find a place to stay."

"I told you, you can stay with me."

The butterflies danced across my gut this time. "I can't stay with you."

"Why not? I've got a spare bedroom, if that's what you're worried about. And anyway, I need to talk to you."

His brilliant smile almost melted my heart and I was tempted for a moment. "What do we have to talk about, Anibal? Lura's gone, the case is solved. I need to go home— I have a detective agency to run."

We walked along a tree-lined street in a colonial neighborhood. Many of the mansions and their tall, broken-glass studded walls were painted brick-red and trimmed in white. Windows were covered in iron grillwork and the street was paved in square-cut cobblestones. Everything I saw looked well maintained and the ambiance genteel and rarified like the atmosphere in a museum. I peeped into windows and doors, straining to make out the dim entries that intersected the sidewalk. The high walls hid marvelous mysteries.

"I need your help," he said, his voice pitched slightly higher than normal.

"I need to go home," I snapped. Changing the subject, I asked, "Say, where is Frida Kahlo's house from here?"

"It's nearby, but you're ignoring me." His eyes were hard and his jaw set, pulling his full lips into a tight line and wrinkling his clean-shaven chin. What was he up to?

"You're not hearing me. I'm tired, I'm sad. I don't belong here, Anibal. I don't belong with your family. I need to go home." Suddenly, I really did need to go home. See my houseboat, my parents, the fog creeping down Mt. Tam into Richardson's Bay. I needed to tend my orchids and relax on the deck of the Sarasvati with a glass of Zin and watch the sailboats and seagulls glide by. Tears welled up behind my sunglasses and slid down my cheeks. I was homesick—I was heartsick. It was Dex I wanted. How could he dump me in a parking lot? In a foreign country! He'd taken care of me for a decade and now he was gone.

Anibal's voice turned hard. "We've got to avenge her, Jade."

I spun toward him, grabbed his arm. "We who?"

"Look, I'll explain it all to you tonight at my house." He forced a smile and softened his tone.

"You really keep a house in Mexico City? I didn't think you came here that much." Something didn't add up. "What's really going on, Anibal?" I demanded. "Can't you stay with your family when you're here?"

"Right, I'll stay with darling Aunt Lidia. She always keeps a room for me—in the servants' quarters. Or maybe you thought I'd stay with my loving brother, Polo? The doorman at his building in Polanco has standing orders to turn me away," he finished dryly.

I didn't know what to say. He sounded bitter, angry, but I knew how it felt to be an outsider in your own family. Luckily, we arrived at the *combi* and I didn't have to respond. Instead, I unlocked the door and slung it open to Pepper furiously wagging his tail and panting from the heat. The solar fan I had installed before leaving California wasn't sucking the warm air out fast enough. I grabbed the leash from its hook and clipped it onto his collar then let him jump out. He made a beeline for a skinny jacaranda planted in the tree lawn and lifted his leg. He trotted back and woofed hello to Anibal, dancing around him happily.

"Hi ya, Pepper. You glad to see me, boy?" Anibal squatted to pet the dog.

Watching Pepper and Anibal greet each other with such obvious pleasure softened my resolve to keep my distance from the Aguirre clan—Anibal, at least. How could I reject Anibal when Pepper adored him? All right then, I'd listen to what he had to say, but I wasn't going to stay at his house. I sure didn't need the aggravation of a new man in my life right now. I had thinking to do—wounds to bind.

Lidia's compound dominated the end of a *callejon,* a Mexican cul-de-sac, with a police *caseta* preventing unauthorized entry. Iron gates set into the high adobe wall opened, admitting the VW into a service area where the storage buildings, tanks for the natural gas that all Mexico City runs ran on, and what looked like water tanks were located. I supposed that water would be precious in a city of over thirty million souls.

"Go that way." Anibal gestured to the left fork in the driveway, which led past a column of Italian cypress trees and a rose garden to the front of the house, then looped around an island of rocks, trees, flowers, and ferns and rejoined itself at the roses. Their scent wafted through the open windows. It was truly amazing that in the thick of a smelly, polluted city, we could find such grace. I parked behind the limo that had transported the rest of the family from the church.

"Well, we're here." Anibal's voice sounded flat.

"They're your family."

"That's the problem, JadeAnne—the Aguirres are my family, but except for Uncle Beto and Aunt Molly, I'm not their family."

"What about Alex and Jason? Aren't they your family?" I looked directly into his almond-shaped eyes.

"Yeah. But I mean..." Anibal cast his face downward.

I could see that his rich *cafe-con-leche* complexion was turning rosy.

"You mean Polo and that little black crow he calls 'Mother'?"

"Something like that," he mumbled in a thickened voice.

I leaned over the armrest of my wide leather seat, took his hand, and said with more conviction than I felt, "Oh, Ani, I know how much you loved Lura. I know how hard this is but it'll get easier—you'll see." I tried to believe my words.

As he lifted his head, I could see his tears and wanted to gather this handsome, bereaved man into my arms and comfort him. We sat quietly looking at one another. Pain radiated from him, clouded his eyes, and tightened his jaw. I watched his grief solidifying into anger.

He broke the silence with a slight groan. "Let's go, then —to the she-coyote's den." He patted his eyes dry with the handkerchief I'd seen in the church, but now it was wrinkled and soggy. He shoved it back into his pocket. With a deep breath, he sat up tall, pushed open his door, slid to the cobbled driveway, and slammed the door shut behind him, shaking the old bus so much the windows rattled.

"Hey, watch it, Anibal!"

"Sorry. Shall I let the dog out?"

"Okay." I fished around the dashboard for my purse and a pocket-sized packet of Kleenex. No monogrammed handkerchiefs here. I blew my nose and swiped my lips with the Revlon Hot Chili lipstick that matched my nails, newly painted in Acapulco on the way to Mexico City. I swiveled the rear view around and checked my hair. It looked pretty much like it always did except my usual auburn had lightened up in the tropical sun to a golden strawberry on top, and it felt stiff like hay. Maybe I'd find a *salon de belleza* while I was in town and get a deep conditioning. I patted down the flyaway strands and tossed my brush into my bag. This was it. I felt like I was about to walk the green mile. Unlike Anibal, I could have stayed at the beach, but it was too late now.

"Ready," I chirped, a phony smile on my freshly painted lips.

I walked around the front of the *combi* and stepped onto the walkway. Anibal had clipped Pepper onto his leash and the two waited for me, Pepper—obediently sitting at attention, ears perked, head cocked to one side, his anticipation obvious in his expression, and Anibal—despondent and slouching, loathing etched across his face.

"Okay, boys, lead on." I forced my voice into a cheerleader peppiness and linked my arm through Anibal's as I took the leash from him and tugged us toward the entry.

The two-story stucco house glowed a peachy-pink and had natural stone trim around the doors and windows. The ubiquitous iron grillwork over the windows, found everywhere in the city, looked more decorative than a feature of safety. The property reminded me of a European estate with the Italian cypress, roses and circular drive, and ivy growing over much of the walls. The foundation plantings reminded me of English cottage gardens, not what I'd seen in Mexico. But what did I know? I'd spent very little time in Mexico City's suburbs, especially the suburbs of the *gente de altura sociedad*, of which, I was certain, the little crow believed herself and Polo to be members. I rang the bell.

A pretty, young servant, radiant even in the dowdy starched apron and cheesy black uniform dress she wore, opened the door. She tossed a flirtatious glance at Anibal. I cleared my throat and she averted her eyes and held the door open for us.

"Buenas tardes, Señor Anibal. Yo se que es una gran perdida para usted. La familia se espera en el salon."

"Gracias, Luci. JadeAnne, you can put Pepper in the backyard. Come on, I'll show you. And leave your bag over there." He indicated a spindly-looking table mounded with purses.

I dropped my bag on the pile and followed Anibal through an archway that led to the yard. Identical white West Highland terriers sat at the door. They jumped up at our approach and started to wag their fluffy little bodies. Both had grins on their faces and their black button eyes shined. The male stood up on his hind legs and scratched rapidly at the door.

"Pico, get down." He shoved the door into the two little dogs who yipped in pain.

"Anibal!"

"I can't stand these yappers. They're Aunt Lidia's."

"So I assumed," I said as I crouched to pet them, handing Pepper's leash back to Anibal. "What're their names?"

"The male is Pico and the female is Mimi, but I can't tell them apart."

"Hello, Pico. Hello, Mimi." The little dogs jumped up on me, wagging and trying to lick my face. "They're cute! Doggies, this is Pepper. Pepper, Pico and Mimi. Be nice," I warned him.

I unclipped Pepper's lead and let him through the door to meet the terriers. He wagged and they all sniffed, the little dogs crouching, with tails between their legs and only the tips moving. Pepper licked Mimi who bounced up happily. Pico nipped at Mimi and the two raced circles around Pepper and each other. Mimi shot off into the garden, Pico on her heels. Pepper woofed once and bounded after them. Anibal and I watched the three dogs chase each other up and down the broad lawn.

"I guess Pepper likes the little ones. I was a bit worried. Shepherds aren't always nice to other dogs," I said.

"He probably thinks they're wind-up toys. Wait till he catches one. He'll rip it apart," Anibal said, his tone snide.

"No, he won't! That's rude, Ani. What's the matter with you?"

"Isn't that what dogs do to their toys?"

"Drop it, Anibal. Let's go in." He was acting like a spoiled child who wasn't getting his way. "Cut the attitude, dude. If this is how you always act, I can see why these people don't lay out the welcome mat."

He frowned at me and stalked back toward the front hall. I followed along, feeling mean for what I'd said. But jeez, I was feeling out of place, too, and he was making it worse.

Anibal stomped into the living room and flung himself into an easy chair facing the fireplace without saying anything to the assembled mourners. I paused at the door expecting Lidia-the-crow and found a sophisticated and gracious hostess instead. At the church, swathed in black drapery, Lidia Sotomayor de Aguirre had appeared ancient—wizened and frail—but in reality, I estimated her to be a spry grand-dame in her mid-to-late sixties. She was tastefully dressed in a white chiffon shawl-collared blouse that peeked from her pastel-blue, raw silk cocktail suit. Pearls the size of my prized turquoise Clambroth shooter saved from my marble-playing days ringed her long, crepe-y neck. Her hair had been coiffed in a lustrous silvered chignon, which emphasized her exotic features. I was impressed by her flawless olive skin and wagered that she'd never been in the sun. Her hands, now uncovered, appeared smooth and manicured. She was elegant and graceful. A socialite shining in the midst of her elegant friends. It made sense that she would leave Aguirre's father on the marijuana plantation in Michoacán after her daughter died. No, I couldn't see this woman on a farm.

Lidia rose and crossed the room, extending her hand as she reached me. "Miss Stone, welcome to my home," she said with little warmth. "I think I speak for my family when I thank you for all you did to try and prevent Daniel from harming his wife. My son has informed me of your investigation and your efforts on behalf of the Aguirre family." This time she took my hand and drew me into the living room before dropping it. Good thing I had my nails done.

"Thank you, Señora Aguirre. I appreciate your kindness. I became fond of Lura in our brief acquaintance and I am truly sorry for your loss," I said, my debutante manners kicking into high gear.

We crossed a thick oriental rug to a grouping of couches and chairs.

"My niece was pig-headed and followed her own path. She chose life on her own terms, with full knowledge of the consequences."

"Yes, she loved her job, but I can only imagine how you and your family must feel. My prayers are with you."

"We all can benefit from prayer," she replied, acidly. "Please make yourself comfortable, Miss Stone. Alejandra, dear, help Miss Stone find some refreshments and introduce her to our other guests," she said as she passed me off.

Alex, Lura's sister, flew off one of the couches where she had been talking with a stylish young woman, "Of course, Aunt Lidia. I'll be happy to," she replied with a strained smile. "JadeAnne, welcome. Let me introduce you to Loli Buendía, our cousin."

She turned toward the woman seated on the dusky-blue couch. Loli might be Lura's age, mid-thirties, attractive with tawny skin, dark hair, and the clan's almond-shaped eyes. She wasn't as sumptuously dressed as some of the mourners I had seen in the church. I attributed that to either good taste or lack of wealth.

"Hi, JadeAnne," she greeted me and stretched out her hand to shake. Her wedding set was old fashioned and crusted with diamonds. A couple of them were really big. I dropped the theory of less wealthy. Her smile radiated warmth and I liked her immediately.

We made small talk as the maid served a tray of *botanas*, bite-sized stuffed chilis. I put in my drink request with a waiter who appeared once I settled into the U-shaped cluster of couches and chairs that faced out the windows into the garden. A floral patterned Persian rug tied the grouping together. I noticed that only women and girls sat in this area. The men, including Alex's husband Jason, congregated near the doors leading to the dining room and conversed in low voices over cocktails and cigars. Aunt Lidia and several black-clad crow-ladies sat in another cluster of plush furniture and drank tea. Lidia hadn't bothered to introduce me to her friends. I must not have been wearing enough jewelry. I didn't see Aguirre or Lura's parents.

"Alex, how are you holding up?" I asked her.

"I'm good. Aunt Lidia was right about Lura being strong-willed and aware of the consequences. We talked on the phone that night, you know. She told me all about you. Lura was very fond of you. She couldn't wait to get home and introduce you to us."

"She talked about you, too. Lura loved her family, especially you, Alex."

"She practically raised me. Mom has a career. Then Ani came and she took care of both of us." She looked toward the fireplace and Anibal, who sprawled inelegantly in a chair with a glum face. "This is killing him—I've never seen him so down. Lura was everything to Anibal."

Her voice trailed off and she started to cry quietly. Loli passed the box of tissues and I smiled sympathetically then sipped the vodka tonic the waiter handed me. Alex needed a moment.

"I saw her just the week before when she and Anibal came through Mexico City on their way to Polo's farm. They stayed with us. She was worried about something—an investigation she was working on—and anxious to talk to Polo. It never occurred to me that she could be investigating Danny," Loli said.

A pudgy woman on the wrong side of forty with short red-dyed hair, wearing a fashionable but clashing pink suit and gaudy diamond earrings, leaned over from the matching couch and whispered conspiratorially, "I never liked Daniel. There was always something dubious about him. I could tell."

"Oh, right, Consuelo, you were the one mooning over him, always jealous of Lura. I heard you made a habit of visiting him at inappropriate hours in the night. I'd be a bit more careful in front of this family if I were you," Loli replied, and turned her back on the woman.

Consuelo opened her mouth to say something, but Alex had turned away too. The red-head huffed, got up and drifted toward the men.

Worthington had a lover? I relaxed back into the stack of soft pillows. It probably wasn't important now, but I filed Consuelo's name away into my memory. Maybe she knew something that could benefit Lura and Daniel Worthington's survivors.

CHAPTER THREE

The Saint

The waiter reappeared, a bar towel draped over his arm, champagne flutes on a round silver tray in one hand and a bottle of Dom Perignon in the other. The redhead signaled and he bent to accept her used Old Fashioned glass and poured a flute, which she snatched without a thank you.

The cousins had been conversing in tones too low to follow, but my ears pricked up when Loli asked, "Alex, who are Lura and Daniel's heirs?"

Alex's face pinched and she clenched her hands together for a moment before speaking. I wondered if either of them had a will. Surely not Ani.

"I don't know about Danny, but Anibal and I inherit from Lura. She had her own money before they married and she was careful to keep her assets out of his reach. Also, she held a percentage of Danny's bank in Panama. I guess Ani and I own that too."

I pulled myself out of the brocade couch pillows and leaned toward Alex, now all ears, "What will you do with the bank?" I asked.

"I won't make any deposits into it, that's for sure," she said, tears brimming from her eyes. I handed her a box of tissues from the side table and she dabbed the moisture, careful not to smear her makeup. Eyes lowered, she agitated her wine glass as she spoke, watching the garnet-colored liquid as it swirled one way and then the other.

"Lura told me about her investigation. Danny was laundering money for cartels and that consortium from Texas that's bucking to buy PEMEX."

Surprise. "You know about that?" Worthington was an idiot. A dead idiot.

"*Claro que sí.* The whole family does. Danny was a total blabbermouth. A big-time social climber, and he couldn't stop himself from boasting. He bragged about the rich politicos and high-society financiers that were relying on his Panamanian bank to step in when the deal was struck. He thought he'd made it to the inner circle of U.S. finance." Alex suddenly raised her head, her eyes hard. "I thought he was a fool."

Consuelo, hovering nearby, shot daggers at Alex and gulped a fresh cocktail when she noticed me watching her. I turned back to Alex. "And Lura's investigation into a counterfeiting scheme led her to her husband's money laundering."

Alex's jaw tightened and her full lips flattened into a prim line. "Exactly."

"Where are all his powerful friends now?" Loli asked, in her soft accent, a trace of disgust sounding in her voice. She hadn't liked Daniel Worthington either.

"I bet they're wondering how they're going to get their money out of Panama," I said, hoping to keep my sarcasm under wraps. "Won't the government seize everything until the probate is settled?"

Alex looked away and placed her wine glass carefully onto the coffee table with a shaking hand. "That's Panama— who can say?"

Alex obviously was uncomfortable with the topic. Did

Anibal know he owned shares in the Panamanian bank? I let the conversation drop.

And who, exactly, owned the rest of it?

I relaxed into the cushions to contemplate answers to these questions. The room glowed softly golden as the late afternoon rays streamed through the mullioned windows and diffused in the hovering dust motes. The women around me spoke in soft voices about children, nannies, schools, and servants as they sipped their sherry, Campari, or white wine. I didn't have anything to add to this conversation, and was feeling too exhausted and too emotionally drained to feign interest. Why had the family insisted on me coming to this gathering, anyway?

More well-wishers arrived. The living room filled up with fancy-looking people, and the men and women began to mix. I wasn't going to solve any puzzles sitting here, so I thought I might as well mingle. Otherwise I would fall asleep.

Anibal still sprawled in the mauve wingback chair by the fireplace. His glum face and posture screamed, "Leave me alone!" I didn't know anyone else to talk to so I ignored his body language and leaned over his chair.

"So, Ani, who are all these people? Were they all at the church?"

"Huh?"

"All these guests. They all knew Lura?" I asked again.

"Don't know." He answered in monosyllables and turned away as though to look over the room.

"I haven't seen Polo. What happened to him? How did he escape the long arm of Lidia?"

"Don't know," he repeated and closed his eyes.

I shrugged and moved off toward a table set with tea and biscuits. For someone who wanted to talk to me, he sure acted like an ass.

A liveried servant sounded tones on a small chime with

an even smaller mallet. "Dinner is served, Madam," he announced.

I looked across the tea table to the group flocked around the crow. Lidia gracefully rose to her feet and gently clapped her hands three times then started moving toward the dining room door. Her flock twittered and pecked along behind her, heels and canes clacking on bare patches of hardwood floor. The cigar-smoking men parted in a wave to allow the crones to pass though their midst into the *comeador*; a hush fell over the rest of the room. I couldn't hear anything more than the clink of ice against crystal, spoons set onto bone china saucers, and the swish of silk on silk.

I glanced back at Anibal but he slouched lower in his chair, facing away from the party. I wanted to catch his eye to encourage him to go in to dinner with me. I was starved. I'd eaten very little lunch in my haste to arrive at Lura's funeral on time. I nodded toward the dining room. Anibal ignored me. Over the top of his head, I noticed the door open to admit three newcomers to the party. It was one of the men in sunglasses and his two trained gorillas from the church— still scanning the crowd. Looking for someone or just looking heavy? The sunglasses, the pencil-thin mustache and Fu-Manchu beard, the western-cut suit and body bling all screamed "dealer," and I was pretty sure he wasn't dealing used autos. He removed his sunglasses and waved-off the goons, who retreated back into the hallway, closing the living room door behind them. The man stepped further into the room and his gaze appeared to alight onto Lidia who was just about to pass through the dining room door. She turned, saw the man, and smiled. He crossed to her.

The man gave me the creeps, I'd never liked the Fu-Manchu look. He must have felt me watching him, because he looked directly at me and stretched his lips into what I could only call a sneer as our eyes met. My breath constricted and I looked away, but I heard his laugh, a nasty high-pitched sound, and watched as Lidia took his proffered arm and allowed him to escort her in to table.

I bent toward Anibal's ear. "It's the hood from the church."

He tensed. "I figured he'd show up. We've gotta get out of here."

I looked wistfully toward the dining room, thinking about the feast inside. "Why? I need to eat first." The spicy odors of mole and tortillas wafted across the room and my stomach growled.

"Where's Polo?"

"I asked you that ten minutes ago."

"Then I don't know. C'mon," he said, leaping from his wingback chair and tugging my arm. "Hurry."

"Tell me what's going on!"

"I'll explain it tonight—he's part of it. We have to leave, Jade."

A familiar voice broke into our conversation. "Anibal, JadeAnne. Thank you for coming. Will you join us for comida?"

"Polo." Anibal's voice sounded flat.

"Senator, you're too kind."

"Shall we go in?" He spread his arms to herd us told the dining room.

"Sorry, bro'. Gotta go. JadeAnne?"

I was practically knocked off my feet as Anibal sprinted toward the door, yanking me by my arm. I fell into step with him as we speed-walked down the hall toward the front entrance to the house, the goons nowhere in sight.

"Wait, Ani! Don't forget Pepper," I gasped and veered down the bisecting passage to the garden door. My boy sat on the doormat patiently waiting with two little white balls of fluff asleep between his paws. He jumped up at my approach and barked. Pico and Mimi woke up and began a chorus of obnoxious yapping.

"I see what you mean," I admitted to Anibal, who had followed me. He opened the door and pulled Pepper into the house, using his foot to block the little dogs.

"No, Pico, No, Mimi. Stay!" he yelled and slammed the door shut. "This way." Anibal turned away from the front door.

"Ani, my bag!"

"Get it. I'll meet you at the *combi*. Hurry."

"Why? What's going on?"

"Edgar Santos Guerrero Félix—The Saint."

"Oh, that means a lot to me. Anibal, what on earth are you talking about? The creepy man who came in just now?"

"Just hurry up, Jade. Get your *bolsita* and hurry," he called over his shoulder and turned the corner, vanishing from view.

I clipped the leash onto Pepper's collar and went back to the entry hall to retrieve my handbag from under a mound of Prada, Coach, Ferragamo, Kooba, and I didn't know whose labels. I felt like the poor relation fishing my vinyl Hansen and Hillard out of the assemblage. Well, I thought it was cute when I bought it.

Outside the temperature cooled as afternoon gave way to evening. I guessed it must be about four-thirty. I didn't see Anibal outside the *combi*, but remembered I'd left it unlocked and figured he'd be inside.

The driveway was jammed with expensive vehicles and drivers lounging, smoking, and polishing the paint. None of them looked particularly suspicious or threatening, but they all checked me out, making me feel slightly grimy. Thank God none of them whistled.

Anibal was not in the cab of my bus. Damn him, what now? I was beginning to feel manipulated. What was he up to? Pulling me out of the gathering right when the food was served. My stomach howled, outraged, so I opened the side door and rummaged through the cabinet for something to eat. Pepper jumped in to check on the possibility of a handout and sniffed at a pile of clothes and bedding I'd left in a heap on the *combi's* floor. The pile moved.

"Ani?" I said and climbed in.

"Shhh. Drive. Get us out of here."

"Anibal Aguirre—enough of this cloak and dagger shit. Get out of my laundry and direct me to a restaurant. I'm starving."

"Quiet. They'll hear you," he replied, casting his eyes toward a pair of thugs lounging against a black Escalade, as he edged toward the door and shoved it closed, almost catching my hand.

"You're doing a fine job of pissing me off. Why should I want to do anything with you? Now you're trying to smash my body parts. What's up with that?"

"Get into the driver's seat and drive us out of here before his bodyguards turn up. Santos can't know I'm gone."

My stomach lurched. "Why not?"

"Later, Jade. Get us out of here."

"Only if you promise to take me to a restaurant."

"Fine, we'll eat as soon as my meeting is over."

We heard footsteps on the walk outside and I backed out of the interior, a package of cheesy Gansitos clutched in my fist.

"*Buenas tardes, señora,*" the heavier of the two bodyguards greeted me. The other craned his neck to see inside.

I nodded in their direction, slammed the door shut and turned to round the vehicle to the driver's door but the men blocked the walkway. I pulled the keys out of my bag, locked the doors, and turned back toward the house, brushing past the stocky gorilla with a curt, "*Permiso.*" He stepped aside and I bolted around my *combi*, jumped in and slammed down the door lock. My heart pounded in my chest and my hand shook so badly I had trouble getting the key into the ignition. What did they want? The heavier man rattled the locked passenger door, while the gorilla came around to the driver's side as the engine turned over. I cranked the wheel to the left and lurched away from the curb, just about running him over.

He smashed his fist into the side of the *combi* with a loud thud and shouted, "*¡Chingao!*"

The bus rocked. I stepped on the gas and rumbled away from them. I saw the heavier man talking into a cell phone through the side mirror before circling behind the shrubbery and heading toward the gate. My veins turned icy. Were these Rodriguez's men sent to kill me?

CHAPTER FOUR

Gandhi

I flipped on the blinker to change lanes and inched over, sandwiching the *combi* between an exhaust-spewing city bus and three green and yellow VW bugs vying for the same space in the lane. They all honked.

"Watch out, JadeAnne—you almost side-swiped that *pesera.*"

"Where are we going?" I yelled over my shoulder. Anibal sat with Pepper on the backseat.

"San Angel. Get in the left lane and turn right onto Miguel Angel de Quevedo. Then we'll turn left again in front of *Vips* and Walmart Supercenter. Then look for parking," he said as he moved forward and made like he was going to climb over the seat.

"Don't climb over that cabinet; you'll rip down the curtain." I saw Anibal's frown in the rearview. Tough. Who gave him the right to ruin my bus?

"Left. Left!"

I stepped on the gas and swung across the oncoming traffic on the tail end of the light.

"I can't believe Walmart is here in Mexico."

"It's everywhere, Jade, but that's not where we're going.

I've gotta stop at Gandhi. I'm meeting someone."

"Is there food where we're going?"

"Yeah. Coffee and pastries. That okay?"

"Ani, I'm really hungry. Can't we go to a restaurant?"

"Just find a parking space. Parking is difficult in this neighborhood."

"Why would you make an appointment during Lidia's gathering? Lura wouldn't have called that a wake."

"Not a wake. A *vigilia* or *velatorio*, maybe, and Lura would've hated anything at Aunt Lidia's. She couldn't stand her."

"Why? She loved Polo so much, practically idolized him. I'd have thought she'd be close to his mother." I was talking to myself more than to Anibal. The noisy trucks on Quevedo drowned out my voice and whatever Anibal replied. No noise pollution laws here, I supposed. Or smell pollution laws, either.

"P-U. What on earth is that stink?"

"There must be a gas leak somewhere. And sewage. Pull over—a space. Gandhi's only a couple blocks ahead. See, *Vips* and Walmart." Anibal pointed out my window as I nose-dived into the parking space.

I avidly avoided driving in reverse. I couldn't see out of the *combi*, not even with the mirrors, and I worried about crashing the gas cans mounted on the back into a telephone pole or a truck or whatever. That would be just what I needed to make my day—a little explosion and fire. God, I'd had enough explosions to last a lifetime. I rocked the bus back and forth in the space that was really only long enough for a sports car until I'd maneuvered the *combi* to the curb and stopped the engine. Anibal slammed the door shut before the last cough of the engine faded away. The crappy *magna sin* gas didn't agree with the *combi*—this gas was the reason Lura, Zocer and Daniel Worthington died? The whole twisted plan struck me as a travesty.

I briefly considered the effects of the bombing in Zihua while I gathered my bag and camera. Certainly Aguirre wouldn't have any reason to vote for privatization now, but with Worthington dead, would the consortium look for a new laundering lackey? Or was the cash locked in Banco PanAmericano down in Panama City and irrecoverable? Or better yet, being divvied up between Anibal and Alex Radcliffe. Ha! That was probably more naïve thinking. The investors were capitalized, probably shareholders, if indeed the group was as connected to the top echelons of U.S. industry and politics like everyone thought. They weren't letting their money go, will or no will.

I turned around in my seat and pushed aside the curtain. "Peppi, boy, it looks like you are going to stay here," I said to my dog. "I bet you're hungry."

He wagged his tail and woofed. I knew he needed to get out, but this didn't seem to be the place. I hoped Anibal's neighborhood was quieter. This was a congested city during rush hour—or I guessed it was rush hour. From the driving I'd done in Mexico City, I'd say it was rush hour all the time. I checked the side mirror for large vehicles coming my way and gingerly pushed open my door. The smell was everywhere, thick and awful, like overcrowded feed lots. I gasped. Anibal, who had disappeared, expected me to walk two blocks in this stench? Where was he? Where was this Gandhi place? I cracked the side door enough to crawl in, and pulled it shut behind me. There was some incense tucked into the cabinet I was rooting around in. That might cover the stench. I lit it and fixed Pepper a bowl of crunchies. He dug in, and I lay back on the seat and stroked him with my bare toes as he ate. I could fall asleep, I thought, closing my eyes.

The grinding sound of the door sliding open on its track jerked me awake. Anibal stared at me, impatience playing across his face. "JadeAnne, what the hell are you doing?"

"Um, feeding Pepper. Where'd you disappear to?"

"Gandhi. My contact is waiting. Hurry up."

Contact? I patted Pepper, slipped into flip-flops, grabbed my bag and jumped out. "Let's go then."

Anibal strode across the uneven sidewalk and disappeared behind the taco vendor on the narrow, car-choked street. I locked the bus. The foul stench had dissipated while I catnapped and was now the usual stench of exhaust, dust, and tacos from the corner vendor's *comal*. My stomach growled and I hurried after Anibal, slowing only to check out the strings of intestines coiled on the wide lip of the pan, waiting to be chopped and turned into rough lumps of what appeared to be carbon, gently bubbling in a pool of oil. Yeach.

Librería Gandhi, it turned out, was a bookstore. A really big one, with nine branches in the city. This branch in Guadalupe Chimalistac, near San Angel, was two stories and had a café. The place bustled with shoppers browsing long tables and shelves laden with books. I passed the new releases on the way to the stairs—all the same titles I'd see at home in Book Passage, but in Spanish. I ought to buy some books and work on my Spanish. I'd picked up *Harry Potter and the Deathly Hallows* before crossing the border and finished it. I thought about the new Nora Roberts but decided she wasn't an author I was willing to pursue in a foreign language. God knew I had enough trouble keeping track of her point of view shifts in English.

Anibal thundered up the glass-and-steel staircase and vanished into what looked like a university library. After wandering through the stacks for several minutes, I bumped into a kind gentleman dressed in a slouchy tweed jacket and black beret, who pointed out the secret door to the café in French. I love Mexico—nothing is what you expect, or where you expect to find it. The café spread out behind the narrow order counter onto a balcony overlooking Gandhi's main floor. People sat singly and in small groups, drinking coffee and reading or chatting. Few worked at laptops, but enough to make me think the store was wired. I looked around for Anibal and found him at a tiny metal bistro table in the back corner with a youthful-looking man. The man's sandy-colored hair curled over his neck and ears, and he wore a powder blue sweater over fashionably faded and tattered jeans, with red Converse high top sneakers. I noticed he wasn't wearing socks. It was very warm outside—he must be out of his mind to wear a sweater. I perspired through my sleeveless shift.

I ordered a double cappuccino and a *torta sincronizada* for starters and dawdled over the displayed pastries. Maybe I'd try one after my ham and Swiss on a fresh *telera* roll. There was no reason to hurry over to the table. Whatever Anibal was up to wasn't my business, and I didn't really care at the moment.

He was such a turn-on in Ixtapa, but he'd understandably changed after Lura died, becoming tedious, sullen, and angry. I'd been so hot for him, scheming on how I could string him along until I settled things with Dex. Well, Dex sure solved that problem. Did he really dump me on a pier in a foreign country? Then the bomb—as if breaking up wasn't bomb enough.

Lura dead, Zocer dead—well, possibly dead, I could swear I saw him at the funeral—and the Aguirre men blaming me, even though they'd apologized today. Did this put too much strain on what amounted to a minor flirtation with Anibal? Maybe I'd won the bet with Lura. Whatever had been between us in Ixtapa hadn't lasted. So what did he want from me now?

The counter server passed over a tray with my food and I shoved twenty pesos into the jar by the register. I'd ask Anibal what the customary tip percentage was in *La Capital* when I sat down. The place had gotten more crowded in the short time I waited for my food. A harried waitress almost knocked my tray out of my hands, but I steadied myself and safely made it to the table.

Both men stood at my approach. My, my. What manners.

"Let me help you with that, señorita," Anibal's contact said, slipping the tray from my hands and placing it on a neighboring table. He pulled a chair up for me from the same table, seated me and handed me my sandwich.

Anibal flopped back into his seat. "JadeAnne Stone, Fernando Torrens. Fer and I were just finishing our conversation," he said, giving Fernando a look that said *scram.*

"I'm happy to meet you, JadeAnne. Are you American?"

"Yes, Californian," I said, as shook his hand. I'd noticed that the Mexicans shook hands more than we did in California. "Don't let me interrupt your meeting, gentlemen."

"No problem. Aguirre and I are finished. How do you like Mexico? Perhaps I can show you around one day?"

Fernando's smile was as disarming as his line was smooth. What an operator.

"I don't think so, Torrens. JadeAnne isn't here to sightsee."

"What a lovely invitation, Fernando. I'd be honored to have you as a tour guide. I'm assuming you live here in the Distrito?" I smiled with what I hoped was a gracious and sincere expression. Frankly, the thought of spending a day with this Fernando character made me gag, but getting Anibal's pompous goat would be worth it. I'd bow out before the actual date. Fernando made me think of smarmy gigolos from the movies, or that weasely informant, Pepe, from the old *Miami Vice* shows, despite his amazing blue eyes.

"Yes, in the north of the city. I grew up here, *soy cien por ciento mexicano,* one-hundred percent *chilango,*"

Fernando said, grinning in a less than friendly way at Anibal.

Anibal's eyes closed to slits and I watched his jaw clench and his shoulders set. I wagered he was clenching his fits under the table. Through his teeth he murmured, "Jade, we're going to be busy for the next week. If there's time, I'll take you to see some sights."

"Hey! I'm on vacation."

"Then it's settled. I'll show you all around *Chilangolandia*. Shall I call for you at your hotel later?" Fernando asked me.

"Actually, take my cell number," I said, as I passed him a business card. "I'm not sure where I'll be staying yet."

"*Muchas gracias, señorita*. Aguirre, I've got to get back to my trainers," Fernando said and shoved away from the table. He stood up, tossed down a couple of bills and gathered his battered-looking man-bag, a thick, zippered leather rectangle with a wrist strap. He smiled at me and nodded curtly toward Anibal.

"Ciao."

Anibal watched Fernando pass out of the café then rounded on me,. "Look JadeAnne, you don't know what's going on here. That man is bad news. You can't—"

"Look yourself. If you don't tell me what's on your mind, how do you expect me to play along? Why did you bring me in here if you didn't want me to meet your friend?"

He scrutinized the café patrons suspiciously and lowered his voice to say, "Torrens is an informant. He had information for me. Stay away from him—he's as sleazy as they come."

"Give me a break, Anibal. An informant? What would an economic think-tank geek need an informant for? You dragged me here. Begged me to come, and I'm tired of your cloak and dagger bullshit. Who are you?"

"I don't think this is the place—"

"Either you tell me what's going on, or I'm outta here!" I

braced forward to push myself to my feet. "Find your own way back to whatever rock you crawled out from under."

He clamped a hand around my forearm.

"Stop it! You're bruising my arm." I raised my voice and several diners looked our way.

"So sit down and shut up." He dropped my arm and forced his lips into a smile that didn't make it to his eyes.

I slumped back into my chair and the neighbors turned back to their espressos and *pan dulces*. "No more crap, Anibal. I really will leave and you can't stop me."

"Keep your voice down."

The drone of conversations, the hiss of the milk steamer, the clanking of plates and glasses and flatware rose around us. I waited silently, letting the café noise build before looking Anibal in the eyes. He held his head cocked slightly to the right, his eyes were soft and his lips parted into a sweet smile. I melted under the warmth and caring—like on the beach in Ixtapa before Lura died. I slid my hand across the small table and he clasped it, eyes locked to mine.

"It's true, I'm Lura's cousin and Polo's half-brother. But I don't work for a think-tank, and I'm not in Mexico for a vacation to see my family. I'm on assignment."

I knew it. "To do what? Bust Polo's operation?"

"To take down the cartel operating out of Mexico City that controls the Guerrero opium and some South American cocaine that's moving through Panama to the Gulf Coast cartels and on to Florida, Texas, and the other southern States," he said, his voice snapping into a businesslike cadence.

Panama again. Things were starting to line up. I dropped my voice. "I made you for a professional—DEA, right?"

Anibal shrugged, coloring slightly.

I leaned in and whispered, "It was the two-way radio that gave you away." I grinned.

"That obvious, huh?"

"Well, it didn't say Radio Shack on it." I leaned across the table. "And this Fernando character? Where does he fit in?"

"He's a dog trainer."

"Well, that explains everything." I tipped my cappuccino back to drain the last drop of frothy milk and scraped my chair back from the table as I stood up.

"Attack and guard dogs."

"Exclusively for the cartels." I finished for him.

"*Pues, eso.*"

"So what did he tell you? Wait—let me get another coffee. Want something?" I leaned over, fished my tote from under the table.

"Get it to go," Ani said and stood up, too. "We'll finish the conversation at my place, then go get some dinner. I know a great little bistro near the house."

CHAPTER FIVE

Disclosures

When the *combi* topped a rise, I noticed the lights of Mexico City twinkle east as far as I could see. Anibal drove. It seemed easier since he knew where we were going. The dashboard clock read 7:36, and against the now black western peaks, striations of mauve layered in the haze. The Anillo Periferico choked with traffic. Vehicle emissions eddied in the depressions every time the highway dipped down. I rolled my window shut.

"Aren't there any controls on car emissions here?"

"Sure. Don't you buy Magna Sin? It's lead-free gas."

"Then why does it stink so much?"

"Diesel—and most of the cars have their catalytic converters removed for better gas mileage. First thing they do after stealing them in California and hot-footing it across the border." Anibal chuckled.

I smiled. At least five guys had offered me pesos for the combi. Everyone wanted a car from California— "You can legalize it easy—*mi cuñado*...." Amazing how many brothers-in-law work for the government. But I wasn't selling, not even if the damn thing did belong to my ex. I paid too high a price to get it here.

I leaned my head against the cool window glass. The heat of the day had mellowed to a comfortable temperature. I relaxed and went back to reading exit signs.

Constituyentes exited right. Two lanes exited, joining two more to make four lanes to the right of the Periferico, separated by a cement median with a cyclone fence—the lateral. *Peseros*, buses, delivery trucks and cars inched on or off the highway—a mess. From past experience I knew that just because I saw the exit sign, it didn't mean I should take it. The Mexicans liked to announce exits several times before the real one came up—sort of a practice exit. Take the wrong one and you could end up in Colonia Doctores having your car stripped of parts and your purse lifted in less time than it might take to find a parking spot in downtown Sausalito.

Constituyentes for the third time.

"Pay attention, Jade. We're taking the Constituyentes exit *oriente*. Got it? East. We'll drive east down the mountain and land in Colonia Condesa at Eje 2 Sur. Stay off Constituyentes during the day, though. It's the main artery leading out of the city to Toluca. It can take hours to move a block."

"So how is it you keep a house here?"

"I inherited it. From Anahí, my mother."

"Oh, yeah, the Aguirres bought her a house to keep her away from your uncle," I said, remembering the stories Anibal and Lura told me about the family out on Sunset Point the night we'd met.

"She worked for Lidia; ran the house and did other things—correspondence, booked appointments, kept Lidia's calendar—and other activities," he added, voice dropping.

"Oh? Like what?"

"Errands. Clean-up. Listen to me, JadeAnne, we can talk about all this over dinner," Anibal said, and turned from the busy street into a neighborhood.

Didn't Lidia have enough staff to cover cleaning? "What

42

do you mean—clean-up?"

Anibal down-shifted, his attention on a snarl of honking *peseras*.

"So, where are we?" I asked. as we cleared the jam and passed a brightly lit taco joint open to the street. My mouth watered at the sight of the tacos al pastor, scrumptious red-tipped layers of meat turning slowly on the rotisserie spit. I cracked my window, the cabin flooded with the rich scents of roasting meats and my stomach growled. Coffee and *sinchronizadas* almost an hour ago weren't doing it for me. I wanted to eat. "Stop!"

"Not here, Jade. There's a better place. Let's go home first, have a drink and a shower. You want tacos? We could go to El Tinzoncito—best *alambre* in the city. It's open late, but I was thinking about taking you to a little Spanish place I like."

He was driving me nuts. *Wait, wait, wait.* I sighed. "Whatever. I'm starving."

"Señora Pérez left us a plate of *botanas.* Some of her famous bite-sized *tamales*, I think. And I've got a great bottle of wine from Sonoma—a gold medal Zinfandel from Miro Vineyards. Do you know it?"

"I know I'm hungry," I grumbled as the *taquería* disappeared from my side mirror.

"We're home." Anibal's voice startled me out of a doze. "Come on," he said, opening my door open.

"Pepper?"

"Holding the elevator." Anibal gestured toward the side of the garage with his head.

Pepper was, indeed, sitting plunk in the middle of the elevator doorway wagging his tail, my suitcases stacked behind him, while the metal door jerked in its track, trying to close.

"I thought you had a house," I said.

"It is."

"With an elevator?" I asked, squeezing into the two-man lift with my dog and bags.

"Sure. Four stories, including ground level. The guest suite is on the fourth level. My suite is on the third."

I felt a little sinking sensation in the pit of my stomach. What was that about?

We crowded in. Anibal pushed the top button on the panel and the elevator groaned and clicked into lift-off, grumbling as it slid up its shaft and clanked to a stop.

"Here we are. I'll help you into your room and meet you in the kitchen for a drink. Just push one on the panel when you come down. PB means ground floor." He pointed to the control panel then grabbed my bags and swung them across the hall, balancing the smallest on his hip while he opened the door. I pulled it away from him and was rewarded with a grin.

"Your suite, señorita," he said and swept the room with his open palm. Pepper trotted in and began investigating the corners for dog-attracting smells.

"That's the bathroom. This buzzer calls the maid." A smile played across those full lips as he pointed to a black button set into a brass plate by the door, "but don't use it unless you want me." He winked. "I don't keep a live-in domestic. Only Señora Pérez, and she comes during the day."

Anibal's face had lost its hard edge now he was home. And he was flirting with me. I smiled in spite of my misgivings.

"How fancy is the restaurant? Do I have time for a shower?"

"Sure, do what you need to. I'll clean up, but it's not fancy. Hey, we're in Condesa, not Polanco."

Whatever that meant, I thought as I turned a circle to

look at my new abode. I guessed I'd find out soon enough.

"Thanks, Ani, this is lovely," I said, taking his hand. I didn't want him to leave. "I won't be too long."

"I'll take Pepper and show him the yard. Come on boy," he said, letting go of me and backing out of the room. "You can have your tour later." His voice sounded husky.

The room pleased me in a girlie, old-fashioned sort of way. Rectangular, it took up most of the street side of the fourth floor, with tall, multi-paned windows opening onto faux wrought-iron balconies big enough for a few dry pots of scraggly geraniums. Old wallpaper with what looked like fading baby-blue roses covered the walls, but hard to tell because the room's lighting was more atmospheric than utilitarian.

Filling one end of the room, a magnificent wardrobe made from rough-hewn dark wood faced the camelback sofa perched on its dainty claw feet and covered in what may have been china-blue silk. Small chairs and tables clustered about in a completely random arrangement. A monstrous console TV topped with a copper lamp and rabbit ears took up one corner. I bet it was black and white.

A massive Spanish colonial-style bed dominated the other end of the room. I hauled my big suitcase over, swung it up, and unzipped it in one motion. My clothes were a mess, crammed in at the last minute before leaving for Mexico City. I shook out the wrinkles before hanging them in the large closet. I wondered what would be appropriate to wear to dinner. Nothing in this bag. I picked up the next, hoping to find a pair of silky pants and matching kimono jacket, but found the book I'd been reading before any of this adventure began. Since Dex left me, I'd barely had the will to read, usually a favorite activity of mine. For the last week, I'd cried and moped in my room at the Hotel Club Papanoa, only appearing for short escapes to the beach to bake in a tan and keep up with Harry, Ron, and Hermione at

Hogwarts then eat at the local fish restaurant. A week was all I could take of that "poor, poor pitiful me" attitude and I'd finally mobilized myself into action—once I'd made sure Harry and friends would return for another adventure. And here I was in Anibal's guestroom shower in Mexico City.

A scratchy voice hissed into the room while I dried myself. I looked around, trying to locate the source of the noise. It sounded like old-time TV on its late night sign-off, but the TV eye was blank, a blind sentinel to the clothing mayhem I'd created on the bed. And still no kimono although I found the pants.

"Jade. Jade!" There it was again, the static charged voice, which sounded like Anibal in a tunnel with a subway car rushing past. Maybe there is a metro here. Did he go for take-out? Or had I turned my cell on by accident?

"What are you doing up there? Hurry up!"

This time I could clearly hear him, and he wasn't coming from my phone, which had gone dead.

"Well, I'd answer you, Ani, if I knew where the intercom hid," I said.

He must have read my mind.

"On the wall in the bathroom, by the door—push the button," his voice scraped.

The apparatus reminded me of the butler calls in my grandparents' house back in Marin. The buzzers had been converted to an intercom system. Clever. But was I about to get a shock when I pushed the metal button? I'd dripped all over the floor.

"¡Hijole! Answer me." He sounded annoyed. I pushed the button.

"Hello?"

"What are you doing up there? I thought you were hungry. It's almost 9:30. The restaurant won't be open all night."

"I'm still looking for something to wear."

"*¡Mujeres!* Just throw on anything."
"Roger that. I'll be right down."

The *huachinango*, red snapper, baked in salt at El Racó Catalan far exceeded my expectations of dinner. Even the salad was to die for. Anibal and I sat at the window overlooking a dark, tree-shrouded Parque Mexico. Although there were several tables filled with diners, the ambiance was hushed, candle-filled—*romántico.* Anibal reached across our tiny table and took my hand. The monarchs at rest in my solar plexus stretched their wings. He smiled and looked directly into my eyes. The butterflies rose like a cloud of down, and fluttered inside my chest. I half-heard the music playing in the background— "*...mariposas bialan en me pecho...*" and looked him right back, eye to eye. The sweetest heart attack.

"JadeAnne," he said then paused.

I put my fork neatly onto my plate and pushed it aside. "Yes, Ani?"

He lowered his voice. "I have to be able to trust you. Completely." His gaze bored into me, sending shivers along my spine.

"Of, course, Ani, and I, you," I whispered, smiling.

"I have to know you've got my back. It could be life or death."

I almost choked.

"The mission, Jade. Are you with me?"

I pulled my hand from his. The mission? Anibal wasn't talking about us. This was something else entirely. I lowered my eyes. Thank God it was dark because my face burned. What an idiot.

"I, I...uh, sure, Ani. What exactly do you mean?" My voice rose. Not my smoothest recovery, but Mom always did call me Grace. I covered my confusion with a long sip of wine.

"Keep your voice down," he said, casting his eyes around the room. A middle-aged couple sat at the next table.

"JadeAnne, before I divulge this information, I must have your word that you will never repeat any of it—ever. Do you understand me?" He had that same stern expression my tenth grade geometry teacher used when he wanted the class to take his theorems seriously. I almost laughed.

"Wait a minute, I can't agree to anything before I know what I'm agreeing to. What's this mission? What does it have to do with me?"

He lowered his voice to barely a whisper. "You don't want to let the men responsible for Lura's death go unpunished, do you?"

His tone was accusing. If I said yes, I'd be colluding with the bad guys and insulting the memory of his beloved cousin. If I said no, well, let's just say it was the proverbial between a rock and a hard place.

"Daniel Worthington is dead. You shot him." I stalled.

"There was more to it."

"Like?"

"Why do you think Rodriguez's outfit was involved? For senate votes?"

"For control of the heroin in the area."

"Good girl."

"Don't patronize me." I plunked my wineglass onto the table and sloshed wine over the cloth. People at the next table turned toward us.

"Ooops!" I took a deep breath and let the waiter refill my glass. More gently, I said, "I'm not a mind reader, Ani. Tell me what this is about."

The waiter interrupted us again, "*Señora y señor,* would you care for dessert?"

"How's the flan here?" I asked.

"The *flan de coco* is a house specialty," Anibal said. "Two, please."

48

"An excellent choice, señor. Coffee?"

"Not for me, thanks," I replied.

"I'll have coffee, waiter. And the check."

"Very well, señor."

Dessert arrived. I savored the delicate coconut flavor and silky richness of the flan on my tongue. When I finished, I sat back and waited for Anibal to tell me what he was up to. The delicious meal and exhaustion rooted me into my chair and I drifted into that Thanksgiving kind of feeling—sated— a little too full and a little too played out. Candlelight reflected on the tall windows, flickering, hypnotic. The room receded.

"…Jade are you listening?"

" Hmm? Oh, sorry. What did you say?"

"Are you falling asleep on me?"

"No, enjoying the dinner, that's all. So, what don't I know about Polo and Rodriguez? Which cartel does Rodriguez belong to?"

"Rodriguez is a player in the Beltran-Leyva Organization, a splinter from the Sinaloa federation. He inherited much of Zihuatanejo from his family, but he doesn't have a strong local organization. He wants Polo's action and Polo's holdings."

"I gathered that. What does this have to do with you?"

"I want Polo's action."

The sharp tone in Anibal's voice unsettled me. "Say what?"

He leaned toward me across the table and lowered his voice, "I'm not into drug trafficking. We think Polo is a capo of the Sinaloa group, one of the most ruthless and violent drug cartels in Mexico. I'm undercover on a joint task force between the DEA and AFI to take it down. I teamed with Zocer. Lura didn't know. She was a perfect foil. She believed that I work for a think tank. She thought she taught me to shoot— *Dios*, I miss her," he said, his eyes clouded over, looking like rain.

I reached for his arm. "Don't think about her, Ani. Give it some time."

"We don't have time. I was assigned to Mexico because of my family connections, but you well know I'm not the favored brother. I need you to get me into Polo's inner circle."

"Me? Good lord, Anibal, Polo blames me for Lura's death. How can I possibly weasel my way into his confidence? And if you wanted me to find out what he's up to, then why drag me out of the party?"

"That guy Santos who came in? He's an enforcer. His mother's brother is Manuel Torres Felix, a high-ranking lieutenant in the Sinaloa Cartel. He suspects I'm law enforcement."

"I read about that cartel. All the more reason to play the loving family member, don't you think? Why is he hanging around Lidia?"

Anibal tossed a wad of *pesos* onto the check and pushed away from the table.

"*Vámonos.*"

I hesitated. Was Anibal asking me to infiltrate a drug cartel to spy? I would have to think about this.

Outside, the crisp night air smelled cleaner than during the day. The quiet residential streets had a magical glow about them. Condesa felt more like a forest than a city. A forest jammed with cars along every inch of curb and a constant low din that reminded me of beehives. I stumbled over uneven paving and took Anibal's arm; he clasped my elbow protectively. I wanted to ask a million questions, but my brain had had enough, and we strolled the several blocks back to his house in silence with a comfortable intimacy. I'd forgotten that sense of ease and well-being that comes when you're secure with your place in the world. I hadn't felt that often in my life, and not with Dex for a long time. I didn't know what would come of Anibal and me, but I agreed—Lura's death shouldn't go unpunished.

CHAPTER SIX

Bulletproof Couture

Thursday, August 9, 2007

I clunked my clay mug of too hot café de olla onto the table and reached for a concha from the napkin-lined basket in front of me, then broke off a piece, and dunked it into the strong, sweet coffee before shoving it into my mouth.

"We're going where?" I asked, after swallowing the sweet bread.

"I told you. Miguel Caballero in Polanco—near Polo's condo," Anibal answered. "You need some protective clothing."

"What do you mean—like a gas mask to protect me from the air? Is it going to be this smoggy all day?"

"Welcome to the morning commute. It's even worse in the winter when the thermal inversions hold the crap down, but it will start to lift—" he glanced at the clock on the stove — "in another hour as traffic dies down and the day heats up, but Mexico is in a bowl and there's nowhere for it to go —it's one of the big problems here."

It was already ten. I'd slept in late, tired from the emotional strain of the last week. "Rush hour lasts until eleven?"

"Well, actually all day, but it's heaviest between seven and ten. Then it all happens again between two and five, and there's a mini-rush between seven and nine when the people who actually went back to work after their comida go home."

"How can anyone live in this?" I waved my hand toward the sooty window and the visible air beyond. If the patches of sky I could see peeking between buildings and treetops showed blue, I'd believe I sat in a kitchen in Europe, except that the oily-bad stink of the smog permeated everything here.

"People either love Mexico or hate it, but whatever your feeling, you can't deny it's an exciting place. You'll like Polanco. Great shopping, if you have the cash."

"You didn't answer my question, Anì. So who's Miguel Caballero?" I blew across my mug of coffee— too hot to drink. "Which cartel does he run with?"

"Not a he—a what. The store is named after the owner, a Colombian who made his first fortune in Bogotá dressing government officials when the Medellin and Cali cartels were killing everyone. Now he's got branches here, Guatemala and Johannesburg—he's probably opening a branch in Baghdad right now. You know, hot couture for the hot zones. I saw the Caballero line in Harrod's catalog recently. Look—" He jumped up from the table and disappeared through a door, returning moments later with a tuxedo and pants carefully draped over hangers.

"Okay, now you've really confused me. Why would I need formal wear?"

"No, Jade, it's bulletproof. Feel the jacket." He held the hanger out to me and I ran the fabric through my fingers. The jacket was smooth to the touch like fine wool gabardine, but thicker and stiff, lacking the suppleness and drape of fine wool or cashmere. I pictured a room full of men with shoulders that looked as though they'd been botoxed, socializing with their frozen-faced wives. Now that sounded charming.

"I've got a bulletproof tux shirt too—certified for a 9mm like Lura's Glock." Anibal sucked in a sharp breath with his mention of Lura, but he controlled his voice and continued, "And even a mini-Uzi—a lot of *los narcos* like the little semi-automatics for around town. I'm going to buy a couple of casual pieces today. He's got polo shirts and a hip military-looking jacket."

"Give me a break, Anibal! You're into Kevlar? I heard of rubber fetishes, but—"

"No, it's a special fabric Caballero created that actually is rated for efficacy by the National Institute of Justice. The guy won awards for his stuff. I heard the Sinaloa boss, El Chapo, ordered bedding from Caballero, but that's just a rumor."

I laughed. Bulletproof bedding? "So what am I supposed to wear?"

"Bulletproof lingerie." Anibal said, a leer spreading across his face.

"You're kinky." I tried to scowl, but giggled anyway.

"So what's the problem?"

I laughed again and it felt good. The weight of life eased off my shoulders and for the first time since Dex left me, I felt like myself—just for a moment, but that was enough to remind me that how we feel is a choice, not a circumstance. My sister once told me to paint a picture of the life I wanted, then step into it. So I'd better get out my paint box, because moping around and feeling abandoned wasn't cutting it.

A buzzer rasped loudly from the direction of the pantry, and Pepper lumbered to his feet from under the table, ears raised and head cocked.

"Señora Pérez is back from the market," Anibal said when I turned to investigate. There was an old fashioned bell panel for the maid by the pantry door. One position lit up as the bell buzzed a second time. "I'll help her carry the food up."

Pepper took advantage of the open door and bounded down the stairs with Anibal. He hadn't been out yet.

"Don't let him into the street," I yelled after them.

Bulletproof evening wear, I mused. What'll they think of next? I watched shifting rays of sunlight play across the brightly painted wooden breakfast table. The old-fashioned kitchen, along with the servant's quarters, occupied much of the second floor of the refurbished building. Anibal's Colonia Condesa gave off the air of stability, duration, and decaying gentility. It was so quiet, if the guidebook hadn't said so, I'd never guess I was in the world's tenth largest megalopolis with over twenty-two million residents.

The setting was deceptively pleasant. I wanted to sit outside in the sun on the beautiful tiled balcony enclosed by wrought iron railings. The balcony housed a brilliant display of flowers and yellow-blooming succulents, ferns, purple princess trees, and orange honeysuckle vines all spilling from old *cazuelas* and Talavera flowerpots. Unfortunately, only the honeybees bobbing in and out of the flowers could tolerate the pollution. The yellow miasma hovered in the leafy canopy, shading much of the block, and it clung to the mix of 19th century, art deco, and mid-century style buildings, leaving a greasy dark stain across everything that wasn't freshly washed or painted.

Footsteps clumping up the narrow wooden stairs from the street door interrupted my reverie. Anibal slammed into the kitchen laden with Superama shopping bags, which he dumped on the floor by the refrigerator. Señora Pérez, a stout, middle-aged woman with a short-cropped coiffeur dyed an unnatural red, huffed in behind him. She wore the typical pinafore-style *bata* of the housewife covering her polyester blouse and skirt, and she hefted two green plaid plastic baskets bulging with food and fresh flowers. I caught the scent of hot tortillas and my stomach growled.

"Señora, this is my guest, Señorita Stone. She'll be staying in the guest room for the next few weeks," Anibal said in Spanish to his housekeeper. She looked at me with a guarded set to her mouth, but replied to Anibal as he moved toward the table where I still sat.

"Sí, *señor*."

"Jade, this is Señora Pérez. She'll help you with anything you need while you're here," Anibal continued without acknowledging her acquiescence.

His thoughtless manner toward the woman surprised me. I made a mental note to ask about the relationship. Perhaps she was another of his dysfunctional family, or maybe it had something to do with the established protocols between servants and served—something I knew little about.

"Thanks, Anibal," I said, then to the woman, "*Muchas gracias, Señora Pérez. Mi perro se llama Pepper y espero que* we aren't much trouble." I smiled warmly. She responded with a grin and began to unpack and stow the groceries.

Anibal snatched his mug off the table and refilled it. "More coffee, Jade?"

"Actually, I'm a bit jittery from the caffeine and sugar. May I have some of that papaya?" The housekeeper had retrieved a huge fruit that smelled sweetly ripe from one of her bags.

"Señora, cut some papaya for the señorita," he said, then in English, "I've got some work to do. *Mi casa es tu casa.* Help yourself to whatever you want. We'll leave for Polanco in an hour."

He left the room and I got up to prepare my fruit. The housekeeper had enough to do without adding my breakfast, and she smiled appreciatively when I motioned her away from the task. I cut off a section, scraped the glossy black seeds into the garbage, found a strawberry yogurt in the fridge, and made up a plate. Pepper woofed from the garden, reminding me he needed to be fed. I filled his bowl and ran downstairs to the garden door to let him in.

"Come on Peppi, race you up!"

I slammed the door shut and we thundered up, Pepper, of course, the winner.

Señora Pérez had vanished—probably in fear of the dog. Pepper went straight to his bowl and I to my fruit. When we finished, we trudged up two fights to our suite on the fourth floor for the exercise. It was time to get ready to buy bulletproof clothing.

"*Desculpe, señorita*," a soft voice followed her gentle knock on my door. "Señor Anibal is waiting for you at his car."

"Is that you, Señora Pérez? Just a minute, I'll be right there." I rushed to find my shoes, purse, and the leash. My things scattered across the sitting room where I'd tossed them when Anibal showed me to my quarters the night before. I'd been anxious to change and eat, planning to settle in after dinner. But his revelations and the scuttlebutt on his investigation into Polo's cartel delivered over Kahlua in his comfortable living room distracted me and I'd neglected my housekeeping before dropping into my very comfortable bed. Now I couldn't find anything.

The knock sounded again and moments later, I heard beeping coming from the street, and looked out the window. Below, Anibal leaned through the front window of a black Mini Cooper double-parked in front of the house and blasted the horn.

"Coming," I yelled out the window. He looked up with one of those clichéd expressions men reserve for women. "I'm coming," I repeated.

When I opened my door, the housekeeper was, once again, gone, but the door to the elevator stood open at the end of the hall. Mrs. Pérez was certainly a spook, I thought as Pepper and I got in and pushed the button marked PB: *planta baja*—bottom floor. The elevator groaned and swayed and clanked its way down the shaft. I hoped Anibal had it inspected and serviced every year. I'd hate to be in it when the cable broke, and it sure sounded like it was in its death throes. But we landed safely. I pulled the squeaking gate open and stepped into the tacky foyer across from the front door.

Anibal rose from an upholstered bench next to the door. "It's about time. What've you been doing up there?"

"Getting showered and dressed. Is that what you're wearing?"

He had on faded black jeans with a ratty t-shirt that said "From 0 to nasty in 7.5 seconds" and expensive-looking German mocs. In contrast, I had put on a short flowered skirt, a white tank appliquéd with lace, and my sexy sandals for our trip to the up-market shopping district.

"What's the matter with my clothes? You look pretty." He eyed my roomy bag suspiciously. "You're not carrying, are you?"

"Should I be?"

"No. They frown on guns in Miguel Caballero," he said as he locked the door behind us.

"But Pepper can come, right?"

Anibal looked at the dog obediently waiting at the car, leash in mouth. "We'll see. Get in." He handed me into the passenger seat once Pepper was settled in the back, and closed my door.

A water delivery truck came up behind the Mini and honked. The driver got out of the cab and yelled something at Anibal before hauling one of the big bottles out of the rack. Anibal jumped in behind the wheel, laughing, and started the motor. We roared off down the tree-lined street.

Avenida Presidente Masaryk, the main street through the shopping district of Polanco, was tree-shaded and noisy, congested with expensive cars, SUVs, taxis, delivery trucks, and the boxy *peseros* that transport the working classes around the city for *pesos*. All crawling through the grid spewing exhaust. All honking, vying for the same postage-stamp sized parking spaces. Trains of Mercedes and limos triple-parked in front of Casa Vieja, blocking the street, while their owners took a leisurely lunch. Chauffeurs chatted in groups or caressed a gleam onto the hoods of their charges with blackened rags. Ani inched the Mini toward Manuel Caballero, and I gawked at the glitzy stores and the beautiful, well-dressed people.

"Where are the Mexicans?"

"These are the Mexicans," Ani said.

"No, the fat little ladies with aprons and plastic shopping bags."

"Not here. This is Polanco. Masaryk is called the Rodeo Drive of Latin America."

"Look Ani, Roche Bubois, Etro, wow! Let's shop after Miguel Caballero. Where is that, anyway?"

"Aristotoles—there." He pointed to the next street on the left. "Traffic is always bad here because of the restaurant. Keep on the lookout for parking."

Oncoming traffic broke. Ani maneuvered us around the corner into Aristoteles. The atmosphere changed. The street was narrow and made more so by the cars parked everywhere. We pulled up in front of number 92. A valet hurried to help us out. Anibal waved him away. "This is it. Get the dog and wait for me, I'll park."

Pepper strained to get over the seat. I flipped it forward for him and he tumbled out onto the shaded pavement. The valet backed away from the grinning dog as I sprang after him to clip the leash onto his harness.

"Shut the doors!" Anibal yelled after me, but the valet sprang into action before I could respond, and I heard the tinny thack of the passenger door slam, then the grumble of low gear as Ani pulled into traffic. Straightening up, I noticed the valet sidling toward me. What did he want?

"*Gracias*," I said, and smiled.

"*Por nada*." He smiled back, but didn't move.

Pepper and I headed toward a building with blue awnings and matching Miguel Caballero sign. The valet followed after me, keeping an arms-length from Pepper. Ah, that was it, a tip. I wondered how much you gave for closing a door. Change jingled in my pocket and I fished a ten-*peso* coin out, tossing it to the man. He grinned and hustled to the front door of the clothing store, holding it wide.

"*No gracias*, we're waiting for *el señor*," I said, and turned toward the display windows. Each of the side windows sported an armless male torso wearing jackets or shirts. In the first, the mannequin modeled a handsome suede chestnut and saddle-colored jacket cut to look like western wear, in front of a blow-up of horses. The next showed a smart black leather model that would fit in at any Polanco restaurant. The third displayed a red-hot parka against a photo of vertical cliffs—not what I'd expect to see anyone wearing here. The last window advertised a white *guayabera* style shirt, a baby-blue polo shirt, and a pin-tucked tuxedo shirt, complete with pearl cufflinks. The clothes looked well made, and not really all that special, but this stuff was supposed to stop a bullet, or a spray of bullets. I wondered why more of the drug people didn't wear bulletproof clothing. Or maybe they did.

I moved around the corner to check out the front windows. A couple of posters presented more of the elegant country living, with horses and women in puff vests and leather jackets. What on earth did Anibal think I'd be buying here? I hardly needed a bright red vest. Or maybe I could paint a bull's-eye on it to make me easier to find, if anyone wanted to find me. I'd listened to Ani's story, but it was almost too far-fetched to believe. A little voice in the back of my mind nagged: was Anibal's hatred of his half-brother clouding his judgment? After all, Polo was a senator. But beyond Anibal's motivation, I thought, what was mine?

"You coming in, Jade?"

I jumped as Anibal interrupted my thoughts. He took the leash from my hand and gave me a quizzical look, then guided me to the street entrance.

We were greeted by a locked door. Anibal slid a card through the reader and the door clicked open to a brightly lit hallway with a uniformed guard at the end of it.

"An armed guard?" I asked.

Ani lowered his voice to a whisper "Miguel Caballero claims to discourage *el narco*, although I don't know how they do that. Most of the police and much of the government in this country are working for the cartels, anyway."

"They don't mind if Pepper comes in?" I asked again, turning side to side to see the advertising posters lining the walls. More of those horsey folks.

"*Pues, no sé.* We'll find out. Maybe they'll have a vest for him, too."

"You're kidding, right?"

"*Buenas tardes, señor, señora,*" the guard said, eyeing Pepper. He held his arm out to stop us and pointed at the dog. "*¿Muerde?*"

Pepper growled.

The guard trained his revolver on Pepper. "Halt! Raise your hands into the air!" the guard ordered in a voice that scared me. I dropped the leash and my purse and threw my hands over my head.

A side door banged open and two more vested guards, weapons drawn, poured into the vestibule.

"*No muerde. ¡No muerde!*" Anibal shouted. "The dog doesn't bite."

All the weapons lowered and the two back-up guards melted back into the wall.

"Your things, Madam," the guard said as he handed me the leash and my purse. He opened the door and Anibal yanked me through into an upscale, attractive showroom. Immediately two sales clerks came to attend to us: a man and a young woman. I recognized the clothing they wore as Miguel Caballero products and asked in English, "Ani, do you suppose these people aren't safe working here?"

He shrugged and replied, "Probably not."

"How may we be of service to you señor?" the sales clerk asked.

"I'm interested in that suede jacket." He pointed to a mannequin on the far wall. "And the señorita wants to look at some jackets, too. What else do you have for women?"

"If you will come with me, please," the young sales clerk said. "*¿No muerde el perro?*"

"No, Pepper doesn't bite," I said, and returned the collar to his neck.

"Okay. Soy Jazmín, *para servirle*. Come this way." Jazmín led me to the back corner of the showroom where a few garments for women hung on racks. "You about size six, *sí?*"

The girl wanted to practice her English. Was it that obvious I was American? Anibal's salesman was speaking Spanish. I could hear them discussing the slightly boxy cut of the suede jacket and how satisfactorily it concealed a weapon. Was that the cut I'd get? Great. Boxy—one of my best looks.

"Here, señora," the girl said, handing me a quite stylish cropped jacket in buttery black leather. "This one good for restaurant."

"Restaurant?"

"You no be standing up."

I got it. The jacket protected my chest and the table would protect the rest of me. "I need something longer. Like that." I pointed to a blow-up on the wall of a model and her horse in a tanned western cut blazer. The horsey crowd was never my "thing," but neither was the narco crowd.

She handed me a size eight jacket. I could store my entire arsenal, if I had an arsenal, under there. The tiny Semmerling didn't need such an elaborate holster.

"Hmmm, no thanks." I handed it back. "What else is there? Something that fits a little better."

"I show you."

She went to another rack, pushed through the clothing, scraping the hangers as she flipped past jacket after jacket until she found one she liked. The soft, low hip-length leather draped beautifully, the collar pulled up high under my chin and it fit like a glove. I cinched the attached belt and gave myself a bit of figure. And I could carry my gun with no problem in the deep pockets sewn into the seams. The only bit I didn't like was the lining. Although, satin-lined, the batting felt stiff, something akin to the fabric used for heater vent filters.

"You like? It rated for mini-Uzi 9mm."

"That's why it feels stiff?" I admired my reflection in a long mirror.

"Yes. I take to *cajero*."

"Wait. How much is it?" I asked and shrugged the jacket off to check for the price. No tag. I glanced around the racks. None of the garments had tags.

"Don't worry about it, Jade. I've got an account. That looked great on you," Anibal said, and nodded to the salesgirl who took the jacket from me. "*También señorita*, the *señora* also needs a vest. High rating."

Jazmín scurried off with the jacket and returned with a tape measure and told me to hold my arms up. She took measurements, bust, shoulder to waist, under arms to waist, my waist circumference. I was unhappily surprised to see that my waist had expanded. Beans and tortillas. I'd better watch it.

"How long will it take to get the vest?" Anibal asked. "We need it right away."

"*Ahorita. Esta tarde.*" This afternoon. I wagered that meant three days minimum. In Mexico, I'd learned, *ahorita* meant anything from "I don't know" to "I'm putting you off because I can." It never translated to "right away" even if that's what the word was supposed to mean.

"Jade, you should get that first jacket, too. It would look great with a pair of tight jeans. And shoes. You're in the city; you'll have to dress the part." He gave me the once-over, frowning. "We'll check out Kulte, maybe Melba. Señorita, get the little jacket," he added.

Jazmín grinned. She was going to make a fat commission off me, I guessed, and while we spent an undisclosed fortune, why not protect Pepper? 1

"Can you folks make a vest for my dog?"

"That's a special order, Jade. I've already taken care of it. A tailor will come by the house later to measure him. We'll have it tomorrow."

Amazing. I'd been kidding. "Peppi! You're going to be bulletproof!"

Pepper grinned.

CHAPTER SEVEN

Fifteen Love

Brow furrowed, the guard assessed me through narrowed eyes. The frown suggested I was in the category of the potato bugs that occasionally dropped down from the skylight in the hall between my sister's and my bedrooms growing up in Mill Valley.

"Yes, JadeAnne Stone. S-T-O-N-E. I told you, I'm here to visit Senator Aguirre."

"*Espérense.*" The burly man punched a button on his Nextel and turned his back. From his tone, I surmised that he did not reach Aguirre directly. He spoke machine-gun rapid Spanish in a snide tone and once glanced back at me, running his eyes up and down my body until he realized I was watching him and turned away quickly. But not before I saw his look of disgust. What was wrong with me? I thought I looked pretty good, and if not good, expensive. My new jeans, low-rise indigo wash with silver studs, molded to my body and looked great with the little cropped jacket from Miguel Caballero and black patent pumps that were killing my beach-spread feet. I fished for my ID in the oversized leather bag Anibal insisted I buy. Señor-Thinks-Too-Much-Of-Himself barely gave it a glance—I could have pulled a mini-Uzi out, but maybe he was daring me to let him try out his bulletproof vest. Does everyone in this city wear protective clothing? Other than the vest, he wore jeans and a blue oxford-style shirt with a name tag that read "Horacio."

None of this indicated why he thought so poorly of me. I was buried under dozens of brightly colored blooms, a sort of Walking Wood of Polanco. Perhaps he didn't like flowers. That must have been it; he thought I was concealing the Uzi under my condolence gift for Aguirre. So frisk me, asshole. If the condo association could panel its two-story lobby and entryway in mahogany, surely it could afford a metal detector wand.

Sure enough, his phone tooted, he grunted into it and pulled the wand from behind his counter and waved it over me like a demented fairy godmother—of the Shrek variety. The wand started to sing as he ran it over my pockets. Maybe all the studs attached to my jeans were a mistake? No way was I going to take off my pants. But the ogre reset his wand to stop the whine and motioned for the bag. I tossed it in front of him and he carelessly dumped it out, turning quite red when he found the lingerie and feminine products Anibal slipped in. I smiled and shrugged. Shrek aimed his thumb at the middle elevator.

I got in and realized I didn't know what floor Polo's condo was on.

"Hey, Horacio, what floor?" I called back to the guard.

He sneered at me again and said, "Push the button." There only was one button. I heard his, *"Pinche gabacha..."* as the door slid closed. Ah, just didn't like Americans.

In a moment I landed, and, like the penthouse at Hotel Kristal, the door opened to a beautifully appointed vestibule, rich with art and antiquities—and Shrek 2, who motioned me to step out of the elevator. These guys must be twins. This one wore a nametag that read Omar, and was whispering into his Nextel. He pointed to a spindly chair and told me to sit down, "The senator will be with you shortly."

I sat.

Perfume and pollen wafted from my bouquets. These weren't any hothouse dahlias and marigolds, but real field grown flowers, and by the time Polo's assistant came for me, my eyes were itching and my nose ran.

"Good afternoon, Miss Stone. My name is Señora Arias de Barrera," she said, in slightly British accented English and extended her manicured hand. I reached to shake but sneezed ferociously instead. A tissue appeared and the woman handed it to me.

"The senator will see you now. Please come this way."

"Thank you, señora," I croaked and followed her into Polo's spacious living room.

Señora Arias de Barrera gestured toward the sofa and said, "Please make yourself comfortable. The senator will be with you in a moment. Why don't I put your lovely flowers in a vase?"

I sneezed again and handed over the stinky weeds. Señora Arias de Barrera glided out of the room, her diminutive size made smaller by the bundle of flowers. My eyes stopped watering.

The room mimicked the layout of Aguirre's living room in Michoacán but for the east-facing floor to ceiling windows. Impressive. The condo even boasted a huge fireplace—large enough to roast a pig. Of course, the tables were scattered with the little copper figurines Aguirre loved. Why did those old indigenous folk make so many of them?

I moved to the windows and gazed across the small balcony at the expanse of Mexico City, stretching far into the distance. The snowcapped peaks of Popocatepetl and Iztaccíhuatl rose above the yellow-washed landscape. Most of the city lay flat, low and rectangular. Here and there, a pod of tall buildings jutted above the cement and rebar sea like orbiting downtowns spun off the main center. And everywhere ,church spires poked into the dusty sky, beacons for the faithful. I could see what I thought was El Centro Histórico.

"The senator apologizes, Miss Stone. His phone call is taking longer than he anticipated," the soft voice announced. "May I offer you coffee or tea while you wait?" It was the woman again. Behind her, a young man dressed in a starched waiter's jacket wheeled a massive clay bowl arranged with the flowers I brought.

"Coffee would be lovely, señora. Thanks. You must work for Senator Aguirre," I said, hoping to start a conversation—the reason I'd come.

"Yes. I am his personal assistant. I manage his appointments and correspondence as well as his home while he resides in *La Capital*," she said, draping a brightly woven cloth across the baby-grand piano that dominated the far corner of the room.

"Your English is great. Did you study it here in the city?"

"*Sí*, to begin, but my family sent me to the United States for high school and I took a year abroad during university, in England."

The young man hefted the arrangement onto the piano and Señora Arias de Barrera sent him for my coffee. "Do you speak Spanish?"

I nodded. "In California, everybody speaks some Spanish. I studied, but I don't speak nearly as well as you do English. Did you make that arrangement? It's gorgeous."

"Thank you, señorita. Yes, I did. I enjoy flowers. Now, if you will excuse me, please, I have other responsibilities to attend." She smiled and slipped out of the room.

"Miss Stone, how kind of you to visit me. I hope the visit was your idea, not my half-brother's attempt to assuage his guilt for running you out of the gathering yesterday." He chuckled and settled himself into an easy chair drawn up to the end of the coffee table.

"Senator, you snuck up on me. Hello. Yes, I wanted to offer my condolences personally." Boy did he nail that. "The truth is, I ran Anibal out." I lowered my gaze and spoke in a hushed voice, "I felt awkward—it was a family time, but I want you to know how deeply sorry I am about everything. I wish there was something I could do. I brought some flowers." I gestured toward the piano and hoped I didn't sound too lame. I wasn't exactly sure what Anibal wanted me to do. Certainly I wasn't Aguirre's type and I'd never been much of a groupie. On the contrary, I'd always been on the fringes of things—a watcher.

"Miss Stone, I'm glad you've come. I wish to apologize to you for my unconscionable outburst that last time we met. I have regretted my words since. In fact, I considered visiting you at your hotel in Papanoa to set things right."

How had Aguirre known where I was?

He read my face. "Yes, I knew you went to Hotel Club Papanoa, Miss Stone, as did Rodriguez. Did you think an American woman, traveling in a *combi* with a trained German shepherd, would not be noticed?"

"I didn't really think about it, Senator," I lied. "What do you care about me, anyway?"

"I remain duty-bound by my agreement with Trouette to protect you, but out of respect for your privacy, I directed my people to keep their distance. I would prefer that you and your beast return to California. I am a busy man and have better things to do with my time than look after a headstrong woman poking her *nariz* into things that she shouldn't," he said and tapped the end of his nose.

"Senator Aguirre, I am truly sorry that Lura was killed. I brought you those flowers…" I gestured toward the piano, "and my condolences. That's all I've come for, and I don't want or need your protection. Please don't trouble yourself or your busy schedule any further."

I huffed at him as I unfolded myself from the comfortable sofa. How could I trust a man who accused me of causing Lura's death? I could see that this hair-brained idea wasn't going too far.

"No, don't get up. I can see myself out," I said acidly as he rose.

"Sit down." His voice was level, but firm.

I clutched my bag and started for the elevator. "Good bye. Senator Aguirre."

"Miss Stone, JadeAnne. Wait."

It wasn't an order for once, it was a plea. I turned back to him still clutching my bag to my chest.

"I was raised to be polite and show proper respect for people with titles, senator, but you alternate between lying to me, patronizing me, and bullying me, and I really just want to get away from you before I say something rude. Please, senator, let me go."

"You are right, Miss Stone. I have not treated you properly. I—"

"No, you haven't. Starting from just how you happened to kidnap me off the highway," I said. I was heating up under the collar and I knew I should bolt for the door. This couldn't turn out well. My jaw clenched and my knuckles blanched over the chocolate-colored leather. *Run*, my better judgment shouted. *Win his trust*, Anibal's voice whispered.

"May I serve you more coffee, señorita?" The white-jacketed waiter stood by the coffee table with a silver coffee pot poised over my half empty cup.

"Please, Chucho. And I would like a cup, also," Aguirre said.

"*Sí, jefe,*" he murmured and carefully filled my cup to just below the brim and wiped the spout with his towel. I didn't move and Aguirre didn't speak, both watching the young man as he gingerly set another cup and saucer onto the low table and filled it with steaming coffee.

"Cream and sugar, Miss?" His voice startled me, so intent I was on the process of pouring: the susurrus of the liquid falling into the cup and the bloom of rich coffee scent rising on the steam.

"Miss Stone, please take coffee with me and I shall try to be more forthcoming," Aguirre said. "May Chucho offer you cream or sugar?"

"Okay, senator. Sure. We'll have coffee and a chat." Win his trust, I reminded myself. Be polite. "Yes, I'd love some cream, thank you." I did my best to smile at the waiter, but my face felt more like a snarl. Oh well.

The sky outside the window was deepening from the bright haze of the sunny day to a golden color reflected from the slanted rays of the sun as it set beyond the western mountains. Pollution and all, it was a magnificent view. I sat down again in front of my coffee, releasing my purse to the floor with a thump.

"What floor are we on, Senator?" I broke the silence.

"You Americans will call it the 20th floor, although here it is the 19th. This is the penthouse. You are enjoying the view?"

"Yes. It's spectacular. You must enjoy your time here." *Déjà vous.* I had the same conversation with this guy at his Ixtapa penthouse. I never was very good at small talk. Hate it, in fact.

"Thank you for coming, JadeAnne. I may call you JadeAnne?"

I shrugged. Anibal was crazy. This wasn't going to work.

"When is the PEMEX vote?" This should be safe ground.

"We go back to session September 1st. We will discuss the issues and debate before the actual vote. The Legislative system in Mexico works in much the same way as yours. We are a Federal Republic. The privatization vote will take months to debate. We may not see a vote for a year or more. Perhaps not during Calderon's administration. The issue is heated and we both know that a deadly game has begun." He rubbed his forehead as though massaging a headache and rocked forward in his chair. "I will not allow my cousin's death to be in vain." He sat up and slammed his fist into his palm. "I swear on Lura's memory, I'll take that consortium down."

"How? If they're so high up in the U.S. government, just how do you propose to do it? Who are they anyway, besides Daniel Worthington who's dead?" Tip your hand, Aguirre.

"Wealthy American oil magnates, I imagine," he said and frowned. "I will know who they are, and as a legislator, JadeAnne, I'll defeat them across the debate platform. Mexico will do the right thing."

"Hmmmm." No hand tipping.

"You don't believe me. Do you think I will take my army of agricultural workers and invade Texas? Or perhaps I might have your president assassinated? Mark me, he will lose the next election."

"God, I hope so!" I blurted out and clapped my hand over my mouth. If George W. and his greedy puppet master, Cheney, won again, I'd move here. "Speaking of armies of agricultural workers, what is the government doing about all the emigrants to the U.S.? Besides providing them with booklets on how to survive."

"Mexico has programs to create jobs, training, funding for new businesses, better access to schooling. We do what we can, but we are still an emerging nation, that is how you say it, is it not?" He reached over and turned on the table lamp, which cast a halo around my head in the reflection in the window. He thought he was the righteous one here, but the lamp and I knew better.

"An emerging nation. That's an interesting term. Why do you think so many people want to leave Mexico?" I asked.

"People here are poor. They look north and see the United States, the fat neighbor who has everything, and our people want the same. Nice houses, cars, clothes, *celulares, computadoras.*"

"I shopped on Calle Masaryk today. You can't tell me there aren't rich people here. And with all the drugs, Mexico is wealthy."

"Organized crime is becoming our largest employer," he said.

Did I detect a hint of sadness in his voice? "I hear that people are running from the drug cartels—the violence. Do you really think Mexico is emerging? It seems more like the country is imploding. Get rid of the drugs and give your citizens honest jobs."

"My government is waging war on the drug cartels."

I laughed and shook my head. "And how does it expect to win this war when its senators are part of the problem? You gave me a tour of your farm. You traffic in marijuana." I mentally whacked myself upside the head. Me and my big mouth—this didn't sound like the path to friendship and trust.

"There are many things you don't understand. Americans are naïve. In life, nothing is how do you say, white and black. You saw my village, my school, the bananas and other crops. I employ workers. I pay living wages. I help students go to university."

"I did see your village and I saw your jail. Who was the man losing at dominoes? Why did a heroin producer blow up your cousin?"

"There are times when a man must do things he does not like in order to make change. You are a woman and don't have the same responsibilities or education."

"No, I'm not a politician or a marijuana grower, but I received a good education in critical thinking and from my point of view, that's a load of hogwash. And don't be such a chauvinist, senator. That's so yesterday. If women ran things, the world would be very different. Gentler. More efficient." I smiled.

"Where did you study?" he asked.

"Stanford. Just like my mother and father before me. Journalism. But don't change the subject."

A chime sounded from another room. I looked out the windows at the almost dark horizon. "Is it really seven-thirty? I better go." Aguirre stood and helped me to my feet.

"A warning, JadeAnne. Be careful. Things aren't always what they appear to be," he said as he steered me across the Persian carpet.

"Oh, like now you're wearing the white hat?" The man was a piece of work.

"The city has become a very dangerous place and my half-brother may not be the man he claims." Aguirre's tone hardened.

Was this a veiled threat?

We reached the elevator and Aguirre pressed the button. I looked up at him and sniped, "You're the brother who thinks he's going to save the world by growing pot."

"I am the brother who will bring change to my country," he said, softly.

"I don't want to be rude, senator, but I don't see it. Show me you want your country to take its place on the world stage—start by ripping out the pot plants and growing tomatoes. Organic heirloom tomatoes. You'll have a huge market in California."

He laughed. "I'll take that under advisement. Thank you for dropping in, JadeAnne. Give my regards to Anibal."

The door slid silently open on its track. I expected to see Shrek 1 or 2 hulking by the control panel, but the car was empty. I stepped inside.

"And thank you for your hospitality, Senator Aguirre." I pushed the down button and the door began to close, but I stuck my arm in the way and it opened again. "Say, how would you like to come to dinner tomorrow night? Say eight-thirty?"

"I would be delighted."

The elevator door closed and I started to go down. "Fifteen-love, Aguirre. My point."

CHAPTER EIGHT

Like a Ship on an Ocean

"Ani, is it safe to walk around here at night? Pepper's been cooped up too long." Pepper thumped his tail at the sound of his name, or was it his favorite word, walk? I reached under the kitchen table and scratched his ears.

"Wear your jacket. And stay out of the park," he grunted over his evening paper.

"Do you really think someone will come gunning for me? Or are you just saying that?" Did they have drive-bys in Condesa? How much did I really know about Mexico City? I knew about the taxi kidnappings, and was glad I had my own transportation, but I needed to go for a run.

"Jade, Polo knows you're here with the dog. He's not stupid, he'll figure out you're going to walk him." His coffee cup clinked into its saucer, empty. I followed his gaze to the stove. The French press appeared empty too.

"But he agreed to come to dinner tomorrow. We're patching up your relationship." I winked at him, smiling. "He can't shoot me before we eat."

"I'm still puzzled why you invited him." He looked at the stove again.

Was I supposed to make him coffee? I already buzzed

from caffeine. I better run it off now that the evening commute was done and the pollution had settled.

"We went over it, Anibal. What don't you understand? Someone had to be the bigger man and open the door to the possibility of healing the pain and resentment between you two. I'm that man." I grinned, but his pleasant expression soured.

"Don't worry, I'll cook—and clean up if you want."

He shook his head, but I saw the twinkle in his eye. "I hope your plan works."

"Yeah," I agreed, serious. "So do I. But if we're going to infiltrate, we've got to build trust. What better way than breaking bread?"

"Take the dog for a run and give me some time to make some bread."

Pepper was up like a shot when he heard the "R" word.

"Okay, buddy, let's go. Where's your leash?"

Pepper trotted to the stairs door and whined.

I pushed up from the table and yanked the door open. "Race ya!" I yelled and sprinted into the stairwell ahead of Pepper. This was a game we played. Pepper would give me a half flight handicap and then barrel up behind me—usually winning. I thundered up the carpeted risers, but a couple weeks of inactivity and restaurant meals got the best of me, and Pepper shut me down. I started to puff by the third floor landing. That was Anibal's floor, and I pondered why he hadn't showed me his suite when he gave me the house tour as I puffed up the last flight to my floor.

"Pepper, you win. These stairs are steep."

"Woof." Pepper plopped down in the hall and panted.

Yes, even he was winded. Blame the altitude. Ani said Condesa was over 7,000 feet, and I sure felt it now.

"Do we really want to go for a run?" I asked. Pepper nudged the closet open and pulled out one running shoe and dropped it at my feet. "I guess that's a yes?"

"Woof."

"How about a nightcap?" Anibal asked, when we rejoined him at the kitchen table.

"No thanks, just a glass of water."

Pepper lapped from his bowl, splashing water on the floor. Sra. Pérez was going to love that.

"Glasses over there," he waved vaguely in the direction of the pantry. "Use the bottled water. Always use bottled water in *La Capital*. The water is bad."

I opened a cabinet and found stacks of plates. All kinds from barro, the rustic low-fired clay, to brightly painted Talavera. I'd always wanted a set of Talavera dishes. I made a mental note to look for a lead-free, oven and microwave safe set while I stayed in Mexico.

"Next cabinet."

I sat down with my water. "Get a lot of work done?"

The French press steamed next to Ani's full cup and a spray of sugar crystals melted around a dirty spoon, otherwise no evidence of activity cluttered the space. Not even his Blackberry.

"I've been thinking." He pierced me with his coal black eyes.

I felt like a bug on a pin under that stare. "Shall I guess?"

He regarded me somewhat as Horacio had earlier. Did I have a big zit on my nose? I gulped a swallow of water and it went down the wrong pipe. I coughed. Anibal continued to inspect me. Darn, I couldn't think of anything witty to say and surprised myself with "And when I am pinned and wriggling on the wall, then how should I begin to spit out all the butt-ends...." His stare melted into incomprehension and I silently thanked T.S. Eliot. Another opportunity to put my expensive education to use. I must write home and tell Dad.

"So what were you thinking?" I prompted him.

"What we need to do. You may be right. We'll infiltrate socially. I hadn't thought of making friends."

"Then what did you want?"

"I-I thought you could go hang around in his office."

I squeaked, "And do what?" Deep breath, I ordered myself. I hate when I get excited—I get all squeaky. "Order his office supplies? Do his filing?"

"Jade, we need to get proof that he's affiliated with the Sinaloans, or controlled by El Chapo or whoever. We need to know who else is involved and we need to find out their plans. There's a safe house—maybe two. One might be in Coyoacan and Zocer thought the other might be in Tepoztlán. The cartel moves people, drugs, and arms through them. Zocer said they use one for meetings with all the lieutenants. He had intelligence, but..." Anibal's shoulders sagged and he slumped onto his elbows. "...well, I owe it to him. I was his partner, Jade. I let him down," he finished, voice cracking with emotion.

So that was it. He wasn't just devastated about Lura, but he felt guilty about Zocer. I bristled—Anibal had me pull into the barbacoa joint and spy on his partner. He lied to me. I flushed, angry. Could I be the bigger man in this situation? They had been partners, and now I was his partner and I wanted the same loyalty.

I took a deep breath, letting it out slowly, and steadied my voice. "Ani, I need to know the truth. Zocer—you knew who he was all along. How can I trust you?"

He exhaled a sharp blast of air and straightened up. His lips parted as though he were about to speak, but he remained silent. His eyes pleaded with me to understand him, and I leaned forward, wanting to, no—burning to—kiss him. I pushed back in my chair. What was I thinking?

"I'm sorry, Jade." He mumbled into his coffee cup. "What could I do? Lura didn't know either. She thought she'd teamed with him. But forget it, he's gone. And—"

"Let's just go forward. We're partners." I held out my hand.

"Should we spit first?" The twinkle was back in his eye and he let out a low chuckle as he spat into his palm.

I spat into mine and grabbed his hand. "And you have to say, 'cross my heart and hope to die, stick a needle in my eye' too."

"Partners, Jade. I've got your back, and you've got mine."

"Forever." We shook. He was so darned cute. I needed to go to my room before I made a fool out of myself. Partners, guarding each other's backs. Not what I envisioned.

"I'm tired, pardner. I'm going up. Come on, Pepper."

He smiled at me, but his eyes looked lost. "Good night JadeAnne. Sleep well."

A faint glow from the streetlamps filtered into my room —Anahí's room it turned out. Anibal started his life in this bed, I considered, settling into the fragrant sheets. I didn't know if I should feel honored or insulted he'd given me his mother's room. Well, the house and everything in it belonged to Anibal, Anahí died a long time ago. I shouldn't put too much weight on his choice of rooms for me. Anahí's bedroom was far nicer than the cramped servants quarters behind the laundry on the second floor and I didn't see any other guest rooms. I wondered again what his third floor was like.

Chop, chop, chop. Someone was chopping wood. Chop chop chop chop—Jade!

Jade? Chop, chop, chop. Someone wanted me to help chop the wood. Someone was out there and wanted me—I needed to wake up and chop the wood.

"Jade. It's me, Anibal." Tap, tap. "Jade, can I come in?"

Tap tap tap.

Pepper pounced onto the bed and nudged me with his cold nose.

"Huh? Wha—chop wood? What?" I swam up to consciousness and floated on the dark raft with my dog.

Tap-tap. "Jade, it's me."

Pepper whined and I came fully awake. Anibal! I padded to the door.

"What happened?" I asked, cracking it open, alarmed.

He pushed through, drew me to him without a word and kissed me sweetly. I kissed him back; I feasted on those plump lips—nibbling, licking, sucking on the spongy flesh until I'd made his mouth mine. I could feel his heart pounding, pacing me beat for beat, and it made me bold. I wanted this man. I wanted him now and again, and again.

He embraced me more urgently, so tightly I gasped, but he kissed me even deeper and danced me across the room, sinking us to Anahi's creaking bed. His lips never lost mine. I pulled away and kissed his face, his neck. He slid his hands under my camisole and caressed me softly, gently, like he was handling a newborn babe. His lips followed his hands, his tongue left hot trails of tingling along my chest and stomach. I felt electrified.

His hands caressed down my legs, up my thighs—kisses right behind. I felt my panties slide away, but I was floating on a rolling sea. I was a vessel on a running sea, rocking, tossing. A slick of sweat spread between our bodies and we slipped and slid into one another until we were face to face, breath to breath—one body pitched by the wild rhythm of the waves. I heard gasping and sea slapping against hull. We bucked and turned through the peaks and troughs. The wind of our breath howled.

"Come on, Jade. Baby, come on!"

His hands were everywhere at once, hauling the sheets, raising the sails; I heard inhuman mewling, the wind gone feral. The wind nipping, scratching, tearing at the sea—we, a single ship in a tsunami—the wave flooding us, washing us away.

Castaway onto shore of Anibal's chest, I wept, spent. Our thundering hearts slowed down and we nestled together, fitting our bodies around each other, and slept.

CHAPTER NINE

Fresh Baked Bread

Friday, August 10, 2007

Loud snorts woke me up. Deep in sleep, Pepper's chuffing saw normally soothed me, and I slept through his snores most of the time. But not this time. I opened my eyes to the watery morning light, and the unfamiliar horns trumpeting from a tangle of bedclothes on the other side of Anahí's big old bed. I eased out of the sheets and padded across the frayed carpet to the bathroom.

What had I done? I inspected my face in the mirror. Spots showed up on my face like grey cancers—the mercury flaking from the mirror back. This must have been an original fixture. Ani should update; my mind strayed from the conundrum before me. What—had—I—done? I'd ruined everything, probably. Never sleep with a co-worker, a friend, or a man you barely know—the cardinal rule, and now I'd broken it. What was he going to think of me? I'd flirted with him shamelessly in Ixtapa then pushed him away when my ex, Dex, showed up. I was back, hanging all over him after the explosion and then I ran away. Push-pull. Push-pull.

I'll just move on, back to biz, I told myself. I pretended

not to want more, admiring his angelic sleeping face from the bathroom doorway. Who was I kidding? I felt electric.

It was still early. I would slip out for exercise with Pepper. Let Anibal sleep. A jog and maybe coffee at one of the myriad coffee houses in Condesa would give me some time to think. Mull it over. Ani had given me a key the day before, and I figured that meant I could come and go as I pleased, and I liked that I could run in the park over on Avenida México just a few blocks away.

I'd stop in Superama and see what looked good for dinner. Aguirre was coming. I wanted to impress him with my famous Thai green curry with shrimp and vegetables. Maybe a pad Thai. If I could find ingredients. How do you ask for lemongrass in Spanish?

Pepper's tail beat against the bathroom door as I pulled it open, dripping into my towel. "Shhh, don't wake Anibal up." I put my finger to my lips as I shushed him. He grinned and woofed.

"He already did. Come'ere," Anibal said. He lunged toward me, grabbed my wrist and pulled me to him. I almost saw the sparks jump where he touched me, my heart flip-flopped. "*Buenas días, mi Reina*," he said, smiling. "Sleep well?"

My Queen. I liked the sound of that, even if I shouldn't.

"I did. You?" I leaned into him from the edge of the bed, and he drew me into his arms, kissing my neck, my shoulder, lips like a red-hot brand. Marking me. I felt my resolve to get back to business sliding away along with my bath towel.

"Ani…"

"*Sí, mi reina?*" He effortlessly flipped me over onto my back and pounced, tickling me in all my secret spots. Pepper jumped up on the bed and barked while I giggled hysterically and tried to tickle Anibal, but he pinned my wrists over my head and I ended up writhing in sweet agony, screaming with laughter.

"What's the matter, *Reina*? Can't talk?" He let go of my wrists and smothered my face with his mouth, kissing me deeply, sweetly, then rolled over and sat up. "I'm going down and grabbing a shower. We've got a big day. Gotta find that safe house."

"How are we doing that? I thought I'd go for a R-U-N, " I spelled, not wanting to excite my dog with the "R" word. Pepper jumped off the bed and bounced around, barking.

"He can spell. Smart dog."

"Okay, okay, Pepper, calm down. We'll go," I said to the dog. To Ani, "Your brother comes for dinner tonight. I thought I'd make Thai curry. Anywhere I can buy Thai ingredients?"

"Yeah," he said, drawing out the syllable, his smile turning to a frown. "I don't think that's such a good idea— Polo coming for dinner, but Thai food sounds great. You cook?" He forced a bright smile back to his face, but it was obvious he wasn't happy with the plan.

"Sure, when I'm inspired. He's already invited. I thought you wanted to reconcile your relationship. We talked about this last night."

His lips narrowed, turned down, and his eyes shone hard. "Not reconcile, Jade, and not here," he said in a flat tone.

"Why not here? What difference does it make?"

Anibal paused, head cocked to the side as though thinking, *yeah, what difference does it make*? then answered in a voice so hardened by hatred it sounded like bedrock grinding against itself as it rumbled up from deep inside him and filled the room. I clutched the sheet around me.

"He's scum."

His words sucked the air, sucked the life, out of us—a black vacuum. My travel alarm ticked over another minute and the room reappeared. Pepper yawned. I gasped, stunned.

Another minute clicked over in the silence.

"So, call in a *brujo* and give the house a *limpia* when he leaves," I quipped—my programmed reaction to intensity. More softly I added, "I have some white sage in the *combi*. It's blessed."

If he didn't smudge, I would. Anibal had loosed a demon into my bedroom. I felt tremors ripple through me. How could anyone hate so deeply? What had Aguirre done to Anibal? My mind flashed to my own family and my gut clenched. This went far beyond the resentment I held for my dead sister—my perfect dead sister. What was I getting myself into?

"Hey, ouch! Let go, Jade." Anibal yanked his arm out of my grasp. "It's okay. Relax. I'll call a witch doctor if you feel that strongly about it." He smiled and that ray of warm sun beamed over me. "Come on, let's get up. I need some coffee."

He picked up my towel and chucked it into a rumpled heap onto the bathroom floor. "Where are my sweats?"

He was a god, a David, and I relinquished the pants I fished out of the comforter with reluctance.

The morning was warm and smoggy. Pepper and I trotted around the lake in the park a couple of times. I got a kick out of the nymphs with their water jugs that flanked the clamshell-shaped bandstand. The weeds sprouting through the concrete testified to the abandoned nature of the Amazon-sized water bearers and their stage, but the tall trees and leaf-lined path made for pleasant exercise. After we ran, we cut over onto Amsterdam and I checked out the Superama. Pepper stood outside the door with a forlorn look on his face, his leash held in his mouth. Shoppers skirted past him, keeping as much distance from him as the narrow entry allowed.

As I suspected, we could buy fresh Pacific prawns, but we weren't going to find Thai ingredients. I bought a kilo of shelled prawns and a can of coconut milk. I'd figure something out. Ani said I could send Mrs. Pérez for anything I wanted. He'd actually said Mrs. Pérez could make dynamite *camarones a la diabla*, if I'd get the shrimp. And her tamales were Aguirre's favorites, as was her *arroz con leche* with a secret ingredient. She should know, Ani, emphasized—Señora Pérez was his aunt. Anahí's sister? For a family who hated each other, they sure stuck together. Like mine, I thought. Well, I supposed that if I wanted to impress Aguirre on behalf of Anibal, I'd do best to serve a meal he enjoyed. It sure would be easier to let someone else do the work. But how could anyone not like Thai food? I wondered as I turned the key in the street door.

"Polo can't come. He's got business," Anibal shouted when he heard me tromping up the stairs. Anibal's voice scoffed at the word business. "About what I expected..." he was muttering as I trudged through the door and dropped into the nearest chair at the table and spilled my packages across the red printed oilcloth and next to a neat stack of clothing boxes.

"The vests," he said, and nodded to the boxes.

"Already? That really was '*ahorita*' for once," I said.

Pepper was lapping water noisily from his bowl. I watched the drops fly.

"Peppi, you make such a mess," I said.

To Anibal, whose eyes scanned down a column of the morning *Universal*, I asked, "Did he say when he was free?" I didn't want him free. I wanted to pry into that "business."

"Actually, he invited us there. Eight o'clock," he said, sounding distracted. "Hey, listen to this..." He dropped the sweet roll he was about to bite into back onto the platter and gripped the newspaper with both fists. "Law enforcement agents detained five men and two women for questioning last night at a home in the elite Bosque de Pedregal district in the south of the capital. An informant identified the residence as a safe house for the Beltran-Leyva Organization (BLO). The BLO is reputed to be the second most vicious organized crime gang in Mexico. Veracruz based Zetas, the former paramilitary arm of the Gulf Cartel is the deadliest. AFI is launching a full investigation. No arrests have been made."

His mouth twisted. Not into a frown, but into something ugly and cold. The harsh gleam of triumph shone in his eyes.

He crumpled the paper onto the table, pushing up in the same motion. "Get your gun and your vest." His voice hardened, all humanity flown out of it, he said, "Right now —no nonsense."

I tensed; he scared me. Pepper growled low in his throat and moved to protect me as I stumbled out of my chair, still holding the mug of coffee I'd poured; his snarl a warning: stay back.

"Cool-it, dog," this stranger's voice commanded, and he lunged forward reaching toward me? Pepper?

"Stop it, Ani. You too, Pepper." Man and dog swung their heads up and glared at me. "What's the matter with you, Anibal?" I shrieked.

The high voltage tension dissipated from the air. The stranger slouched into the doorframe and it was Anibal once again. He hung his head. "Sorry. But what's with this dog? He was going to attack me."

"What did you expect? You threatened me then threatened him. Never lunge at my dog, Anibal," I warned him. "Who was that person you turned into?"

"Look, we're losing time," he said, his voice placating. "We've got to get there before AFI covers up the evidence. Or steals it. Hurry up. "

"Are you always this bossy?"

"When I'm team leader on an investigation. Meet me on the street in ten minutes. The dog stays here."

Fifteen minutes later a bread delivery truck pulled to the curb. The driver waved to Anibal, turned off the ignition and dove into the back, reappearing in the doorway with a tray of fresh bread. The white vehicle was boxy in the style of a UPS van, although smaller. It said PAN in red letters with a telephone number painted below a selection of loaves and a couple sprigs of wheat.

Anibal jumped onto the running board, shook hands with the man then stuffed a couple loaves into a shopping bag. "Jade, run up to the kitchen and bring Señora Pérez down with her purse."

"I thought we were in a hurry," I said, smiling past Anibal at the deliveryman.

Something didn't add up. The man had on a delivery uniform, but the pants were wrong.

"Yeah. When you come back, step ahead of her and into the back of the truck. I'll be waiting for you."

Mrs. Pérez waited just inside the entry, purse in hand. She drew me into the vestibule and shut the door.

"*Espérense, señorita.*" Seeing my incomprehension she added, "*Un momentito solamente*—just a moment."

We stood in the vestibule staring at each other until she said, "*Ya, vamos,*" and barreled out the front door, a battleship, her prow splitting the air. I scurried ahead a little tugboat, hopped up the step, and slipped into the truck's cargo hold.

Anibal sat on a bench bolted to the floor in front of a bewildering array of electronic gear. I recognized switches, wires and pliers, but the rest was a jumble. One side of the truck held floor-to-ceiling racks, presumably to hold trays of bread, but other than a few dozen loaves, the racks were filled with an assortment of gizmos, tools, weapons, boxes, containers, and I wasn't sure what all. Anibal now had on a white deliveryman uniform like the one worn by the driver, who was chatting with Mrs. Pérez about the fresh bread she bought. I perched on a seat just back from the door with a perfect view through the windshield and eavesdropped. A late model VW drove slowly past and parked. The woman driver got out, looked at the truck, waved hello to Mrs. Pérez, and let herself into a house two doors down.

Mrs. Pérez said, *"Gracias, joven,"* and sailed off down the street toward her friend's house, carrying her bread in a plaid shopping bag.

The delivery driver sat back into his seat, turned the key, eased the old truck into gear and pulled away from the curb.

"Jade, here, put on your uniform," Anibal shouted at me over the rumble of the engine and the truck's farty backfiring. I could barely hear him so I scooted over to his bench. Were the guns assault rifles? I recognized pistols with suppressors. Was I going to carry one of those?

"What is this, Ani? Surveillance equipment?"

"Yeah. Put on the uniform jacket. And the hat. Get your hair under it."

I slid my arms into the jacket he held out and buttoned it over my shirt. I wore my new Miguel Caballero vest under that. It chafed at my skin. Lura's Glock banged my ribs from inside the purse I'd slung on my shoulder while I tried to stuff my ponytail under the cap.

"So, is this an undercover operation?" I yelled into his ear.

He grinned. "Yeah. Slick, no?"

"Where'd the bread truck come from? The driver doesn't fool me. He's not a delivery guy."

"I'd tell you, but then I'd have to kill you. Let's just say there are agencies who are willing to loan out their assets for a good cause." Anibal's face took on a conspiratorial look and he wiggled his eyebrows.

The truck swerved and shuddered, farting like mad when a bus cut it off. I gripped Anibal's arm to steady myself, and coughed as a cloud of diesel exhaust billowed through the open passenger-side window. He hugged me to him and kissed my neck.

I raised my eyebrow. "Where's the bread come from?"

"Superama." He laughed.

I was grinning too, the excitement of the operation not quite pushing out of mind my misgivings over the earlier incident. Anibal's transformation in the kitchen scared me. He acted normal now, but what had that been about? Pepper had been ready to attack Anibal, and I was ready to have him as my boyfriend. Some sort of disconnect played out in my brain paths. I might be in over my head.

I stared out the windshield as acre after acre of graffiti-crusted, half-finished cement boxes flashed along the Periferico, one stacked on another.

"Tell me where we're going," I shouted.

"Bosques del Pedrigal. South on the slope of the volcano, Ajusco," he shouted back.

"To do what?"

The little Anibal was willing to say consisted mostly of an environmental impact study on the *mancha urbana*, urban sprawl of Mexico City. I didn't pay close attention until he said that the development was built amid lava flows. This I had to see.

The CIA agent, or so I presumed, steered the bread delivery truck through a portal into a residential neighborhood. I moved forward to see better. Marvelous modern homes sprouted out of dark swaths of volcanic rock. Some of the homes we passed were constructed from the same material. All appeared to be fortresses with their high walls, wrought iron gates, heavy wooden doors. How did Anibal expect to get into one of them? Duh, he's got a truck full of tools, I told myself.

"Is this Bosques del Pedrigal?" I asked.

Anibal had come up behind me and circled me in his arms. I didn't need to shout. The truck rumbled slowly through the streets and we could almost talk in normal voices.

"Yeah. In the early '70s it was a collection of squatters living in corrugated tin shacks," he said into my ear. "Ten years later, the *medio clase* took hold and turned it into an architect's dream community. But it's an area where you can fully see the disparity between classes. Look—" He pointed to a hovel crowded against the wall of a whitewashed Mediterranean style mansion. A ragged child and a skinny mutt crouched in the dirt in front of the door.

"I don't get how you can be so sure of this house," I said, looking up over my shoulder at him.

He replied right into my ear. "After the bomb—after Lura and Zocer..." his voice quavered, "died, I found Zocer's laptop in his car. I hacked his files. You were working it out with your ex—at the Krystal. I was there in the parking lot lifting his computer. I tried to catch you, but you just drove away."

We swayed around a corner onto what the sign said was Calle San Augustine.

"That's the house, Jade." He nodded toward a split-level that may have been carved out of the lava ahead on the left. Pockets of emerald green grass and stands of avocado, jacaranda, and giant crotons contrasted with the black rock. No more smelly exhaust, the air smelled of the pine forest that covered Ajusco. I took a deep breath, savoring the freshness.

"Are you sure?"

"Zocer described the house. Anyway, this is the address."

"It doesn't look like a drug house to me. It's pretty posh."

The driver continued beyond the house and pulled over in front of a neighboring property. He stopped the truck. The sudden quiet was a blessed relief even if I still vibrated, an after-effect of the uncomfortable ride. Birds twittered in boughs overhanging the high wall. It seemed a peaceful neighborhood.

The agent picked up his clipboard and appeared to read a delivery order.

Ani whispered, "Jade, Not a word. Just do what we say," and pulled me away from the opening.

In a beat, the agent joined us in back and gestured that I go up front. Me?

"Take the tray," he mouthed.

"Bread?" I asked, confused

"You'll see. Slide over into my seat, Miss, and look like you're checking your delivery."

He handed me a clipboard and a heavy metal tray, surprising because it was empty. I slid out to the driver's seat, lodging the tray onto the dashboard, inspected the clipboard and waited for instructions. Anibal followed me into the cab, carrying a larger tray of loaves and rolls in varying shapes and sizes, and topped by a cheap dishtowel. A mean looking revolver lay on the dishtowel in its holster. If I had bread delivery in Sausalito, it wouldn't come with a gun.

"Picnic lunch?" The bread smelled so good, it was all I could do to keep my hands off it.

"Can't have it. It's undercover bread. Or 'covering over' bread." He lifted the towel and I saw a mound of cigarette lighter-sized devices, pill-sized disks, lock picks, screwdrivers. I remembered Lura's sexy two-way radio and realized where it came from. Well, why wouldn't I believe the State Department outfitted its agents with state-of-the-art equipment? "Ani, don't we get little two-way radios like Lura had?"

"Of course. Here. Just push this button when you want to talk." Anibal adjusted his chestnut curls over a wire running from his ear under his jacket. "Ten-four, Mike. Loud and clear. Now, Jade, stuff some of these into your pockets," he said, handing me some of the gizmos. "Where's your gun?"

I gestured the clipboard toward the back. "In my purse."

The purse slid into the cab, a smear of dirt grinding into the light colored straw. Surely the DEA reimburses for cleaning?

"Be able to reach it fast," Ani said.

I put it into my waistband—a real cowgirl bandido.

Anibal took the clipboard and looked it over as he spoke. "Follow me. We're going to ring the front door and hope no one answers. If someone comes, you stand behind me and stay quiet. Look like an assistant. If nobody opens the door, hold up your tray and turn to face the truck. Like this." He demonstrated, holding my tray shield-like. "Take up as much space as you can and protect us. I'll pick the locks. When you hear the door open, lower the tray and carry it as though something were on it. Here." He tossed me the towel.

He'd pocketed the rest of the equipment from his tray while he talked. "If there's shooting, hit the floor and shoot back. Look, like this," he said and chambered a round. "Just this trigger." He wiggled his finger over the trigger.

I got the picture.

We climbed down out of the cab and crossed the street. My heart beat arrhythmically, skipping about every third beat, and the jitters in my gut morphed into swarming termites. What was I doing breaking and entering a known drug house? What if the police came? What if the Saint came? What if Polo Aguirre showed up? How would we explain what we were up to? And what if I had to actually fire the gun and kill someone?

CHAPTER TEN

How to Bug a Safe House

The heavy front door probably came from a church. At least the dousing of guilt felt the same as I marched across the threshold bearing the sacramental bread on a bulletproof shield. This B & E was far more audacious than fearless, and I, for one, quivered in terror. An army with guns could be waiting behind the massive door. My intrepid leader moved cautiously, gun ready. His shoes made faint plopping sounds against the stone-tiled floor and echoed up the bare vestibule walls. Bad *feng shui*, but possibly appropriate for a cartel safe house. The energy felt stagnant, like a swamp, something akin to wading in a murky bayou complete with crocodiles submerged just below my vision. I hoped one wouldn't surge forward and grasp me in its saw-toothed jaw.

Anibal checked every room and closet as we crept deeper into the house, Anibal slapping listening devices or tiny video cameras anywhere he could in the empty house. No wonder the neighbors were calling the police—or was it the neighbors? Who else would report illegal activity? Anyone could see in—there weren't even curtains on the windows. But why? Nothing to steal except maybe the bugs.

We circled the main floor. No gun totin' drug cowboys

jumped out at us. The garden outside was empty as was the pool. Anibal motioned for me to stand guard at the top of the stairs and handed me his little Uzi.

"Can you use it?" he said in a whisper.

"Pull this." I wiggled my index finger over the trigger. "And brace for the kick."

"Yeah. Keep down—over there." He pointed his chin at a shadow cast by the edge of a large wardrobe. The first piece of furniture we'd found in the house.

I tiptoed past him toward my post, but he halted me with his hand, raised his gun, and crept up to the wardrobe. I held my breath. We listened for a moment and he flung open the wooden doors. Nothing. I stood my watch and Ani disappeared through the first door in the hall.

The house buzzed and groaned. I identified the whirring of the refrigerator and the clunk-clunk-clunk of cubes cascading from the ice maker into the bucket. I heard the creak of weight on wooden flooring, but since this house was tiled throughout, I assumed I imagined it. Just like the sound of the heating system kicking in. So far, I hadn't seen a floor register in Mexico City, and guessed central heating wasn't a big item. What did people do when it got cold?

A bird called in the distance. Nothing moved in the house. No, wait—what was that thumping sound? And there, the creaking again. Yes, I could hear it thump-thump. Thump-thump. I stiffened; my stomach clenched. The creaking stopped. My hands shook. I stilled them and listened. Thump-thump. Thump-thump. I felt lightheaded. I swayed. Then the creaking again, an odd crick. Where was Anibal?

A door puffed open and Anibal poked out. "All clear," he mouthed.

My heart pounded and I motioned him over.

"I heard something. Thumping and a floor creaked."

"Could have heard me."

"No, unless you walked on wood floors."

He shook his head. "What do you mean, creaking?"

"You know, that crrrit critt sound of bones—" I stopped with the embarrassing realization that I'd been listening to my own bones in the silence.

"And the thumping—something like a heartbeat, right?" He stifled a laugh. "Always happens when it's this quiet."

My face and ears heated up. I was sure I turned deep scarlet. His grin widened and he winked.

"Come on, Red." He pointed up. "Roof."

We repeated the procedure. I stood watch at the top of the stairs and he explored the flat roof. It had several small cinderblock buildings constructed on it, containing the usual utilitarian items: the gas tank, the water reservoir, the air conditioning unit, electrical panels, etc. but the cement box closest to me was a bodega and I could see through a grimy window that it contained furniture and stored items. I was glad to be outside in the warm sun, even the pollution on the horizon looked inviting. The house gave me the creeps.

Anibal stepped into view and sent me the "all clear" sign. He led us back down the stairway in silence, his handgun drawn. When we reached the main level, he motioned me toward a door off the pantry. I hadn't noticed it on our earlier pass through the kitchen, but I was beginning to get the hang of this business.

I noticed, when I ran my fingers along a window ledge, that the house had been cleaned—dust free. In Mexico City, this was nigh impossible. The air pollution dropped particles onto everything all the time. Wash it clean and in ten minutes a thin film re-deposited across every surface. I figured this accounted for why so many people employed domestic help. The dusting never ended. For a nanosecond I was bowled over by homesickness—my Sarasvati moored at Varda Landing, the clean evening fog tumbling down Mt. Tam, its cotton threads raveling into scuds across the deep blue of the sky. I reached out to stroke Pepper—my anchor to life back home—before I remembered he waited in Condesa.

Ani motioned. I swung the little Uzi up toward the ceiling and grasped the handrail. The steps dropped steeply to another level, and these were wood. I stepped into the stairwell and sniffed. Damp, earthy air. A whiff of mold. Automotive oil. A garage. It was dark, too dark to see more than a shadow of Anibal's back as I peered ahead, but I followed the soft screak-screak of his footsteps down the stairs and bumped into him at the bottom. The dark enfolded us, and I lost my balance, thrusting out my arms to break my fall. I hit rock—rough, volcanic rock.

"It's a cave," I said in a voice barely audible to myself.

Ani's warm breath tickled my ear, "The house was built right into the lava flow. Hold on to me, I'll go first. I've got an LED light on my phone."

"Crazy, this is crazy. Let's go back."

"Jade, it's a garage—look. Here's the light panel." He flipped a couple of switches and the lights flooded on.

He was right. It was just a garage. An empty garage bigger than any I was familiar with. The six bays could hold a dozen cars, attested to by that many oil stains. The cement slab stretched back along the lava wall and narrowed into the shadows.

"It keeps going," I said, under my breath.

Anibal stopped short and put his finger to his lips. I held my breath. I heard it too. He pointed to another light panel near the passageway and we glided single file along the wall toward it. The sound continued, low, metallic, rhythmic. Then muffled thuds. A tattoo like an SOS. He flipped on the lights to the passageway and we saw a metal gate padlocked closed several meters into the tunnel at the terminus of a rail line. I hesitated. What if…?

"Come on. Someone's down there."

"No, Ani. Let's go back."

"Can't," he said. "Cover your ears." He shot open the lock and swung the gate wide. He was almost running, dragging me by my jacket sleeve. My shoes slapped the paving and the sound bounced along the rough stone walls as they closed in on us.

I gasped for breath. The space was too tight—no air. I needed air. "Really, I have to go back," I said in a gasp. Anibal pulled me forward into the dark.

The narrow tunnel twisted into the mountain and the lights shone farther apart. I slipped on the rail track and skidded to my knees. My throat tightened up a little more; I labored for breath. Anibal wrenched me to my feet and yanked me behind him. Faster, he moved faster into the rock. Another metal door—solid. We stopped.

My heart beat too hard and the darkness and dankness smothered me. White showers of light streamed in front of my eyes and my legs bucked.

Anibal caught me and slapped my face. I inhaled sharply, swallowing a deep gulp of the clammy air.

"Get a grip, JadeAnne," he said, his voice Gollum-like, distant.

"Claustrophobic—I'm claustrophobic!" I sucked in another breath.

The door felt like Zamboni'd ice—smooth and freezing. The strange noise tattooed behind it. Affixed to the rock, a lighted button shone red. Anibal hit it with his palm and the light turned green. I rasped another breath and slumped against the door. It gave way, letting me fall into darkness. My gun spun out of my hand and skidded across the floor, then silence. We froze, Anibal barely a silhouette in the doorway. He dropped beside me in the blackness and we lay still for several heartbeats.

A breeze rushed passed us into the tunnel—fresh air— and the sound of the ventilation system. And the metallic clanking, louder now, echoing around what I judged to be a cavern.

I grabbed Anibal's pant leg as he eased up to his feet, gun ready, and whispered, "Listen."

"I hear it."

It sounded like the theatrical production *Stomp* Dex and I saw but with many drummers. I pictured Dex taking charge, wished he were in the cavern. Protecting me.

"Find my gun," I said.

"I've got it. Get up and stay out of the light."

I scrambled to my feet using the wall as a crutch. The cavern illuminated—I'd hit the light switch. A huge cave spread out before us. Around the walls, shelving had been installed that stored crates and boxes, equipment, plastic sheeting, and containers of liquids. The odor of chlorine hung in the air near where I stood, and I noticed that some of the cartons claimed to hold muriatic acid, others sodium hydroxide.

Pallets marked TEDRAL 50 mg. INDIA stacked up one wall next to cartons of nasal inhalers and cases of rubber gloves and surgical masks, if I read the graphic correctly.

"What the—?"

"It's a meth lab," Anibal interrupted.

Down the middle of the cavern, a clutch of tables held bowls, beakers, and glassware. I gestured toward the work area.

"How many...how much...?" I wasn't even sure what to ask. This was way out of my league. Now and then a boat exploded on Richardson's Bay when a meth lab blew up, but I'd never seen it. I shivered. That beating metal irritated me. It sounded louder.

"I understand the ventilation system now. Jade, check out the rail system. ¡*Hijole*! this is a sophisticated operation."

"Where are the workers?" I asked, as we circled the lab, following the tracks.

"I don't know. Better question, why didn't the police find this yesterday?"

"Maybe they did."

"No way. This place would be smashed up and the stock would have been hauled out. Or there would be guards." He paused, staring absently at another metal door.

I glanced at the door. "Ani. A cell door." It had two grates—one at eye level and a lower, larger aperture—big enough for a food tray. I shoved the top grate open. The banging went ballistic.

CHAPTER ELEVEN

I Thought it was a Drug Cartel

The pounding metal on metal, sounded frantic, and now I could hear high-pitched screeches.

Ani drew his gun. "Try the door."

"It's electronic. Help me find the panel."

My heart thundered in my chest as I scanned the walls surrounding the metal door. Rock; nothing but rough rock. No wait—wires.

"Ani," I shouted, pointing to a thin black cord running a couple hundred feet into the shadowy recesses of the cavern from the door and disappearing behind an industrial shelving unit. I bolted to the unit and found a fuse box. Which switch?

"How do I know which switch?" I said.

Anibal called back to me, his voice eerie as it bounced off the rock, "Trial and error. Leave it alone; the noise stopped. I think it's a machine in there, cycling. Maybe the ventilation system. We don't want to turn that off."

"You're wrong." I felt it in my bones. "Try the grate again—it's what set them off before," I called back.

"Let go of it, Jade." His voice held a warning. I decided to ignore him and trotted back to the door, brushing him aside. I rattled the peep-gate and produced the shrill scree of metal grating on metal. The metallic banging started up again. I stood on my tiptoes and pressed my ear to the opening. Faintly, a harmonic counterpoint to the beat-less drumming, I heard human voices and spun around to face Anibal.

"It's people. Listen." I pulled him toward the aperture.

He leaned down and put his ear to the opening. The banging petered out. I sawed the narrow flat cover in its groove, the discordant squeal of a beginning violinist pierced the cavern, and sure enough, the pounding started again, louder.

"It's women—no, Dios, Dios!" Anibal stepped back, his hands thrown to his head, his voice a croak, "It's children."

A wave of nausea burned up my gullet and I tasted bile. "Kids?"

"Stand back, Jade, I'm going to shoot the door open."

I staggered into action. "No, Ani, too dangerous. Help me figure out which switch it is. I can follow it into the box. Come on." I grabbed his hand and tugged him toward the fuse box.

"We need a circuit tester. You can't figure it out without testing—or flipping all the switches."

"Look," I said and flung open the cover. "Here's the wire coming in. It's the only one like it."

The box looked old, industrial. It reminded me of a rat's nest, fibrous and matted together. Except for one new-looking black cord running into the box with the bundle of raveling, fiber covered wires, and snaking through the rows of terminals and breakers. "What happens if we flip the wrong switch?"

"Well, that's the question, isn't it, Jade."

"What could happen?" I probed the box with the eraser-end of a pencil I'd fished out of my purse. "What's this? Shine your LED here." I tapped the lip of the hinged cover.

He shined a concentrated beam of light into the cover.

"*Pues*, who would have expected it to be labeled?" He flipped the bottom left circuit breaker. A bare bulb mounted over the locked door shown green. The heavy door rumbled in its track as it opened. The banging and cries of voices were clearly audible as I ran toward them.

"Jade, stop. Stop. We have to clear the room. Follow me," he said, his gun ready.

I drew my Glock and followed Anibal into another cavern much smaller than the meth lab and illuminated with glaring florescent tubes. He crouched, and cautiously surveyed the room. No one was there, only the piercing din of metal pounded on metal. I couldn't bear the screams and yelling that radiated into the harsh-lit cave. This is what hell sounds like. I hurried past Anibal and racks of cardboard boxes toward a small slate colored door. I barely noticed the worktables arranged in the center of the room.

"Jade, look at all the money!"

I glanced around and saw a dozen tables covered with bound bundles of paper money and several machines that I guessed ordered the loose bills into stacks, since one had a hopper filled with U.S. bills. The king was in his counting house, counting all his money. Then it hit me. The stench. The caves had smelled musty and damp as we entered, but here, by the door, I smelled the stink of misery.

Anibal caught up to me. "Dios, what's that smell?" he yelled over the incessant clanging.

The air was heavy and thick in this part of the cave. The ventilation system must not reach this far into the tunnels.

"We've got to get them out. Hurry!" I tapped my gun against the door. The clanging stopped. I tapped again. "We're going to get you out of here."

Anibal shoved back the old fashioned bolt and, gun drawn, pushed open the door. A cloud of vile stench billowed over us. I stepped back and yanked my shirt over my face. If it sounded like Hell, then this must surely be the odor of

Hell: vomit, feces, urine, rotting food, dirty bodies, blood. I gagged and choked my breakfast back into my stomach.

Several naked bulbs dimly revealed a low cave about the size of my living room back on the Sarasvati, maybe twelve feet by twenty feet. The uneven rock floor held mattresses and jumbles of bedding and clothes and, in the midst of the tangle, cowered a couple dozen filthy children, now silent, squinting into the beam of Ani's flashlight. I threw up.

Twenty-four blackbirds baked in a pie. Their ages ranged from tiny—four, six? To near adult—fifteen or sixteen. I wasn't sure as the little ones hid behind the protective arms of several skinny, haunted-eyed girls. The prettiest of them, both girls and boys, were near naked in dirty shifts and briefs. The others, mostly girls, reminded me of the children I'd seen all over the city selling Chiclets or newspapers, washing windshields, begging. Dirty, tattered, and often wearing the satiny pinafores or plaid *batas* matching their mothers and grandmothers, also begging or selling trinkets or foodstuff on busy streets. But these kids also wore the dull expression of despair.

"That bastard. That sick bastard. I'll get him for this," my partner muttered, clenching and unclenching his fists.

My voice quavered. "Who are they? How did they end up here? I thought it was a drug cartel," I whispered to Anibal, who stood in the doorway, speechless. My blood thundered through my veins, pumping anger throughout me so forcefully that I was afraid I might fly apart. Ani thought Polo was involved in this—did he traffic in more than drugs? I'd never felt like killing anyone before, but I was staring at evil, and murder seemed too good for whomever left these kids here.

"We've got to get them out," I said.

"Jade, we're in real danger here. They won't just leave them, or the money. If someone flips that fuse—"

"Who are you?" I asked in Spanish.

Twenty-four pairs of eyes bored into me, but none of the kids spoke. Their fear palpitated in the heavy, oxygen starved air. I lowered my gun and Anibal followed suit. A collective sigh escaped from the group and they all began talking at once. When the pie was opened, the birds began to sing.

I heard Spanish, something Slavic sounding, an Asian dialect, and Oh my god! English, in a distinctly Californian accent. I turned toward the American accent. An older girl, blonde and shapely in her frilly nightie, clung to a budding, curly-topped ten or eleven-year-old girl in soiled panties and a thin camisole.

"What are you doing here? How did you get here?" I almost shrieked.

The girls cowered and the older girl mumbled, her nails digging into the soft flesh of the younger, "Help us, please."

I inhaled a deep breath of the foul air and forced myself to calm down. These kids needed help, not a hysterical woman scaring them more than they already were.

I looked at Anibal, who had made his way to the other side of the cave and squatted, cradling a tiny boy, and whispering to the knot of children surrounding him.

"We'll get you out of here and back home," I said.

But how were we going to do that?

Anibal got to his feet, still holding the child, and organized them into pairs, holding hands as though it were a school outing and the kids were going to cross the street. He took the hand of the oldest boy and they started the procession out of the cell. My pair watched wide-eyed.

"We're going home," I said, and took the girl's hand and guided us toward the line of kids snaking past the prison door.

"We don't have a home anymore," the girl whispered.

I squeezed her hand. "We'll find you one—a safe home. I promise," I said and glanced at her face. Tears created muddy runnels as they washed down her cheeks. The little one put her hand on the elder's cheek and rested her head on her shoulder, eyes blank. I realized they must be sisters.

"I'm JadeAnne. What's your name?" I whispered, as we brought up the rear of the silent file, passing the tables of money and stacking machines. I wanted to shout, "Take all you can carry!" but money would have been a sad compensation for the trials I imagined these kids had endured.

I barely heard the girl's response. "Lily. Evie, my sister."

"How'd you get to Mexico, Lily?"

The girl shrugged as we passed into the meth lab. "This is Mexico?"

Anibal halted the march and said something in rapid-fire Spanish. The kids turned away and covered their ears. Ani ran to the fuse box, flipped the switch to close the metal door to the counting room and let fly several rounds into the fuse box. The girls and I gripped our ears too, as the shots echoed throughout the cavern, growing quieter until silence.

Anibal trotted past me to the head of the line and moved us out.

"That'll slow them down. Let's get out of here," he said in English.

"The man, Mr. Lobo, he said he'd help us," Lily said, breaking the silence in the safe-house living room. The kids clung to one another, still in pairs.

Anibal spoke on his Nextel. "...money and kids. Yes, kids. We need a detachment...a bus, a chopper," Anibal said and lowered his voice.

"Mr. Lobo said I could be in the movies and...and ..." Lily trailed off, turned away from me, and gazed out the window over the swimming pool. This was difficult for her.

"Where was your mother?" Lily cast her eyes down and

clamped her jaw shut. "Lily..." I reached out to her, smoothed her matted hair. The set of her chin told me she wasn't saying anything more.

Evie spoke for the first time. "Our mom's boyfriend did things to us." Her voice, the resignation of a used up life.

"He hurt you?" The tear streaked faces in front of me colored under the bright afternoon glare in the curtain-less room.

"Mommy got a job at a restaurant and he had to take care of us at night. I hate him. I wish he was dead."

"Evie, shut up." Razor sharp, Lily's voice cut through the air.

So the bastard was molesting these girls. These kids weren't going to trust me just because I said so, I would have to earn it. The people who count the most had betrayed them. What was I going to do with them?

"Girls," I said, and extricated my hand from Lily's vise grip. She paled. "I'll be right back. You'll be able to see me —look, there's Anibal." She stared, a rigid cutout of a teenager, and watched me as I walked up the steps leading to the entry hall.

"Ani," I spoke in a low voice, "what're we going to do with them?"

"A team is coming. They'll be here on a few moments."

"Moments?" Why did it take us almost an hour to drive to the south of the city?

"Helicopter. The team will cover the kids as they get on board. They'll be taken into custody until this mess is sorted out and some agency claims the Mexican kids."

"Custody? Whose? What about the foreign kids? They need to go to their embassies."

"I really don't know, Jade. Let my superiors work it out."

"I don't even know who your *superiors* are. I can't just send these kids off to a new prison."

"No choice, woman. Get the line moving up the stairs," Anibal said.

My body tensed. My breath came shallow and ragged. How dare he order me around? "We're taking my girls with us," I said.

"What?"

I glared at him. "Yeah, Ani. We're taking them."

Anibal's ring-tone sounded. "Yeah...okay...we're moving."

I heard the unmistakable thwump-thwump of helicopter rotors beating the air and looked outside in time to see three transport helicopters sail overhead.

"Okay, kids, we're going to the roof," he called out. "Come on, bring your *pareja*. The helicopters will take us home." Anibal spoke soothingly to the children as he tapped his way down the row and buddied up the kids into line. "Ready? Okay, let's march!" he said and led them toward the stairs to the roof. They followed like calves to market, bowed and bawling, or stonily silent.

I cut the Americans out of the line. "You're coming with me. We'll go to the American Embassy," I said and bustled them up the steps to the front door. I opened it a crack and searched the street. I had my cell phone, but had no idea how to reach the unnamed agent in the *panadaría* truck that remained parked in the shade two doors up, had I service to call. Could he see me?

Deserted, the street remained as we left it when we entered the house, but something didn't feel right. I scanned the neighboring houses. Everything looked normal—no one watching that I could see. A gardener moving a hose, a maid shaking a rug. I pulled out my gun and pushed the door open just a bit farther. A light glinted from behind a window across the way. I heard a crack. Then another and plaster sprayed onto the stoop. I pulled back and pushed the girls aside, hitting the speed dial button on the Nextel Ani had insisted I use.

"Ani, I think some one's shooting from the house directly across the street." I peeked out again. The gardener looked my way through the sights of his rifle, the maid talked into a radio. "Ani, do something."

"Get down, Jade!"

I dove for the floor, dragging the terrified kids with me as the first volley of Armageddon ripped into the safe house.

CHAPTER TWELVE

Ambushed

Bullets thwacked into the thick masonry, miraculously missing the door and failing to penetrate the walls. The rhythmic firing of the guns across the street kept up a staccato braaapp for what felt like eons. Then silence.

"I can't breathe. Lily get off!" Evie gasped.

I let go of Lily. She rolled over and sat up, exposing the child pressed into the marble floor.

Evie gulped the oxygen-thin air. "Are we going to die?" she whispered, sitting up.

"No we're not," I said with as much conviction I could muster, and pulled the girls close to me. I punched Anibal's number again.

"Yo!"

"What's happening? Can we get to the van?"

"Negative. Stay put."

"What's—"

An explosion rocked the house. The girls screamed. I threw myself over them as a rain of plaster and dust clouded the air. Another burst of automatic weapons. I heard the sound of helicopter rotors beating the air. More guns. They must be shooting at the helicopter, but it was moving away and barely audible. I pictured the blades, chopping through the pollution. Was Anibal onboard?

I realized I was holding my breath. I exhaled and gripped the girls tighter. What if he'd left us here? We were supposed to go to the roof, but I led these girls here, to the front door. Stupid. Stupid. Stupid.

"Ani! Ani!" I shouted into the device. Nothing. Was he ignoring me? Had he been hit? "Answer me Anibal," I screamed. Glass shattering on tile echoed sharply through the passageway. "Ani! Ani, the living room windows…"

"Jade," he shouted from the hallway. "Move. Move!" He pounded into the entry, snatched Evie from my arms, and half-dragged Lily to the corner out of the sight line of the hallway. I scrambled toward the corner in a half run, half crawl. Anibal reached out and yanked me the last few feet and folded himself around our human knot.

"Heads down. Cover your ears!"

The house erupted. Flames surged into the entry hall and the oxygen was sucked out of the air. I felt the hair on my arm singe. Squinting, I watched the burning tentacle pull back into the hallway as smoking chunks of stone and cement dropped to the entry floor. Embers glowed across the front door, and the smell of gasoline-laced smoke wafted up from the living room on greasy drafts of air.

"What happened?" I shouted, trying to extricate myself from the heap of girls. They cried and clung to each other and me, their faces bone white, their tears streaking through the fine ash that settled over everything.

Anibal grimaced and let us go. "Is everyone all right?" He was barely audible through the ringing in my ears. I waved "more-or-less," and pulled the girls to me. They shook with fear. I noticed Anibal's arm was burned. The arm he'd held around me. I felt somehow guilty.

"Your arm. I'm sorry, I…"

He half smiled at me and stroked my cheek. He said in

rapid-fire Spanish, leaning into my ear, "Let's just get out of here before the next shell hits. Or worse, the *policía* show up." He scrambled to his feet to peer through the hallway door.

More explosions? If these explosions kept up, I'd be deaf before I turned thirty-five, not the middle-age my father predicted when he caught me cranking up the volume on my rock 'n roll.

"The living room is a crater. We're not getting to the roof."

"Can't we get to the bread truck?" I asked.

"If the chopper covers us," he said, the look on his face belying any hope for that.

"Is it still there?" I heard the panic rising in my voice. The girls whimpered. Spanish or not, they understood.

He shrugged. "No radio. I don't know."

"Anibal, I can't..." Another blast rattled the house and several of the sidelight windows cracked and dropped glass to the floor. I screamed along with the girls, but the explosion hadn't felt the same. It wasn't as loud, that was for certain.

The color rushed into Anibal's face and he threw his head back to laugh without sound. Crab-like, he scuttled across the floor and spied through one of the jagged holes in the sidelights. "We got 'em." He whooped. "Let's go. C'mon, ladies."

I groaned. Standing up took effort, as stiff as I felt from fear and crouching too long. I dragged the girls to their feet and shook out my legs. Pins and needles rushed to replace the numbness and I nearly stumbled to my knees when I tried to walk.

"You girls watch where you're stepping, okay? There's a lot of glass on the floor," I said.

"We are," Lily replied.

We picked our way the few feet across the room to the

door. Anibal signaled us to stand to the side as he cautiously opened it. He drew his gun and peeked around the broad plank.

"Yes!" He pumped his fist in the air. "Okay, stay behind me. Jade, you last. Got your gun?"

I waved it at him and we filed out the door. I glanced across the street at the house where I first saw the sniper gardener. The house burned, black smoke vented through a ragged hole in the masonry and drifted away from us on a slight breeze. What kind of weapon makes a hole like that? And who shot it? I looked up the street toward the bread truck. The agent must have been monitoring us because the engine coughed alive and the truck roared toward us in reverse, gears whining.

Anibal moved fast down the steps to the approaching truck. The girls had to run to keep up, and I saw that Lily was leaving bloody red heel prints on the cement. I cringed.

"Lily. You're bleeding. Wait!" I shouted.

The truck's breaks squealed as it stopped in front of us, and the passenger door grated open in its track. The agent stuck out his head and beckoned us to hurry up. He disappeared and I heard the rumble of the engine gunning. Only a few feet more and we'd be safe in the truck and speeding home to Condesa and Pepper.

Only a few feet more, I thought. Ani lifted Evie into the truck, then Lily. I leapt to the running board. Damn, something stung my shoulder. I dove for the back, soft hands drawing me in, the truck already racing away from the cartel safe house. I heard the zings and thwacks of bullets as they sprayed the back of the truck, and I touched my stinging flesh. My fingertips came away bloodied. I thrust my hands away from my body—blood stains are so hard to remove from clothing...

A relentless white sun penetrated my eyelids but I shivered with cold. My head pounded. I wanted to open my eyes, but the effort was too much. Maybe I'd just sleep in a little longer. If I weren't so cold. Can't someone give me a blanket? I heaved myself onto my side and instantly came awake. Fire seared through my shoulder, settling into a punishing ache as I rolled onto my back. I remembered running to the bread truck, the bees swarming, the sting to my shoulder. I'd been shot.

I shrieked.

A door banged open and rubber clapped over linoleum. I squeezed my eyes against the light and screamed again.

"She's awake," an unfamiliar voice said.

"Jade. Jade?"

Anibal's voice. I cracked open my eyes and squinted into the light. "Where am I?" I croaked. A warm hand patted my good shoulder and I tried to look at who it was but could only see a plain of brilliant snow.

"Jade, this is Dr. Agustin. He gave you a sedative."

The snowy steppes morphed into a lab coat and I could see beady black eyes boring into me from a brown, whiskered face. I shivered.

"¿Como sientas?" he asked, without warmth.

"She's got to get up and get going, Doctor, " Anibal said. "Jade, can you sit up? We're putting Dr. Agustin in danger. We've got to go. Come on, sit up."

"Let her rest, señor. You'll be fine here. No one saw you come in. I'll be in the *consultorio* with my patients."

"No, I'm okay." I swung my feet over the edge of the surface I lay on and levered into a sitting position. "I'm freezing. Isn't there a blanket or something?"

The doctor wrapped a sheet around me. I took a look at my hospital room. We were in a large storage closet. Metal shelving stacked with supplies from toilet paper to medicines and cleaning equipment lined the walls. I saw several brooms and mops propped in a corner by the door. I had been lying on a gurney. No wonder it was so bright and cold —the florescent lighting turned this storeroom into a cinderblock cell.

I shuddered; Movement aggravated my shoulder. I winced and patted the bandage. "We can leave, Ani?"

"Are you ready?"

"She shouldn't be moved yet."

"Thank you, Doctor." Anibal pulled his wallet from his pocket and extracted a fistful of bills. "I think this should take care of it," he said and handed over the money.

Doctor Agustin snatched the bundle, fanning the bills and quickly counting. Dollars. I sucked in a quick breath. A leer crossed his face and the bills disappeared. A magician's sleight of hand. Ani had just handed over more than a thousand dollars. Who carries money like that around?

"Hey, Ani, what did this quack do for that amount of money?" I asked in English. "What happened to me?"

I grabbed his arm and skooched off the gurney. My knees sagged, rubbery and weak, and a dark swarm of flies swirled across my vision. I grabbed Anibal, head hanging. He supported me the few steps into the dim hallway and the dizziness passed.

"She needs to lie down, *señor*. She's lost blood," Doctor Agustin said, his voice sounding unconvincing.

"Tell me what happened."

"Once we're in the car."

"Car?" I was confused. Didn't we come here in a...bread truck? "The girls! Where are they?" I half turned to look at Ani as the alley door clicked behind us.

"Move, JadeAnne! We've got to get out of here and fast," he said, dragging me along the trash-littered *callejon*.

"But, Ani! Where are the girls? Why are we running? Stop!"

We'd reached the sidewalk lining a broad, traffic choked

boulevard in a dismal, grey neighborhood of half-built cinderblock houses and seedy-looking low bodegas. An SUV screeched to a stop in front of us, the door swung open and Anibal shoved me toward hands that lifted me inside.

CHAPTER THIRTEEN

Some Sort of Mexican Stand-off

My head pounded. My arm ached. I'd been dumped into the back seat of a black SUV with smoke-tinted windows by Mr. America—Prison Edition. The ape had deltoids bigger than my buns. And his biceps? Like fence posts, covered in amateur-looking black and blue lichen. A sharp, angular woman glared at me from his shoulder and morphed into an eagle. A rattlesnake clutched in its talons dangled down his arm. He had pyramids and spider webs and strange icons disappearing under his tank top. A stylized number 47 covered his thick neck like a collar. Were these Anibal's friends? Colleagues?

I straightened up and turned to the window. Nothing worth looking at out there. Just dun-colored acres of low, graffiti-crusted warehouses and cyclone fences spreading from either side of a desolate six-lane boulevard. The occasional tree struggling to catch its breath in the yellow air. A cluster of tarpaper and corrugated metal shacks. I found no comfort in this view of Mexico City. I wanted to lie down in my comfy bed and escape the surreal nightmare. Why didn't Anibal sit back here and take care of me? Spit partners forever. I snorted.

The tattooed ex-con swung his bowling-ball head around and grimaced at me. Oh, my god, his whole face was tattooed in tear drops, spiders, something that resembled doors or playing cards joined by a third eye swastika and topped with devil's horns. Yikes. But under the horror, his face looked sweet, probably a liability in prison. I half smiled and he showed me his Uzi.

"Put that gun away." Anibal sounded angry. Pretty much how I was beginning to feel as my head cleared of sedative. Ani sat next to the tattoo freak, dwarfed by his grotesque body and bad art. The devil put the gun on the floor under his hooves, but the man sitting shotgun glowered over the seat at Anibal, his gold jewelry gleaming in the curly forest sprouting from his open collar.

"You're not the *jefe* here, *güey*."

"We're guests, and Thor there isn't acting very hospitable," Anibal replied amiably.

I couldn't see if he smiled.

The tension thickened along with the gloaming in the SUV. Maybe it was late in the day. It was hard to tell through the tinted glass, and I looked forward for the view out the windshield, right into the mean eyes of the driver. From the back, the driver looked pretty normal, what I could see of him reflected through the rear view mirror. A Mexican guy wearing a blue *guayabera* and a military buzz cut. With hard, menacing eyes staring at me. I looked away, chilled.

"Ani, what time is it? We have to be at Polo's by eight. I'm a mess. Can't we go back to your place now?" My voice quavered and squeaked.

"You were shot, Jade. You're really worried about dinner with my half-brother?"

"I just want to go to my room and rest for a while."

"I'm having the house cleared. They'll let us know when it's safe."

I yawned. My head felt heavy and pounded as the

sedative wore off. "Why wouldn't the house be safe at home? We're going to Polo's anyway."

"We were attacked, JadeAnne."

"Not by Polo. He could get rid of us at dinner. Please Ani. Let's go." I reached out to touch him and Shotgun snickered.

"Got yourself a cute piece of ass there, *pachuco*. Cut her out of the stable for yourself? Mebbe you want to share with your brothers?"

The three men hooted. My stomach dropped, nauseating me. I almost wet my pants. Dex would never put me in this kind of danger. I wished he'd ride up on his tarnished steed and save me. Fat chance. The last time I thought he'd come to save me, turned out he'd come to dump me—and encourage me to stay in Mexico so I could be raped and butchered by ex-cons and ex-military thugs. Tears brimmed my eyelids, but I brushed them away. Ani wouldn't let me be hurt. Would he?

"I'll share some of this with you *pinche pendejos*," Anibal said, and grabbed his crotch. The men roared at that. "Carlito. If you don't get us lost, maybe I'll let you have a sloppy second." Anibal laughed, harsh like barbed wire stretching over metal fence post, but turned and gave me a wink.

I leaned to Anibal and asked in a low voice, "Where are the girls?"

"We'll talk about that later."

"No. Now." I spoke rapidly in English, hoping the thugs weren't bilingual. "You said you'd tell me what happened when we got in the SUV. Well, here we are and I want to know. Tell me you didn't turn those little girls over to these monsters."

"Jade, you got shot and passed out in the surveillance truck. The kids were scared. They needed somewhere to go while I got you patched up. Consuelo's was on the way, San

Angel. We dropped them with her and got you to Dr. Augustin. Don't worry. They're safe." His smile radiated, reassuring me. "Consuelo will get them cleaned up, checked by her doctor and to the Embassy. Isn't that what you wanted?" He frowned.

Is that what he thought? I looked beyond him to see the driver's hard grin in the rearview mirror. His teeth were bared. It couldn't have anything to do with my conversation, could it? I felt sick, but maybe it was the sedative. But Consuelo? The cousin or aunt or whatever she was, who'd had the affair with Daniel Worthington? She didn't sound like a responsible caregiver to me. "Take me there now."

Anibal's sweet smile. "This isn't a taxi service, Jade. We'll go tomorrow."

That driver was definitely listening. His eyes said he took great pleasure in this conversation.

"And the others? What happened to them?" I wouldn't be placated by that smile. Or scared off by the other.

Anibal turned away and mumbled what sounded like, "Agency flew them to Social Services. Child Protective Custody."

Why wasn't he looking at me? "Where?" I asked, my voice louder, and glanced at the rearview again. The driver gave a mean little laugh. I shuddered as the realization came over me with a sour taste in my mouth: Anibal was lying.

I needed Pepper, my devoted, steadfast, dog. The only one I could count on. If my "partner" would lie to me, I'd need all the support I could get. No way would I leave those children in danger—at least not the Americans.

"How the fuck would I know? Maybe Chapo got 'em."

"Are you telling me that was a Sinaloa cartel safe house? I thought you said BLO before?" I heard his phone buzz.

He quickly turned away from me. Anibal flipped it open, read a text, and grunted something to the driver that sounded like, "L40." I understood the "head for Condesa" and my heart fluttered. Pepper would be waiting.

"Yeah, okay, *pachuco*," the driver said. "But we've got merchandise to pick up on the way." The driver swung the vehicle in a wide U and shot back the way we'd come, turning left at an intersection in front of a LaLa tractor barreling down on us. The view didn't change, but the tension in the cabin eased. I slumped back against the seat.

Chapo. The name on everybody's lips in this corrupt country. It appeared Anibal didn't want to tell me why he thought it was a Sinaloa safe house now, or maybe he couldn't talk in front of these thugs. Something he'd learned when he hacked Zocer's computer? But why the subterfuge? Why the lie? I couldn't wrap my brain around Anibal hacking anything electronic anyway. I saw him as more physical than cerebral. But what did I really know? Aguirre, his own brother, had warned me that Ani wasn't what he presented to the world.

I gazed into the dusty distance and saw the Cemex bodega. Hadn't we passed that ten minutes ago? Well, circling certainly defined my interactions with Anibal—with most men, it seemed. Spit partners keeping each other's backs.

I closed my eyes. A vision of a refrigerator magnet filled my mind. My sister gave it to me one Christmas in my stocking: The Queen of Choosing Mr. Right with a horizontal flying fairy, brandishing her magic wand at the hopeful-looking woman gazing up at her. My heart sank with the realization that Anibal may be one more in a string of trout, which should have been thrown back. Spit partners forever, my ass.

I opened my eyes as we barreled up a congested boulevard in a tacky, run-down area that had a median strip dividing the transit lanes and sported sculptures in every block. Was that a muffler? In another sculpture I recognized a spoked wheel, a hubcap, what looked like jumper cables. Every one of the several sculptures looked to be made from car parts.

"Ani, check it out. Look. Look at that horse. I think these are welded from car parts." Four heads swiveled left.

The driver said, "We're in Colonia Buenos Aires, the place where the car thieves live. I'm gonna stop, but you have to stay in the car. This is a dangerous *colonia*." His accent was heavy, but it sounded like he'd learned English in the U.S.

He swung left into a narrow street filled with possibly derelict cars and lined with dusty trees. Pink and white paper cutout flags festooned the block as though we'd landed in a little girl's birthday party.

"*Apúrrense coños*," he barked as he double parked alongside a funky truck where a dark-skinned worker unloaded a ton of scrap metal onto the sidewalk in front of a hole-in-the-wall decorated in dented hubcaps. The name of the establishment had faded and peeled from over the door.

Anibal, Tattoo, and Shotgun jumped out, but the driver glared at me through the mirror and hit the childproof lock button. I guessed I was staying put. The rich scent of taco meat bubbling in its fat wafted through his open window and my stomach growled. I hadn't noticed the *taquería* tucked between the laundry and *hojalaterría*.

"Ask Anibal to get me a taco," I said.

"Do I look like your maid?"

"Then let me out and I'll get my own."

"Relax, lady. He's getting food for all of us."

"How do you know English?" I asked, curious, but more to make a bond with this scary man. I'd read it's harder to harm someone you have a connection with.

"I went to high school in Los Angeles. Served in the military."

"The U.S. Army? How?"

"Green card."

"Why didn't you stay there?"

"They pay better for my skills here." He grinned. With the teeth bared like that I expected to hear him growl. I guessed driving wasn't his usual occupation.

"What do you do?" I finally asked him.

He leered at me. "*Sicario.*"

My blood turned cold. I shrank into the seat, heart suddenly pounding in my chest. I wasn't hungry anymore. I was scared. I'd heard the word before—he was an assassin. I snuck a look into the mirror and he was watching me. Bile rose up my gullet. He laughed, a deep mirthless *ga-ha ga-ha ga-ha* and was still at it when someone banged a short tattoo on the sliding door. The driver clicked the unlock button, still laughing. Anibal slid the door open and climbed in with a bag of tacos and bottles of Victoria beers.

"What's so funny?"

"Just chatting with your girl," he said, turning enough that I could see a number tattooed on his chin. What was up with the numbers?

"Yeah, she's a riot. I got *pastor*, *cabeza,* and *suadero*. What do you want? Jade, *Suadero*?"

I nodded and he passed back a little paper boat with a couple of tacos stuffed with chopped onion, cilantro, and my favorite *manzana* chili. The driver liked *suadero* too. Maybe that would keep him from killing me. Yeah, Ani was right—a riot.

We fell to eating. I noticed how, with tacos or quesadillas, or any number of street foods, people didn't converse while eating, and there wasn't the clinking of cutlery. It was like going deaf while you ate, that is until Tattoo and Shotgun wrenched open the rear cargo door and started slamming boxes of I-didn't-know-what into the space.

"*Oye, pachuco.* Pull down that fuckin' seat," Shotgun

demanded.

"Shove over, Jade," Anibal said, swatting over the seat at my thigh. I moved and he folded down a section of my seat and his. Tattoo shoved a long, narrow metal case inside. Ani grabbed the front and heaved then eased back onto the seat where Tattoo had sat.

The back hatch slammed shut, Shotgun jumped back in, slammed his door, and said, "*Vámonos.*"

Ani handed him a boat of tacos and a beer. The driver threw the SUV in gear and backed up, almost hitting a young guy on a bicycle, then peeled out into traffic on the main street. I clutched my lunch in my lap to keep from spilling.

Anibal said, "Hey, *güey*, slow down. We want to get to Condesa alive."

Was that a joke?

CHAPTER FOURTEEN

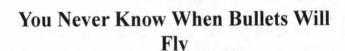

You Never Know When Bullets Will Fly

I climbed out of the Suburban, easing myself to the curb in front of the house, no help from Anibal, thank you very much, and glared at him. But he was engaged in secret handshakes with the creeps in the front seat and didn't notice me, even when I slammed the door shut. I turned around in time to see a dark blur streaking toward me. A perfect strike! and Pepper was in my arms dancing me in circles over the uneven paving, panting and crooning, his tail moving faster than the wings of a *colibri*. I held him tight and buried my face into his neck, while my bandaged shoulder screamed in pain. He barked and dropped back to all four legs then sniffed at me so intently I thought I'd be hoovered right up his long snout.

"It's okay, Pepper." I swiped unbidden tears from my cheeks. "I'm home now." Sniff, sniff, sniff. He discovered my bandage and backed me into the side of the vehicle trying to lick it. Dogs.

"Pepper, no. Sit," I commanded. He sat and lowered his head watching me obliquely, continuing to sniff.

"Let's get inside. That dog is attracting attention." Ani

pulled Pepper away from me, and the Suburban pulled into the street. Pepper snarled.

"Pepper!" I admonished. "Let him go. He's glad to see me and wants to check out my injury. It's what they do." I heard the agitation in my voice. Nothing had made much sense since breakfast.

One hand on Pepper's collar and the other gripping my good arm, Anibal guided us into the vestibule. Señora Pérez closed the street door behind us.

"Señora, please take Señorita Stone to her room, and clean her injury. JadeAnne, I don't really trust that quack. Do you want me to make an appointment with my doctor for antibiotics?"

"No. I'm going to take a shower and get ready to go to Polo's. Then I'm going to feed Pepper. No offense but I don't want Señora Pérez fussing over me. I need some space. You clean up too. You're a mess." I eyed him critically for the first time since the ambush. His clothes smelled burned and I was certain that the brown stains were blood. The spraying glass from the blast had lacerated his scalp, his neck, his hands, a roadmap of scabs. He herded Pepper and me into the elevator behind the housekeeper and pushed our floors on the panel. Mrs. P moved away from me. I guess I stank, too.

"We should cancel. You're in no condition to go out, Jade."

"What, and pass up this opportunity? I thought you—"

Señora Pérez shook her head in my peripheral vision.

"Okay, you're right," Anibal said without conviction, but didn't argue, and got off at the second floor without the servant. How would I get rid of his housekeeper?

The elevator stopped at my floor. I dragged open the gate and smiled at the woman. "I can manage, Mrs. Pérez, *gracias.*"

"No, I will clean your wound and re-dress it as the señor

requested."

"Really, I'm fine," I said and pushed open my bedroom door. Pepper barged in ahead of me, sniffed the air, and jumped onto the bed.

Mrs. Pérez waddled in behind me, scowling. Tough beans if she didn't like dogs on furniture.

"Come into the bathroom and let me unwrap that bandage." She dragged the desk chair behind her and placed it near the sink where the light would be the brightest.

Reluctantly I followed her, peeling off the bread delivery suit and bulletproof vest I still wore, and sat down. In the mirror I caught sight of the blood-stained bandage taped around my shoulder and upper arm. The señora poked around in the cabinets until she had assembled the bandage scissors, gauze, cotton, something that looked like Betadine and a roll of bandage tape with little Yodas printed on it.

Gently, she cut off the soiled bandage, exposing inflamed stitches oozing thick blood. It throbbed like hell. Obviously the pain medication had worn off. I sucked in a breath. At least I hadn't felt it, but that butcher sewed me up with fishing twine and did a lousy job. Now it hurt like hell and I would have a nasty scar. Maybe I should go see the Aguirre clan doctor. I'd ask Polo over dinner. That would get Anibal's goat. Or a reaction out of Aguirre. Could Anibal be right? Was the senator behind the attack?

Señora Pérez inspected the stitches making tutting noises. "Once the stitches come out, I want you to use this crema." She nodded toward a jar of white cream on the counter. "It's *crema concha nacar*, an ancient preparation used to heal and fade scarring."

I couldn't stop my rude outburst. "Great, I'm going to use some Aztec poultice."

She frowned. "This is a special *crema* made from the ground pearlized interior of the nautilus shell and has been used for centuries to fade scars, sun damage, and uneven pigmentation." She inspected my facial skin. "Your skin will look younger."

Did she think I looked old? A cougar preying on her young nephew?

Mrs. Pérez cleaned the wound and wrapped it back up like a pro and started a bath for me. Turned out, she was a pro, an RN. My, my. Hadn't Anibal got an interesting team of helpers.

"Don't get it wet."

"I won't. Thanks for doing that. I'll take it from here."

"I'll help with your hair."

I was supposed to bathe in front of this woman? "I—"

"It will hurt less if you don't raise your arm." She reached into the claw-footed tub and cranked open the handles.

The roar of water drowned out anything else she might have said.

My stomach took a little turn. Mrs. Pérez was hovering. Did Anibal tell her to keep tabs on me? Prevent me from using the phone? Did he know I was anxious to call Qadir, a twenty-something computer wizard, my researcher at Waterstreet Investigations? He'd search-out every shred of info on the cartels' involvement in human trafficking; and certainly the office could find the girls' mother to notify her they had been found. He could contact the Embassy as well. Surely it would send someone to recover the American girls from Consuelo. I fanned away the enervating steam. Or I'd go in the morning.

I felt guilty for letting those kids out of my sight. Aguirre would tell me how to find her house, unless he were behind the operation. But right now I had another problem besides the humidity making me drowsy—Mrs. Pérez. Who did she report to? Lidia or Anibal? Or—?

All right, if the housekeeper was keeping an eye on me, I'd interrogate her, pick her brain while she acted as my warden. She turned off the water to a knocking of pipes—blat, blaat, tat-tat-tat—just like the hot water pipes in Gaga's house back home. I slipped out of my clothes and into the warm herbal bath scenting the quaint bathroom, aching for my grandma. Mrs. Pérez pushed open the window overlooking the street and moist air steamed out.

"Señora Pérez, how did you come to work as an *alma de casa*?" I closed my eyes and inhaled roses and lemons. I sank as far as I could into the warm water and let some of my tension ease while keeping my bandaged arm on the side of the tub.

"*Pues*, after the earthquake—"

"1985?"

"*Sí*. It was a disaster, ten thousand people died and thousands more were injured. I was on my way home from my shift when the quake hit. My hospital, Hospital Juarez, collapsed, killing almost everyone. Most of the city's hospitals collapsed and we lost hundreds of medical staff. But I didn't know until later. My house had collapsed, the whole block came down. My mother and my children were gone. Volunteers couldn't dig them from the rubble in time." Mrs. Pérez sucked in a ragged breath.

"I'm so sorry, señora. Please, I didn't mean to upset you." I reached a dripping hand to her wrist and gave it a squeeze.

"*El muerte* is a part of life. I have accepted my loss. I went back to the hospital to help. Trained nurses were in short supply. The hospital was a mountain of cement and steel—my friends, my patients…and my older sister, a nurse on the day shift. Gone. Everyone gone."

I watched a tear spill from the corner of her eye and became aware of the dull headache I'd carried all afternoon. She cleared her throat and smiled at me, a glassy, sharp look that felt incongruous to the loss she had sustained—her family, her home, her city. All crumbled. "And the Aguirre family?"

Mrs. Pérez lathered my hair as she talked. "We worked around the clock; there were so few medical workers, no water, no electricity; the gas pipes leaked and caught fire. The air was thick with smoke and dust. I listened with my stethoscope for survivors and found few. Rescue workers would come and start to dig. Most died, buried alive, but not La Señora Aguirre. We rescued her five days after the earthquake. I took her home and nursed her back to health."

I felt a draft of steam flowing toward the window.

"La Señora Aguirre? Polo's wife?"

"No, his mother." She deftly held a folded towel over my wound while she rinsed the shampoo from my hair.

"La señora had gone to the opera and stayed over at the Hotel Regis. She was having breakfast on the terrace. Only a miracle saved her. And she saved me. I had no home, no job, no family. Señora Lidia employed me to nurse her and later to care for this house. Señor Anibal's mother, Anahí, lived here. I have served this family for over two decades."

"I thought you were Anibal's aunt. Anahí's sister."

"We became like sisters. Young Anibal called me Tía."

A heaviness settled into the bathroom. For a moment the only sound I could hear was the rhythmic slap of soapy hands as Mrs. Pérez massaged my back. So Lidia had her eagle-eye on Anibal and his household. Did that mean Aguirre knew everything that went on here? And why?

"Jade, are you ready?"

I jumped, startled by the scratchy voice coming from the old intercom. Mrs. Pérez had finally left me to dress and I'd managed to make myself presentable in a black silk skirt and white chiffon blouse that set off my tan and covered my bandage. I peered at my face as I finished swiping on mascara. Fine lines etched my brow. Maybe that *concha nacar* cream might be worth a try.

"JadeAnne!"

I leaned into the bedroom and pushed the speak button. "I'm almost ready. I'll be down in a few."

"Wear your new suede jacket."

I groaned. Anibal could be such an idiot. "Polo is likely to pull an Uzi on us tonight?"

"I'm more worried about traveling on the streets."

"You're scaring me, Anibal."

"Just hurry up. I fed the dog."

I stuffed my flip-flop-spread feet into a pair of pumps, grabbed the jacket, and Pepper's vest. I wouldn't risk it for either of us; you never knew when bullets would fly in this city.

CHAPTER FIFTEEN

The Lion's Den

Shrek 3 had replaced Shrek 2 at the reception desk in the senator's lobby. He glowered at Anibal as he slammed down the intercom receiver after announcing our arrival, growling something only Pepper understood. Pepper snarled back, and the guard skittered away, remarkably light on his toes for a grizzly trapped in a narrow lobby. Anibal snickered. I punched the elevator button and Pepper smiled as we ascended to Aguirre's apartment.

The car stopped and the door slid open. 8:30 p.m. Right on time.

"*Bienvenidos, hermanito*, Miss Stone. Please come in." Aguirre smiled warmly and gestured past the magnificent arrangement made with the flowers I'd brought, filling the entry table.

The houseman stepped forward. "May I take your coats?"

I handed my jacket over readily. The lining was so stiff I felt like the Tin Man trying to move in it. Maybe I'd leave it behind. "*Gracias.*"

"*Hermanito*, I'm happy you've come. I don't believe you've visited my Polanco apartment before?"

Anibal grunted something pleasant sounding. Exercising restraint, I noted. Aguirre led us into the softly lit salon. I could see the city, diamonds sparkling in the window glass. As before, the view took my breath away. I guessed there was something to be said for having a buttload of, probably ill-gotten, money.

"It's a beautiful night. I don't think there was much smog today," I said, as I seated myself on the striped sofa facing the window.

Aguirre stood until Anibal flung himself next to me, and then eased into a side chair. Pepper squeezed in between us, and faced the senator. Aguirre raised his eyebrows and cocked his head toward the dog. I shrugged. The clock ticked.

Chucho appeared with embroidered napkins and a tray of steaming half-moons of filled tortillas. Quesadillas. I could see truffle-like black *huitlacoche* oozing from some of them, and the others turned out to be my favorite: *queso panela* melted over a sprig of *epazote*. He placed the tray on the coffee table in front of me. Pepper's nose peeked over the edge of the table and he sniffed. Anibal lunged for a handful, dripping salsa on the highly polished surface. Aguirre frowned—at the dog? Sloppy Anibal? I helped myself to a napkin and selected a *botana*, nibbling delicately at the gooey cheese. We ordered our drinks and smiled at each other, or were we grimacing?

"Senator, did you know we were attacked today?"

"JadeAnne!" Anibal cut me off.

"Ani, don't you think your brother should know what's going on?"

"What exactly is going on, Anibal?" Aguirre's cocktail glass clunked onto the table as he set it down and shifted to the edge of his upholstered chair.

"I got shot." The words tasted sour on my tongue. Suddenly I wasn't sure I wanted to start anything. The spectacular view, the soft couch, the delicious appetizers—I was relaxing.

"Anibal, did you take Miss Stone to one of the rough neighborhoods? Were you robbed?"

"Nothing like that, bro'. We were in Bosques de Pedrigal. She's fine."

"Is that true, Miss Stone?"

His eyes bore into me. I touched the bandage under my blouse. It felt dry and I leaned toward Aguirre. "It was only a flesh wound, but I got six stitches and a pain not quite in my neck."

"I'm relieved to hear you are not seriously injured, Miss Stone. The city is going to the dogs. It's this war on drugs. We wouldn't see the violence if PRI were still in power."

Aguirre looked a little sad as he sank back into the chair and picked up his drink again. I asked, "Why not? What party is in power?"

Anibal interrupted. "The PAN, *Partido Acción Nacional.* It's a Christian democrat member—conservative. Stands for free-market, small government, and doesn't let employees wear mini-skirts, although they support same-sex unions... just not gay marriage—"

"—the PAN believes that politics shouldn't dictate how a problem is dealt with, but each issue should be looked at individually and the best solution found," Aguirre explained.

The tinkle of crystal sounded from across the room where the houseman waited to usher us into the dining room. Pepper's ears pricked up and he raised his nose to sniff. Good. The quesadillas had disappeared fast. I only ate a couple and Aguirre skipped the appetizers for his second Old Fashioned. Pepper had been the perfect dog guest, minding his manners and his place. He could teach Ani a thing or two. I stood up.

Aguirre held out his arm. "Shall we go in?"

"Sure, I'm starved. What's for dinner?" I asked, as I

crooked my elbow into his. Lifting my arm up like that hurt like hell just as Mrs. Pérez had warned. I winced and gritted my teeth as we began the promenade to the table. Anibal fell in behind us and Pepper slinked along after him, probably not sure he was invited to the party.

"Senator, I'm curious to hear your thoughts on the new president's War on Drugs. What's going on?" I smiled at him over the lip of my wineglass. Cut crystal, of course. My socialite mother would so approve of Aguirre's table—all those lovely cabriolet legs and tile-patterned brocade camelbacks—a modern take on Louis XV.

"I'm glad you've asked, Miss Stone." Aguirre smiled back at me, his forkful of *pechuga con rajas en crema* suspended above his plate. "*Presidente Calderón* has upset the status quo. His administration is no longer willing to let sleeping dogs lie in Mexico."

"The PRI, he means, Jade. His *partido*," Anibal said.

"Yes, *hermanito*, I am a member of PRI. But I am not in favor of allowing organized crime to take over our country." He cut another bite of chicken and daubed dabbed it in the delicate but spicy creamed poblano sauce drizzled on his plate, and neatly placed the bite in his mouth.

"We don't want to see that either," I said.

Aguirre blotted his lips with the monogrammed napkin.

Anibal smirked at his half-brother. "We being the citizens of the good ole U. S. of A." He tipped his glass toward me.

I sighed. "Ani—"

"Yes. You've become an *estadounidense*." Aguirre clucked, a disapproving hen. "Your government—" he emphasized *your*— "has pressured my government for years to stop the drugs crossing into the U. S."

"Polo, *no olvidas, ¡Ya, yo soy cien porciento Mexicano*! I've got dual citizenship. I voted for you."

"Even though I'm a member of the corrupt *Partido Revolucionario Institucional*?" Aguirre laughed with genuine mirth.

"Even though, bro'."

"But what do you think of the drug war? Did you vote for it?" I asked.

"He grows pot, Jade. How do think he voted?"

"It's not that simple, *hermanito*. No, I did not vote for the War on Drugs, but it is because I do not believe interdiction is the answer. The crime organizations have more money and power than the government. We cannot win," Aguirre said, glaring at Anibal as if Ani were making policy.

He swirled his wineglass and studied the legs then sipped before continuing. "What we are seeing is the beginning of a criminal insurgency. If we are to take back our country, we'll hit them where they live—in their *bolsas*. This is why I have assumed leadership of the senate committee investigating money laundering in Mexico."

"So why did you kidnap me off the highway?" My tone sounded more accusing than I'd intended. I gently placed my fork with my knife across the top of the plate from eleven o'clock to two o'clock, just as I'd been trained at Castilleja School. I was a debutant. I can dine with the *alta sociedad* even if I can't hold my tongue.

"I apologize once again, Miss Stone. I hope someday you will forgive me for my employee's error, but yes, my committee was investigating Daniel Worthington. He has been implicated in illegal banking practices and was known to associate with members of the Sinaloa Federation."

"What does that have to do with me?"

Anibal grinned. "Zocer had Danny under surveillance. He knew Danny visited your office. Polo expected you."

So I'd been right. A set-up. "You mean Zocer was working for you, Senator?"

"We investigate many people."

"And that's all you have to say? Did you know I was set-up, Anibal?" I strained to maintain an even tone.

Chucho appeared and began to clear the table onto trays lining a polished sideboard intricately carved in a floral motif, effectively diffusing the volatile atmosphere.

"It's ancient history, Jade. Let's move on. Polo has apologized, Danny is dead. We've got more important things to do, don't we?" He flashed me that dimpled grin and I felt the heat rise into my cheeks.

"We do have more important worries," I agreed. "What about the kids we found in that house? What will happen to them? I think the senator might want to hear about our day, Ani." I watched Aguirre's reaction as I kicked Ani under the table. No accusations, I prayed.

"You found children in a house in the Pedrigal?" Aguirre addressed his brother, a surprised and quizzical look on his face.

Anibal related our adventure in the caves under the Ajusco range.

"Two of them are American citizens kidnapped from the L.A. area. We got them out but Anibal had to leave the girls with Consuelo while I was sewn up. I want you to help me get them back to their family. They're sisters."

"Consuelo," Aguirre said, through tight lips, his voice almost a sneer.

Aguirre didn't like Worthington's mistress.

He continued, "What would compel you to involve that woman in anything?"

"Her house was nearby. My greater concern was for JadeAnne. Consuelo will do anything I ask to make up for betraying Lura."

"Consuelo is a conniving, greedy shrew. She is not to be trusted. Further, I was deeply offended that she attended Mother's gathering. Who invited her?" Aguirre asked.

"Your mother, I expect. I saw several people I considered to be inappropriate to the occasion. El Santo?"

"He and his boys were in the church too," I added. "I can't believe he's a friend of your mother's."

"Nor can I," Aguirre responded dryly. "I've spoken to her. He is not the sort of man a woman of her standing should fraternize with. Unfortunately, my mother does not care to take my advice."

"She better take it, bro'. El Santo is a lieutenant in the Federation. You know his mother's brother is a boss in the BLO."

Aguirre visibly deflated as his shoulders slumped. I could have sworn I felt a rush of air blow by me.

"Yes, I've heard that rumor. And he is Noé Santos Mandujano's nephew on his father's side." Aguirre turned to me. "Santos was head of SIEDO, the *Subprocuraduría de Investigación Especializada en Delincuencia Organizada.*"

"You mean the department of organized crime? That's irony. Does it give him immunity?" I laughed.

"Organized crime is not a laughing matter, Miss Stone."

I blushed and shut up.

"Perhaps you are interested in learning more about the problem?"

I nodded. Anything to get the senator to open up to me.

"Then you will be my guest tomorrow at Hotel Geneve Ciudad de Mexico on Londres in Zona Rosa. I will send a car for you at eight-thirty. Many experts will speak on topics ranging from money laundering to kidnapping to human trafficking, as well as our war on drugs. Presidente Calderon is the—what do you call it? *Claro*, the keynote speaker."

"Wow! Yes, I'd love to come."

"Please carry your passport and visa. And leave your beast at home."

"Ani?" I winked at Anibal. "Sure, no problem, Senator."

"Hey! I think he meant the dog, Jade." He winked back.

"Excuse me." Anibal, smiling, pushed away from the table and headed out of the dining room.

Aguirre and I watched as Anibal disappeared down the hall. He cleared his throat and I smiled across the table. "Pass the rolls, please, Senator."

"Miss Stone, you should not place trust in Anibal. He is not what he claims."

"What do you mean, Senator? He's told me about his education and job."

"I'm sure he has. My brother, you met Beto at the funeral, made sure Anibal received one of the finest educations money can buy. And my *hermanito* is using it to enrich the pockets of the ZETA organization. He is a double agent."

"What? You're out of your mind, Senator. Ani is dedicated to interdiction. He hates what's going on! He'd never—" I dropped my voice and took a gulp of air, scrutinizing Aguirre's face, but it was Carlito the *sicario* I saw.

This couldn't be true, could it? Scenes of the day's events rushed through my mind. I sank against the orange and white back of my chair. How did a DEA agent get hold of assets like the helicopter on a moment's notice? And those tattooed thugs in the van? I groaned and put my head in my hands. Who could I believe? I suddenly felt my energy dissipate. It was like my bones had turned to Jell-O, and were it not for my skin, I'd melt to nothing.

"Go home, Miss Stone. You aren't safe here."

"Oh, sure, you've been trying to get rid of me since you kidnapped me. You're just saying this to scare me."

"You should be scared. I will assign a security detail to protect you if you will not be sensible and return to your home. Now, enjoy our house specialty." He nodded to the kitchen door.

The houseman had appeared in the gilded doorway

bearing a silver tray laden with a delicious-looking dessert. I felt nauseated.

"Is that your *flan neopolitano*?" Anibal plopped down in his chair. "Give me a big slice."

I flinched. I hadn't heard him come in. How much of Aguirre's and my conversation had he heard?

The houseman cut wedges of the smooth custard and served each of us. I drizzled *cajeta* over mine and pushed a bit around my plate.

"So bro', you never did say how Aunt Lidia happens to go around with that scum. Isn't he a little young for her?" Ani sounded contemptuous. "She'd do better with that guy who came in with him, that old *vato*. Although he certainly didn't look like he belongs in Tía Lidia's crowd, either." He looked at me. "Aren't you eating that, Jade?"

I filled my spoon and sucked the sticky, sweet custard onto my tongue. My teeth hurt and I put down my spoon. My mind filled with the image of thugs strutting into Lidia's living room at Lura's Celebration of Life. Like they owned the place. But the old guy? I scraped off the *cajeta* and slipped another bite into my mouth. With the surge of sweetness came the image of a lean, angular man with a stubbly beard, graying hair, and a rumpled linen jacket. I hadn't realized it at the time, but something seemed familiar about him.

CHAPTER SIXTEEN

Soldier of Fortune

Saturday, August 11, 2007

In the car my stomach clenched and rolled with every brake, turn, or stop. Ani drove like a maniac—too fast, too aggressive. Just like every other *chilango* on the busy boulevards. Between eating too much, the over-sweet flan, and Aguirre's accusations about Anibal, my stomach churned. The Zetas? They were the worst of the bunch I'd read about: formed ten years earlier by U.S. trained Mexican Army commandos who later deserted to become the Gulf Cartel's enforcement arm. He couldn't be one of them. He just couldn't.

The car swerved and Anibal lay onto the horn. I grabbed the suicide handle above the window as a bite of flan filled my mouth. I swallowed and gagged. "Slow down, Ani. I'm going to throw up."

He swerved across three lanes of traffic into Chapultepec park and roared to the curb. My knuckles glowed blue under the dash lights from gripping the handles so tightly. "Do it outside, not in my car," he said, leaning across me to push open the door.

Pepper barked and shoved his head over the seats. Anibal shrank away from me. Good dog. "Just slow down. Your driving is scaring me," I said.

"Sorry, Jade. I want to get off the streets as soon as possible. Didn't you see that black Escalade following us?"

A chill ran through me. "What are you talking about?"

"I wouldn't put it past Polo to have us followed." His eyes tracked the taillights of a green taxi that passed. It didn't slow. There wasn't much traffic on this road and fewer streetlights.

"Why, Ani? He knows where you live. You don't make sense. Let's go." I'd let go of the handle and clutched my stomach instead. I could have used a hot cup of ginger tea.

"I don't think he'd care where we went, but you're right. That SUV will circle back and we don't want to be on a deserted road in the park."

"Anibal, if your brother—"

"Half-brother."

"Whatever. If your half-brother wanted to harm us, he could have while we were there."

"Yeah? Maybe that's why your stomach is upset." He gunned the engine into life and accelerated.

I hung on, gorge rising as we shot from the curb, making a U-turn. Thank God there wasn't any traffic coming. "The senator didn't poison me, if that's what you mean. It's your driving. Please slow down."

"I think you'd be stupid to go with him tomorrow. You're just asking to be kidnapped."

Kidnapped? At a public conference? My limbs turned to stone and the cauldron of my stomach boiled and bubbled. What better place?

Anibal entered the Periferico and shifted into fifth gear, leveling out the speed to match the southbound traffic. Fast, but I wasn't pinned to the seat from G-force.

"What did he tell you? I know he said something while I

was out of the room. He wants to poison you against me," Ani said with a petulant whine.

Oh, so that was it. Anibal was worried Aguirre had convinced me of something. Like: he's a Zeta. I clapped my hand over my mouth.

"Don't hurl in my car, Jade."

I took a gasping breath and groaned. I might as well play this up. I needed time to think. "I'm okay. Just get me home."

We swerved onto a *lateral* and fought our way onto Constituyentes through a maze of baffling intersections then swerved onto Avenida Chapultepec. We'd be back at his house soon and I would barricade myself in my room. With my gun.

Pepper visited the garden while I made tea and Anibal went to his office, whatever that meant. I'd never seen his floor of the house. Why not? Because he was a double agent? A traitor, more like it. How could he? But then, look who passed me the information. I snorted at my gullibility as the teakettle shrilled. I poured scalding water over my teabag and trudged down the back stairs to let Pepper in. I peeked into the yard but didn't see my dog and whistled a low note. Nothing. Where could he be? The yard was tiny and fully walled-in with glass-topped stone. There was a gate, was it open? I edged out, whistling again, and heard a soft growl coming from under the balcony. A cat? No, Pepper wouldn't growl at a cat. He'd loved his own tabby, Zach, before he died. Must be a raccoon. "Pepper, leave it alone. Come in. It's bedtime," I sang out into the dark.

A shadow burst from the shrubbery and morphed into a fleeing human with Pepper snapping at his heels. The man cried out, then the gate slammed shut on the dog's nose. He yipped and jumped at it, scratching and howling in frustration and rage.

What the...? I slumped back against the stairs door, washed-out. Someone had gotten into the garden. How? Who? Questions rushed at me. It was impossible, unless the gate had been open. Only Anibal had the key. No one, not even Sra. Pérez was allowed to use it. Unless...

"Pepper, come now!"

I felt my body collapsing as I heard panic rising in my voice. Pepper did too. He left off his harangue and bounded back to me, herding me through the door then bounding past me up the stairs. I pushed home the three deadbolts, slumped into the wall, and steadied myself to follow him up to the kitchen. I jumped, my heart in my mouth when I saw a figure standing by the refrigerator.

"What was the racket, Jade? You can't let your dog bark like that late at night. He'll disturb the neighborhood," Anibal said, sounding mean.

Had the shadow been another of his associates like the thugs in the van today? "There was a man in the garden. Pepper chased him away." I watched Anibal's face darken. His lips flattened into a line and his eyes darted off me toward the stairs door.

"Impossible. No one can get into my *jardín*. It was probably a cat." He glanced at the floor and half turned away from me. "You're acting jumpy. I bet Polo has something to do with that." He swung to face me, blue eyes turned to icicles, piercing me.

"Anibal, a man ran out of your garden through the open gate, and slammed it behind him. I'm sure Pepper bit him. Could it be one of those men from the van?" I stared at him, daring him to tell the truth.

"You've got an active imagination, Jade. Get your tea and go on up. I'll be there in a little while."

No way I would sleep with him tonight. I softened my tone, "Ani, you're probably right about the cat. I feel so sick I'm seeing things. It feels like flu. You don't want to catch this. I'll see you in the morning." I gave him my best I'm-too-sick smile and collected my tea and dog and hustled into the elevator. "Good night."

The door closed on his reply.

A hazy beam of sunshine sliced across the old-fashioned room, turning the pink wallpaper dusty rose. One of my sister's favorite colors. I stretched and nudged Pepper who snored softly next to me then swung my legs from under the covers. 6:17 according to the bedside clock.

"Pepper, want to go for a run?"

My dog leaped off the bed and pulled the leash from where it looped around the closet doorknob, dropping it at my feet.

"I guess that's yes. Get my shoes," I said as I dragged on a pair of Adidas running pants, favoring my injured shoulder. It ached. I had a flash of my sister in a matching pair of pants, only her stripe was purple not blue. As if she ever ran. Especially not with me. I'd been dreaming about her. What was it? She and Anibal wanted to take something from me. Pepper? I dragged on a tennis sock and fished around the bureau drawer for its mate. Pepper dropped my left shoe by my right foot and dove under the bed for the other one. I laced up and we headed out.

Pepper trotted to the stairs door. Would the stairs be quieter than that cranky old elevator? I didn't want to wake Anibal. I didn't need him on this run. Thankfully he'd left me alone during the night, and I'd had a few moments to think about him, his behavior, and Aguirre's warning during dinner. I hadn't come to any conclusions, and wanted to use my run to sharpen my mind. Exercise always helped. Pepper clicked his nails on the door.

I clipped the leash to his harness. "Okay, beast. We'll warm up on the stairs—quietly."

Outside, the cool air smelled stale but looked cleaner than I expected. Patches of blue showed through the trees lining the block. I zipped my key and phone into my pocket and we jogged in the direction of Parque México and the Superama. Nothing moved on the street. I stepped up our pace and we pounded the uneven sidewalk for several blocks.

The park was already a hub of activity. I jogged by dog walkers, young moms out with kids in strollers, food vendors. We turned south and I flung myself onto a green-painted wrought iron bench placed near the restrooms. I let Pepper off the lead and squirted a sip of water into his mouth from my sports bottle. For a short, flat run I'd gotten out of breath. Wow, I had no idea the altitude would affect me so much. Maybe it was the heat? Nah, it couldn't be more than low seventies, but the brilliant day was sure to heat up into the eighties. Whatever, it was a good time to call the office. Qadir always got in by six-thirty.

Qadir answered on the first ring. I told him what I wanted and that I'd call back tomorrow at eight-thirty. He'd be gone today by the time I finished the symposium on organized crime. He wished me good luck and we rang off. I checked my watch and realized we'd have to hurry if I was going to be ready at eight-thirty when Aguirre's car came for me.

Although my shoulder throbbed, Pepper and I jogged around the east side of the park past the pond. Trees and bamboo grew thickly between the water and the path. It was pretty, damp, and the fragrance of green growing plants enveloped me. I relaxed into the rhythmic thud of our feet on the packed earth. It couldn't be possible that Anibal was a double agent, DEA and Zeta. Why? What would he gain? Money? Didn't he already have money? Maybe not. Field agents made a decent wage, but cartel enforcers got rich. I hoped Aguirre was wrong. He'd always resented his half-brother; it could be sour grapes. But that well-equipped bread truck, the helicopter, the weapons. DEA agents on Mexican soil didn't have those kinds of assets, did they? But the cartels had plenty of money, plenty of soldiers, and plenty of assets. Wouldn't a DEA or Mexican military helo have identifying markings on the hull? Maybe I hadn't seen them. Maybe there weren't any. I wondered who I could ask.

I started from my reverie just in time to avoid slamming into a large man blocking the path before it rejoined the main walk. I zigged and he lunged toward me, something flashing in his hand. I sprinted forward, pulling away from him on a surge of adrenalin. Pepper turned and charged the man as I ran full-out into the open park. I heard barking and an angry shout then Pepper galloped by my side again. We shot out of the park at the intersection of Avenida México and Calle Parras and stopped short. The avenue was choked with commuter traffic. I juked between the stopped cars, panting, a stitch in my side. From the opposite corner, I scanned the park for large men. None wearing black. My chest heaved. He'd melted back into the bamboo at the pond's edge.

We jogged back to our digs and thundered up the stairs to the kitchen. Señora Pérez poured me a cup of coffee and I fed Pepper. While he ate, I gulped down a Lala brand strawberry yogurt.

"How was your run, Señorita Jade?" Mrs. Pérez asked, patting Pepper's head as he finished bolting down his kibble.

Nice of her to make friends with my dog, but was that a knowing look in her eyes? I smiled and held my tongue. Could Anibal be connected to the incident in the park? That's two threats in eight hours. I'd find it hard to call them coincidences in normal circumstances, but little here in Mexico could be called normal. At least not my normal.

I grabbed my coffee and we rode up the elevator to our room—noise be damned. I had thirty minutes to make myself clean and presentable.

The doorbell chimed at eight-thirty. True to his word, Aguirre sent a car and driver for the short jaunt to Zona Rosa. I took a last look at my cream-colored dupioni silk skirt and pale pink crepe de chine blouse, adjusted my belt, and slipped into the lightweight gaberdine navy blazer I hoped would turn the outfit into a suit. Weren't suits the expected attire at summits? I frowned at my pumps. The doorbell rang again and I called down from the open window.

"I'm coming."

A man stepped away from the portico and looked up. The scruffy guy who'd come into the Celebration of Life at Lidia's with El Santo. Aguirre's man? But what would he be doing with The Saint? I shuddered. What was I getting into? Maybe Anibal was right, or maybe I was feeling paranoid after being accosted in the park.

"Good morning, Miss Stone, Senator Aguirre has sent me to fetch you to the Summit on Organized Crime." He smiled.

Despite his Miami Vice beard and rumpled dress, he exuded familiar warmth. I still felt apprehensive, but wanted to get to the bottom of this little mystery. He spoke in California-accented English.

"G-g-good Morning. I'll be right there," I stammered and pulled my head back through the window. "Come on, Pepper, let's go. You can stay with Señora Pérez."

Pepper woofed his assent.

The driver held open the rear door of Aguirre's Mercedes while I slid onto the soft leather seat. Nice car.

"Buckle up, please, Miss Stone."

I grabbed the belt and fished around for the latch, spilling the contents of my clutch onto the spotless floor. Drat. No wallet.

"Let me get that," he said and scooped up my cell phone, lipstick, and passport, dumping them into my lap.

"Thank you, uh, do you have…"

The door closed on my question and the nameless driver walked around to the driver's seat and got in.

"I was asking if you have a name," I said, when the door closed. I shifted to eye his face in the rearview mirror. His eyes met mine. My eyes met mine—the exact shade of green. The exact shape. Even his brows matched mine in color and arch. My heart palpitated.

He turned over the engine and, sliding his arm over the seat to reveal a vicious snake undulating from shirtsleeve to his wrist. "Of course I do. I'm Jackman Quint." He jerked out his hand. His brow crinkled and his head cocked slightly —just the way mine does.

Should I know him? I tore my eyes off the ugly tattoo and saw myself mirrored in his expectancy. Did Jackman Quint expect me to shake hands with that striking rattler? What kind of person inked something so off-putting right in plain view? I gasped and shrank toward the door, ready to bolt back into the house. At least my dad's rattler undulated up his arm and the scary teeth hid under his sleeve, even on a hot day. I hated that tattoo and this one looked just like it. I imagined the two entwined, becoming a two-headed snake.

"Why the hell are you stalking me?"

He pulled his arm back and regarded me through the rearview mirror, brow furrowed. "I'm not stalking you. Why would you think that?" Quint asked.

"It was you at the bar in Las Velas. Spying on us. Then at the Celebration of Life—watching me. I recognize the tattoo."

He'd engaged the gears and pulled slowly away from the curb. "Of course you do. It's the mate to Charley's. We got them when you were born."

"Stop! Let me out of here, Jack Quint." I slapped the

back of his seat. "Stop, I say!"

The car stopped and I lurched forward. He twisted toward me again. "Charley never told you about me then," he said, softly. His eyes saddened. "Go on, honey, call him." He reached his cell phone over the seat. "Go on, take it. It's time you knew."

I bristled. Honey? I'm not your honey, soldier. "I don't know a Charley," I said, in the coldest tone my anger could muster and started to get out of the car.

"Please, JadeAnne, Miss Stone, please get back in the car. Call Charley. Ask him who I am. I'm not stalking you, but I've been looking for you since Worthington turned up at your door. I knew it was you."

I felt weak, disoriented, light-headed. The driver was crazy—or was this a ruse to confuse me?

My gut turned over. The rattlesnake tattoo—I had seen it on Aguirre's estate. The prisoner losing at dominos, that was Jack Quint.

"Are you kidnapping me?" I shrieked, as I tried to shove the door open. The locks clicked.

The driver ignored me and continued talking. He sounded like a madman. Something about Vietnam, heroin, Charley. I couldn't follow him. I couldn't breathe. I gasped as my chest heaved and my skin turned clammy. The bright morning faded.

The next thing I knew, the driver was sitting next to me patting my hand and murmuring, "Breathe slow, Jade. Deep. Good. Good. Take another slow deep breath."

I coughed and shook my tingling fingers free of his gentle grasp. "What the hell?"

"You panicked. You'll be all right now," he said. "I'll deliver you to your conference on time. We can get acquainted later when you've had time to call Charley." He slid out of the backseat and resumed his post behind the steering wheel.

I drank in several lead-laden gulps of morning air, calming myself. Was he talking about my father? Did Jack know my real father, the one who died in Vietnam? But I asked, "Charley who?" as the pretty Deco-style buildings of the Condesa slid by my window. I needed to get out of this car and away from this brain-addled Vietnam vet. This one with his cruel serpent tattoo wasn't the shy homeless guy who slept on my dock back home and gratefully accepted a hot cup of coffee from me in the morning.

I tried the window switch. The window cracked open a half inch. I flicked the lock button and my door unlocked. He was pretty stupid if he really was kidnapping me. I could jump out at the next light and melt into the morning bustle on Avenida Insurgentes.

"Charley Stone, the man who adopted you after sending me to Leavenworth. Obviously you don't know your history."

"My father has never gone by Charley."

"Yeah, Charles Smyth Stone—Charley to his army buddies. He's never told you about me, has he?"

I could see him looking at me again through those eyes, my eyes. I shuddered as I recalled a sharp image of that tattoo sinking out of view on the down escalator while I paid for my groceries in the Zihuatanejo Mega. I tucked my bag under my arm and reached for the door handle, ready to jump at the next light.

"You're the man who stalked me in Zihua. Don't deny it. The tattoo. But where's the ponytail?"

The car slowed and I tensed for escape.

"It wasn't what you thought. Have lunch with me and I'll explain. Please, don't jump out of a moving car in traffic. I don't want to lose you again."

CHAPTER SEVENTEEN

My Life has been a Lie

I clutched the door handle, something I was getting good at in Mexico City. A city of suicide drivers. I hoped this Jack Quint wasn't hell-bent on dying, because as far as I was concerned, it wasn't my day to die. A break in the traffic opened and the Mercedes jumped into the left lane and turned ahead of a rush of oncoming taxis then immediately turned right and slowed to a stop in front of Hotel Geneve Ciudad de Mexico.

"Lose me?" I said, my voice a near screech.

"I lost you in 1975. I won't let it happen again."

"You must have me confused with someone else, Mr. Quint. I was a baby," I said, as an attractive man in smart-looking livery opened my door and helped me out of the Mercedes.

"*Bienvenida a Hotel Geneve Ciudad de Mexico Señorita* Stone. Senator Aguirre is expecting you. If you will follow me."

How nice, they were rolling out the red carpet for me after my death-defying ride—or was I being programmed?

"*Gracias*," I said. Did this guy expect a tip? Well, too bad. I hadn't brought any money. I dutifully followed the doorman into an elegant turn-of-the-century library—the lobby—and too beautiful to overlook, dotted with cream, clay, and brown-striped wingback chairs, loads of dark wood, ornate gilt frames, and what may have been a converted gas chandelier. I felt my tension dissipating into the wafting currents of wood polish and old books. I ran my fingers over an antique typewriter perched upon a gleaming mahogany table. The hotel looked like a museum. My kind of place. A place this Jack Quint had no business.

"Miss Stone, thank you for joining me. I trust that Mr. Quint arrived on time?" Aguirre, formal in his blue gabardine suit and school tie, bowed slightly and held out a hand to me. I took it.

"Yes, thank you, Senator Aguirre. But your driver. Is he, ah, crazy?" I didn't want to blurt out anything, but I couldn't think of a more apt description.

A cluster of important appearing gentlemen turned toward us. Aguirre raised his arm sweeping me into his circle of power. "Gentlemen, please allow me to introduce my guest. This is Miss Stone from California, a friend of my late cousin come for the funeral. Miss Stone is a journalist and has taken an interest in our criminal insurgency."

The men drifted closer, smiling. I wrenched my face into what I hoped would pass for graciousness.

"Miss Stone, Senator Rodolfo Bendicias from the State of Mexico."

The young senator took my hand in his. "*Encantado*," he said, holding my gaze a beat too long. As I shook hands, I thanked God my manicure had held up.

"And Mayor Marcelo Fallas." I nodded in the direction of a well-fed belly.

"How do you do, sir."

The third man stood slightly behind the mayor and he jerked his head sideways. "My bodyguard," he said, by way of introduction. "I hope our little summit tells you

154

everything you need to portray our law enforcement in a positive light," he continued, eyeing me up and down.

Dirty old man.

"I'm sure it will, sir."

"Then, shall we go in, gentlemen?" Aguirre smiled at me as he guided me through the door. "And lady." Another nod.

No surprises at the plenary session. Aguirre welcomed us to the summit and spoke on the need for reforms and actions to be taken to safeguard Mexico from the growing threat of organized crime. He then introduced Mayor Fallas who babbled for the next thirty minutes about how Mexico City was so safe the cartels didn't dare come into his town, or the long arm of the law would be sure to pluck them from the population and send them to prison where they belong. He forgot to mention the last Police Chief murdered the month before by the Arellano-Felix gang. Fallas could dissemble with the best of them—I'd give him that, but whose pocket was he in? I'd heard the Zetas had claimed El Distrito as their own. But what did I know. I worried about Anibal's affiliation. I worried about the American girls turned over to Consuelo for "safe" keeping. And I dreaded this business with Jack Quint. Damn, I need to get out of here and call Dad.

Finally the last plenary speaker, some woman whose name I missed while obsessing over Aguirre's bodyguard-driver, finished to enthusiastic applause. I darted out of my seat and up the side aisle toward the door. Aguirre caught my eye and frowned, but I marched on. A man with a curling wire going into his ear followed me out the door. I slipped into the ladies room and locked myself into a stall. How could I pay attention to these talks all day? I already felt wrung out. I flushed and went to the sink to wash up. A woman with an ear wire monitored me from the lounge area. I patted my neck and face with a damp towel, dried off, and smiled at the agent as I left the restroom.

The rest of the morning I attended most of the large group talks on various topics held in the theater, a pretty, sloping room with velvet theater seats. Although I hadn't noticed heavy security, except following me, the first session was a panel on President Calderon's War on Drugs, and surprisingly, the president actually slipped in through a side door and gave a speech. I wished my Spanish were better. How often do you sit in the third row when a president speaks? The panel also featured Aguirre and Mexico's Drug Czar, Noe Ramirez Mandujano—wasn't he The Saint's uncle? I missed the last introduction, Hector somebody, the CEO of some big company.

The mayor was right, though, this would make for an interesting article if I would pay more attention. Especially the Q & A. Oh my god! I couldn't believe how the audience hammered the panel with questions and derision. The CEO, although a smooth speaker, was ignored. His talk—whining about production limitations for lack of workers because the cartels siphoned off the work force through high wages and intimidation, therefore lowering revenues—turned the audience off.

A young man, probably a student, called out, "People are getting killed in this war. Not just the criminals. What are you doing about it?"

Calderon replied, "The deaths in the country are because of the criminal organizations; criminal organizations that are recruiting young people like you, to create addicts and criminal gangs and to kill other young people."

It sounded a bit simplified to me, but the audience, mostly folks in business suits, roared approval.

The president continued, "If you or others presume that the Mexican—my government—would cross its arms and watch as they attack the young people of Mexico, as they kidnap them, as they extort them, you are very mistaken."

"But interdiction doesn't work. We've got to cut off the money," a hipster in the back row yelled. "Why aren't you listening to Senator Aguirre?"

"Stop the money. Good luck! The *gabachos* aren't going to stop buying cocaine. It's the U.S. that should be solving the problem. Country full of drug addicts," another student yelled.

Within ten minutes the room had devolved into mayhem and the president was whisked away. Aguirre promised to report on his committee's findings and what Mexico was doing to "get 'em where it hurt" at the noon session.

I didn't notice a chaperone as I slipped out to call Dad.

I'd complained for eons about the sappy Muzak Dad's firm played while callers "held" for their parties, and it was still playing. What was that, a Donny and Marie song from the seventies? The Umbrella Song?

"How can I help you, JadeAnne?" my father demanded.

"Gag me with a spoon, Dad. You're still playing that awful music!"

"JadeAnne, did you have me pulled out of an important meeting to criticize the on-hold music? How much do you need?"

"I don't need any money, Dad. I need some answers." I watched Summit delegates streaming into the lobby. Must be break.

"Can't this wait until I get home?"

The row of pay phones in the hallway filled up. "No, Dad. I'm calling you from a hotel in Mexico City on my cell and I need to know now."

I heard his exasperated whoosh of breath

"All right, what is so important? Why don't you ask that man you're keeping company with?" Dad didn't try to hide the sneer. "That Dex."

"Jack Quint." Static air sounded on the line. "Dad? Dad, are you still there?"

He cleared his throat. "What is your question?"

"Who is Jack Quint? Why is he stalking me?"

"Call the police, honey. If someone is stalking you, it's the police you need."

"Dad, I'm at a Summit on Organized Crime sitting with the senator from Michoacán and the mayor of Mexico City, but I'm asking you. Why does a man named Jack Quint have the same tattoo as you—"

"I've had it removed, JadeAnne—"

"I don't care, Dad. Why does Jack Quint wear your tattoo and tell me to ask you about him? Answer me." I made my voice as firm as I could. Several of the women snaking through the ladies room line turned to look at me. I held the phone from my ear and shrugged. "Dad. Now is the time."

"JadeAnne, I'm not sure how you've met this character, but you should get away from him as fast as you can. Can't your private detective protect you?"

"He broke up with me. Would you just tell me who he is and how you know him?"

Dad hesitated. I could hear his breath, but the moment had slowed into unreality. I braced against the wall for the blow to come. The truth. I already knew it. My stomach went queasy.

"Jack Quint is your biological father."

His words were a punch to my gut and I exhaled, sagging down the wall and dropping the phone. The man at the closest pay phone handed my cell back to me.

"Dad? Dad I'm still here. You're making that up!" I snapped, red hot magma surging through my veins. "You're lying. You've lied to me for my entire life."

"I wanted to protect you, JadeAnne. He was never to contact you. He abandoned you and I found you. You wouldn't have been placed onto that plane."

He continued—the Vietnam War, the heroin, Jack's arrest and conviction.

"Did you lie about my mother too?" My words sounded aggressive. I'd never doubted my father before, even if I didn't often agree with him.

"No. She died."

"Daddy? What do I do now?"

"I'm sorry, Jade. You're an adult. You'll figure it out."

I fled to the library and sank onto a couch facing an antique typewriter. Wasn't that what I was supposed to be doing? Writing fluff for the IJ? A column maybe? Life in Marvelous Marin. Dad had given up guilt-tripping me for my "expensive Stanford education in journalism" that I never used. Was he right? Had I made a huge mistake?

I felt the hot tears tracking down my face. I'd embarrass Aguirre in front of his colleagues with my mascara dripping off my chin. No, it wasn't really happening. I'd stepped through a rent in reality. This is Mexico after all. Magical Realism—a dead birthfather is the chauffeur. Why not? My real family, my workaholic, distant father; my socialite, pill-popping mother; my perfect dead sister—I belonged to them. Didn't I? I groaned and lowered my face into my hands.

"Miss, may I help you?"

I looked up into the concerned face of a hotel employee.

"Thank you, no. I've had disturbing news from home."

"Perhaps some water and a tissue will help," she said, and scurried off.

"Nothing will help," I mumbled, and wiped my palms across my cheeks. Who was I kidding? My family had made me walk the plank. They'd lied to me for almost thirty-two years. This creepy soldier of fortune with scary tattoos was my father? It explained a lot.

I'd been cut adrift by my boyfriend, by my family. On my horizon, only a suspect senator and his untrustworthy half-brother. Unless someone was lying. Unless everyone was lying. Jack Quint couldn't be my life-ring. Who was I going to trust? Possibly only my dog. I'd better get paddling, then. Before this riptide of betrayal sucked me under. The tears welled up again.

"Here you are, Miss." The employee handed me a box of tissues and set a sweating bottle of water and a glass of ice onto the polished table. They would leave rings.

"*Gracias, qué amable, señorita.*"

"*Por nada.*" Her smile looked kind and a little sad as she retreated back to her work.

I blew my nose and swigged off the Peñafiel. Better freshen up and find Aguirre, my lunch ticket. I stood up and found myself face-to-face with Quint.

"You've talked to him."

It wasn't a question; his voice sounded apprehensive. He must be nervous too. I hadn't considered that.

"Yeah, Mr. Quint, er—what am I supposed to call you?"

"Jack works."

Really? I didn't think I could call my father Jack.

"Can your old man buy you lunch?" He half-smiled. Joking, I guess.

"I'm supposed to lunch with the senator," I replied, a little stiffly.

Quint snorted. "Nah, he's tied up with his hotshot colleagues. Come on. I know a joint with great tacos. Go powder your nose and meet me out front. I'll bring the car around."

Wow, he can just use Aguirre's car? "The senator won't mind?" I asked, stupidly.

"It's your car today. The boss has instructed me to take you to the Pedrigal to check on the girls."

"To Consuelo?"

"Yeah."

"Look, I need to go there, but I'll take a cab. You don't have to take me. Just tell me the address and I'll go myself." I didn't trust this new twist in the day's plans. Another shift in reality. Quint might be my sire, but that didn't mean I trusted Aguirre. He'd invited me to the Summit and now he wanted me to go across the city?

"It's my job to see you safely there and back in time for the afternoon session. You only have two hours. Let's go. We can talk in the car." Quint took my elbow and guided me toward the door.

So much for powdering my nose.

The moment of my abduction swirled through my mind in images. But who was directing this scene? Aguirre? Was I supposed to resist or go along with Quint perp-walking me away from safety? The lobby doors silently closed behind me. The Mercedes purred at the curb, the liveried doorman holding my door, smiling. Quint guided me in; I half expected him to push my head down cop-like.

He bent in and grinned at me. "Buckle up, JadeAnne. We want to keep you safe."

The door clicked shut. I could feel it in my bones. This hadn't anything to do with Aguirre or Anibal. Was this a big set-up to extort millions from Dad? They'd be SOL, shit out of luck. Dad wouldn't pay ten cents to get me back because "I'm an adult, I'll figure it out".

CHAPTER EIGHTEEN

That's Madam Consuelo to You

I had to hand it to Quint. He knew his way around the city, even managing to avoid most of the lunch rush. I wasn't locked in the car, and he projected friendliness and interest as he attempted to initiate a conversation. But I wasn't having any of it. I looked out the window at the passing scene. Even that didn't interest me much. He punched on the radio.

"Not hungry, are you?" Quint's steel-wool voice vibrated over the pop music blaring from the speakers. Cristian. An oldie. *"Si no quieres mi amor, para mi, no me importa, te quiero a morir…"*

Yeah, exactly—he wants me to die. Everyone wants me to die, or at least go away. I was lost, slumped into a Mercedes going who-knew-where inside a potential hornet's nest.

Well, not entirely lost. I recognized the attractive Del Valle district when Quint picked up *tacos suadero* at a street stand. They smelled wonderful and my stomach growled. Time to get over myself and move on. Lunch was here. I sat up.

The stand, Antojitos del Valle, served tiny, steaming

tacos with perfectly crisp *chile manzana*. My favorite turned out to be Quint's favorite too. I guess we had tacos in common. That and dripping taco fat all over Aguirre's car. I wasn't ready to concede inherited genetic makeup just yet and blotted salsa off my blouse instead. I noticed Quint had a blob of fatty meat on his shirt. Slobbery wasn't an inherited trait, was it?

About the time I'd crumpled the tinfoil and greasy napkins into an equally grease-stained bag, we pulled up to another modern split-level house built into the flows of lava. The neighborhood impressed me with attractive homes and gorgeous landscaping all built on, in, and around the lava field, the *pedrigal*. Hence the name: Lomas de Pedrigal. Consuelo's house reminded me of school friends' homes built in the fifties in Kent Woodlands—lots of wood and glass set on large parcels. Not as many trees here, but the plantings in Consuelo's yard looked mature. A few giant cacti poked from the rock along the walkway to the grand front door. I noticed a sunny patio dotted with teak furniture and a pool.

"Quint, do you think that pool is carved right into the lava flow?"

"Nah, it's cement dyed black to look like the rock. I've been here before." He pressed the doorbell.

"You didn't tell me that," I glared at him.

"Hey. I've only known you for a couple hours. Give me a chance, JadeAnne."

I'd upset him. He clenched his jaw and wiggled his left fingers against his thigh, shifting his weight, foot to foot, almost imperceptibly. I should be a little nicer. But it would be good to have the facts before entering the enemy's camp. Or would this be my prison? Would I be allowed to swim?

"I didn't mean to—"

"I was here on some business for the senator. Crazy bitch came on—"

A uniformed maid opened the door, cutting Quint off. She couldn't have been older than ten and wore a typical plaid pinafore covering her black dress.

"Get back to your work, Nedda," a gravelly voice slurred from the hall. The girl cringed and bowed her head. Like the maid at Aguirre's farm. What was up with working children? The little girl shrank away as Consuelo appeared. "Get goin', you lil' rat. Move." She slapped out at the child, missed, and the girl scurried through a doorway out of sight. "These girls," she mumbled at Nedda's retreating back then looked up and started, upsetting her balance. She gripped the door to steady herself.

"Hello, Jack. To what do I owe this lovely s-s-surprise?" Consuelo took his hand in hers, caressed it and drew him into the entry hall. Not even a nod toward me. Piece of work, indeed. And I thought she was so hot on the late Daniel Worthington. I trailed behind them, waving away the bourbon fumes, into a tasteless living room overcrowded with chairs and occasional tables. The furnishings shared a garish cherry color scheme, and a hint of modernity, but competed with the flowered carpet and striped gold curtains. Nothing was where it should be. The cherry-colored couch turned its back to the fireplace and the framed art, if that's what she called it, was either too large or too small for its position on the walls.

Several men conversed at one end of the room. A couple of others read newspapers or spoke quietly on cell phones. All had cocktails and fat cigars in-hand and looked middle-aged, porky even. Consuelo certainly had a bunch of loser gentlemen friends. And the heavy cherry red decor clashed with her hair.

She led Jack through the room to the patio door. "Sit." She gestured vaguely toward a chair. "Let me pour you a drink, Jack."

He waved her off and took a seat in one of the low

chairs. "Miss Stone has come to take charge of the American girls. The senator requests that you turn them over to her now."

"Oh, yes, Miss Stone." Her head swung lazily in my direction and gave me a bleary sizing up. "The American hanging all over the servant's son at Lidia's. Jack, a whiskey?"

She smiled coyly but it looked played out. Practiced.

"It's a little early in the day for me, Consuelo."

"Then I'll jus' go find mine," she slurred. She lit a cigarette from a pack and tossed it onto the table next to her and wobbled across the patio. Having not been invited to sit, I followed her.

Quint's tone sounded threatening as he called behind us, "Bring them to us now, please. Senator Aguirre has made arrangements to reunite them with their family."

Consuelo glanced around at him and lipped something I didn't quite catch. "...wants everyone to think he's such a do-gooder." Aguirre?

I stepped into her personal space, towering over her, hopefully intimidating the drunken woman. She stepped back and almost toppled over one of her little patio tables. The color rising in her cheeks clashed with her hair, too.

"We don't have time to fool around, Consuelo. Get them."

She thumped her wide *derrier* into the chair next to the table and tinkled a tiny bell she'd pulled from a pocket. Nedda appeared.

"Girl, bring my guests a glass of wine." The girl stared at Consuelo without moving. "Are you deaf, Nedda? I said bring our guests wine." The girl's eyes said it all. She didn't understand the order. "The regular girl is off today," Consuelo said.

Quint spoke rapidly. I didn't understand a word he said. It sounded sort of like Spanish, but clearly was not. He finished and the girl nodded and replied in the unfamiliar language. He lunged up from the chair and stood over Consuelo. Jack definitely was menacing. Consuelo cowered, but tried to look defiant. She turned to the girl and waved her away. "Send the cook with the wine." Nedda fled from the room.

"Where did this child come from, Consuelo? Don't lie to me. She's Iraqi."

My mouth fell open. "That was Arabic? You know Arabic? How did she get here?"

Quint's tone and the anger in his eyes brought tears to my mine. "She was sold—"

"What did that lyin' rat of a girl tell you? Is a lie, I tell you."

He clenched his fists as he got right into her face. "Where are the Americans? Get them. Now."

Quint's voice would have frozen the Sahara. The look of loathing and pure disgust on his face sent a shockwave of fear through me. He was just like the tattoo, a rattlesnake about to sink his fangs into the enemy. I shuddered. What if I crossed him? What would he do?

Consuelo sneered at him, clearly lubricated, "I've delivered 'em to the American Embassy. They're gone." The gleam in her bloodshot eyes was of sheer triumph.

"You're lying." He raised his forearm, palm wide.

Consuelo flinched back into her chair, sneer replaced with fear.

Quint pulled his cell phone out of his pocket and flipped it open. "I'll just go ahead and verify that, Consuelo."

"I, uh, I didn't mean I took them to the Embassy personally. I meant—"

"Who has the girls, Consuelo? The senator wants them. Now." Quint spoke slowly, his words measured. Goosebumps tingled along my arms. The calm before the storm.

"Aguirre doesn't need to bother his meddlesome head," she whined, then glanced into her lap and suppressed a tiny smile. "They're gone," she repeated, unaware we'd both caught her moment of triumph. What had she done with the American girls?

Quint clenched his fists. No one said anything. Perhaps I was going to find out what happens when you cross the man purporting to be my father.

A woman appeared with a bottle of wine and three glasses and waited silently for instructions. I heard a voice coming from a nearby window. A girlish voice.

"I have to use the bathroom," I said, and bolted into the living room, almost tripping over the little maid crouched inside. The conversing men looked up. One beckoned to me, a lascivious gleam in his eye. What the hell was going on here?

The child sprang up, crossed the room and jetted down the hall. I followed her. She pointed to a door. It was locked, but I could hear what sounded like sobbing on the other side. It was a cheap lock. I fished in my bag for a hairpin.

Something yanked me off my feet and flung me into the wall. I caromed into the opposite wall and bounced to the floor. The tiny girl flew in front of me, arms out as if to ward off the attacker. Our attacker, a hirsute bulldog, lunged toward her but Quint materialized between us and karate chopped the man's muscular back. He dropped to the floor.

"Are you all right, JadeAnne?" he asked.

"Yeah, I'm okay," I said, as I shook out my limbs and climbed to my feet. "I heard girls crying in there." I nodded to the door.

Consuelo's guard pushed up to all fours, a fighting dog gathering strength for the next round.

Quint grabbed his collar. "Open the door," he ordered.

The man scrambled to his feet and did what he was told. Smart man. Now I'd learned why you don't cross Quint.

The door banged open and a heavy-jowled, ape-shaped, fat man lumbered off a terrified young woman who clutched the bedsheets around her. I backed out of the room feeling pretty stupid. Consuelo ran a whorehouse?

Consuelo stretched on a patio lounge, puffing at a slim black cigarette, her half full, lipstick-stained wineglass in easy reach.

"Where are the girls, Consuelo?" My demand wasn't as dramatic as Quint's, but it would have to do. I felt sick to my stomach. She wanted to turn those little girls into whores.

"I told you, I sent them to the Embassy."

"I don't believe you. What's going on in this house?" I said.

"What are you accusing me of, Miss Stone? Maybe you should ask your boyfriend what he's up to, and with whom before you go pointing your prissy little fingers." A Mexican Mae West, she aimed her stubby legs toward Quint and lolled deeper into the chair, her posture cooing, *why don't you come up and see me sometime*?"

"Anibal rescued those girls."

"What happened to the others, Miss Stone? Picked up in a helicopter? My, my. The U.S. government isn't officially sanctioned to be working here, but it certainly has ass-assets available. Don'cha think?"

"What are you trying to say, Consuelo?" Quint wrinkled his brow and narrowed his eyes. Did he suspect Anibal too?

"Oh, Jack, don't mind me. I'm just going on. Please, enjoy s'more wine." She took a swig off her glass and gave Quint a bleary smile. "Miss Stone, how'd you come to know Danny? Poor Danny. It's so sad. I knew that wife of his would get him into trouble."

"Oh, yeah? What did Lura have to do with it?" I said.

"You know, a wife should stand with her man. Lura didn't. Danny was going to leave her. For me." She paused for dramatic effect, eyes gleaming.

What universe did this Consuelo live in? Certainly not mine—or maybe I didn't belong in hers. Neither Quint nor I responded. She unsteadily grabbed her wineglass and gulped the wine then reached for the bottle. Empty.

"Lura got in the way. She and that Anibal, double agents, I'm afraid. Out to take everything for themselves."

I tensed. That was the second time someone called Ani a double agent. Was he another loser? I didn't want to believe it. I could trust him. Couldn't I?

"Consuelo, sober up. Come on, JadeAnne, let's get out of here." Quint helped me to my feet and guided me toward the front door.

"I'll go to the embassy while you meet with the boss," he said. "Where's Nedda?"

"Shouldn't we take that poor woman—?"

"Too late, JadeAnne, she's an adult."

Our shoes clattered over the polished Saltillo tile in the hall and echoed from the stucco walls. Hollow. Kind of how I felt, leaving without Lily and little Evie. My shoulders tightened with the image of the frightened woman in the bedroom. We were leaving her to endure the degradation of those flabby old men we saw sucking on their cigars in the living room. Had she started out as an enslaved teen locked into a basement or warehouse or a cave? For a moment I hated people and all the greedy evil humans inflict on each other.

We entered the reception hall. Nedda held the door open for us, tears streaking her cheeks. Quint said something in Arabic, she nodded and he swung her into his arms. Nedda buried her face into his shoulder as she grasped him in a neck lock I thought might choke him to death. Nothing was going to pry that little girl off my alleged father.

But it was something else we had in common. I wasn't the only one who saved children. Jack Quint advanced in my estimation. Maybe he wasn't such an awful person after all.

Just maybe.

Quint buckled the little girl into the backseat and walked around to the driver's side door after checking that mine was latched. I blew out the breath I'd held since we left Hotel Geneve. Quint was pulling a child out of slavery and had protected me from the guard.

Give him bonus points.

"Buckle up," he said. I'll get you back and deliver Nedda to her embassy.

"Shouldn't we search the house? Consuelo's lying. I know she's lying—"

Quint keyed the Mercedes's engine. It purred into life. "The girls are gone. But not into safety. Consuelo isn't just a drunk."

I clicked my seatbelt into the buckle and locked my door as the car slid through the Lomas de Pedrigal gates and cruised toward the Periferico. "What do you mean? I get it, she's a madam, but why would she want those American girls?"

"Wake up, JadeAnne. There's something fishy going on. She's not smart enough to have put this operation together; she's working for someone else. Can't you see Anibal's the one who delivered them to her?"

"You're wrong, Mr. Quint. Ani dropped them because I'd been shot. I think everyone is making too much of it. He saved them."

Quint grunted. He didn't share my opinion. Nedda yawned and I turned to watch her slump to the seat, a tiny puddle of cheap clothes.

I shifted to face Quint. "Do you suppose Worthington met her as a customer? He and his wife didn't live together."

He turned toward me. A loopy grin spread across his face and his eyes twinkled.

"What? What's so funny? It's true."

"Your face is so earnest. Just like your mother when she

wanted to change the subject."

"My mother! Tell me about her, Mr. Quint." I fished into my bag for my wallet. "Oh, damn, I forgot my wallet. I have a photo of her."

Quint watched the road for a silent moment, maneuvering the car through a tricky multi-lane highway entrance. A cloud had passed over his face and his grin faded. Was Quint sad? Maybe I read too much into it and it was just the angle of view. I could only see his profile.

"Call me Jack."

I wasn't sure I could. I didn't really think he was out to kidnap me anymore, but I wasn't about to get that chummy with him just because he sired me. He'd abandoned me and my mother, when things got tough in Vietnam—just to make a buck. At least that's what Dad had told me. Odd that he'd care about the Iraqi girl when he hadn't cared about his own daughter. Or maybe that was exactly why—atonement. Either way, why the hell should I trust this man?

A delivery truck cut in front of us spewing exhaust. Quint stomped on the brake, honking. We dropped back and three green and white VW taxis jumped into the space. Quint shot into the next lane, accelerating to speed. Traffic moved but not all that fast. Ahead I could see a major slowdown.

"After lunch rush hour. It's two. You'll be late for the first session."

"Shouldn't we figure out what happened to the girls?"

"The senator expects you, Jade. I'll handle it."

I gazed through the windshield at the ugly polluted city churning by. Everything was the color of yellowish sand. The air, the buildings, the sky. After Consuelo, everything looked slummy and dirty. My skin crawled with the grime. I didn't want to go back to the Summit. I wanted to go back to Condesa, see my dog and relax in a hot soapy tub.

Quint braked, jerking me back to the conversation. "I want you to leave Anibal's house. I don't trust Aguirre's brother."

"Do you even know him? Aguirre has always treated him badly."

Quint's laugh sounded like a rusted hinge. "As badly as any rich punk can be treated," he said.

"Ani works for a living. He doesn't grow marijuana like your employer, Mr. Quint."

"Look, JadeAnne, Senator Aguirre has intelligence you or I can't get. He thinks you're in danger. He wants you to stay at the Polanco apartment until this situation is resolved."

"Oh, right. I'm not falling for that." I glared at him, letting his stupidity sink in. "It's your boss who's in the cartel's pocket." I heard my voice rising. I knew I should shut up, but I was powerless to stop. Anger boiled off my tongue, "Anyway, who do you think you are telling me what to do? You gave that right up thirty-two years ago."

Quint stiffened, his face contorted and burned red. He looked like he was going to cry—or was it rage? He didn't say anything, just skidded to the curb in front of the hotel and sat, staring forward, hands tense on the wheel, head erect, a rattler coiled, ready to spring.

A new liveried doorman opened my door. He was portly and short with a broad indigenous forehead and angled features. I started to slide out of the car.

Quint clamped his calloused hand around my wrist. "JadeAnne. You are wrong about the Aguirres."

I yanked free and sashayed away from the car, head high, feigning a confidence I didn't feel, even as confusion ripped me to shreds. Wrong? Not me. How could I believe him? He'd left me when the Viet Cong captured Saigon, but my heart whispered he spoke the truth.

CHAPTER NINETEEN

A Summit on Organized Crime

The doorman scurried to hold the lobby door open, smiling broadly. His hand begged for pesos. I tossed my head in the direction of the Mercedes. "The chauffeur will tip you." Quint probably would, but I felt stingy anyway. This guy only wanted to make a living and good for him he worked for a hotel, not a crime gang. That alone deserved a reward.

But I was late. The afternoon sessions had started and I hoped I hadn't missed either Aguirre on money laundering or the talk on human trafficking that included agents from SEIDO. I gently pushed open the door to the conference hall.

Aguirre gesticulated from the lectern. A bar graph glowed on the screen behind him measuring by state the estimated billions of pesos in crime revenue laundered annually through Mexico's legitimate business structures since 1989. I sank into an empty seat in the back row. The amounts were awe-inspiring. Especially Sinaloa. No wonder organized crime ran rampant in this country.

"You can see for yourselves that the amount of money laundered each year is significant. I find it strange that the state governments act as if they are free of corruption. How can these drug trafficking organizations operate without the complicity of the government? Nothing is done in terms of financial investigations at the state level." He paused.

A smattering of applause greeted his scowl.

"Only the federal government has bureaus for financial intelligence. How can we, here in *La Capital*, effectively combat money laundering when the money is going for farms in *las provincias* or kindergartens in *los pueblos*?" Aguirre glared into the room again but the hall remained silent. "We cannot monitor these far-flung territories from Mexico City. But my friends...to truly wage war on drug trafficking we must attack the organizations in their *bolsas* —"

The room thundered with approval, drowning out the senator's voice. But I wondered how many of these fat cats were benefitting from the cartel money.

"Take away their money and they lose their power. Take away their money and these drug kingpins will no longer be able to bribe their and their products' safety. Without money? The risks to these organizations increases a thousand-fold. "Let us take these devils down, cutting them off *peso* by *peso* until they have fallen back to the pits where they belong!" Aguirre's voice echoed throughout the theater as the screen shifted to a list of business names and cities. I didn't understand. The sponsors? The list scrolled: Culiacan... Culiacan... Culiacan... I got it—the Sinaloan cartel. The senator was suggesting boycotting any business owned by the organized crime families and tightening up on banking laws. The crowd ate it up. I saw the approval on the faces around me. Was Aguirre going to make a bid for president in the next election?

Again the room erupted into applause and I observed Aguirre smiling from the lectern as he placed his notes into a folder. From the audience response I judged his talk to have been successful. This group would vote for him. He bowed his head to the crowd and leaned into his microphone.

"*Gracias. Gracias.*" He grinned and stiffly waved at the now-standing ovation. His face filled the projection screen behind him then panned back to show him smiling, acknowledging his fans. The perfect presidential candidate.

The projection changed to the schedule. Next up, a panel of professors including an American from the College of William and Mary in Virginia and the American Ambassador, Tito Garza. Sounded interesting, great minds analyzing the terror. I stayed put with most of the previous audience although the Summit offered seven additional breakout sessions. According to the schedule, these would be too focused in scope for me. Why would I need to know about weaponry for law enforcement? I hoped they had bigger guns than the cartels, but doubted it.

The lights dimmed as the panelists filed onto the stage and took their places at the table now dominating the podium. The governor of the State of Mexico moderated. The American professor was called upon to give a brief history of the rise of the cartels in Mexico. This guy was a scholar of the cocaine trade, starting his research in Colombia. Apparently, Mexico took over the South American coke trade in the eighties when the "war on drugs" heated up in Colombia.

"More than ever before, Mexico's security challenge is not one of overcoming singularly powerful enemies, but rather creating a social, economic, and political framework capable of dealing with both the root causes and the immediate manifestations of organized crime," the professor said.

Like cutting off the money. God—and the panelists— knew the demand wasn't going to let up. Pointing fingers north was a recurring theme, but I learned that since the first volley fired in Calderon's war on drugs the death toll had risen one hundred percent, and it was only August. The city of Juarez had become a failed city, a no man's land. The entire border had gone totally out of control and I could just imagine what the U.S. thought about that. How soon would the violence spill into El Paso, Brownsville, Tucson, and San Diego?

The panelists shared their fear that Mexico was imploding into a narco-state ruled by feuding drug lords. One expert reported kidnapping on the rise, even of poor people, and posited that the crimes are not reported largely because of lack of trust in the police—or the reality of police involvement with the crime. Poor Mexico.

Garza explained, "Calderon must, and will, keep the pressure on the cartels, but look, let's not be naïve—there will be more violence, more blood, and, yes, things will get worse before they get better. That's the nature of the battle. The cartels are like cornered animals. The more pressure we put on them, the more they will strike out."

Mexico's future looked bleak. So did mine. Could I really trust Anibal? Not for the first time I wondered why I stayed. I could go home, get back to work at Waterstreet Investigations, find a new boyfriend and tend my probably dead orchids. I doubted Dex was watering them. Damn him. A wave of longing washed over me and I slumped into my seat. I'd have gone home if he'd asked. But then I'd never have met my father. And now Quint wasn't going to want to know his rude daughter, anyway.

The audience clapped and the lights came up. I straightened in my chair and checked my watch. Pepper would want his dinner soon. Would Quint still drive me home?

"Miss Stone, may I invite you for refreshment before the last session?" The senator held out his hand to assist me from my seat.

"Uh, sure, Senator. I'd love a cup of tea."

"Then tea it is," he said and folded my arm into his as he

escorted me out of the theater and to a smaller parlor-like room marked *PRIVATE* where a refreshment station had been set up. The serving man offered me a plate and I realized I felt ravenous. I ordered a hot tea, accepted a few wedges of *quesadilla* and helped myself to my favorite *dulce de leche* candies. I joined Aguirre, now sipping a short glass of *tequila blanca*, on a couch along the wall. Clusters of important-looking people chatted. This was the "backstage" for the speakers.

"Senator, thank you for this opportunity. News coverage in California of Mexico's criminal insurgency isn't that great. I knew there were problems, but I had no idea the depth and breadth of it."

"I'm pleased you are enjoying the Summit, Miss Stone. Yes, my country is in trouble and I don't think we're going to solve our problems without some big changes. We've got to combat the corruption in the government and our law enforcement. But we also need to strike the cartels deeply and swiftly, and I don't think Mexico can do it alone. We need the U.S."

"There was a lot of blaming the U.S. in that last panel. Do you really think the U.S. will stop demanding drugs?"

"No, Miss Stone. I do not."

"So, what can we do? I mean, besides interdiction?"

"People need to know who we are, what Mexicans are up against because of this prohibition. I think if that were the story told in the States by a talented journalist, if a face were put to the horror, your countrymen might pressure your government to change its policies."

My jaw dropped. "You want me to write about the drug war?"

Aguirre smiled. "You have some talent, I've researched your work—"

"years ago—"

"—and you're here. Mr. Quint says you've refused my

177

offer of asylum. If you insist on staying with Anibal, you might as well make yourself useful. Yes, Miss Stone. I want you to research our problems, meet and talk with people, write a comprehensive history of organized crime in Mexico. Give Mexico a face that the U.S. citizen can recognize—" He raised his hand— "Wait, Miss Stone. Without bias, give our problems a face and get that face into the American public's eye. I will make available any research facilities or contacts I possess."

"Did you know Consuelo runs a whorehouse?" I blurted.

"I was aware of that, yes."

"Isn't it a touch hypocritical to talk about reforms and laws but allow her to operate?"

"Then you'll accept the assignment?"

I gazed across the room, thinking. The handsome woman studying her notes at small round table in the corner stuffed her papers into her briefcase and rushed out the door. She must be the next speaker, the one I wanted to hear, Rosi Orozco.

"At least, Senator, I'll go learn what I can about human trafficking."

Across the screen, the face of a young girl. Makeup. Provocative clothing. A hint of a shiner under one eye. Señora Orozco stepped to the lectern and told us the story of Lupe, rescued in a raid on her pimp's Texas operation. Lupe had been kidnapped when she was six and placed as a house slave with a rich Mexican family. When she was about twelve, she ran away and was seduced by a man promising her a good life in another city. She was taken to Tenancingo, plied with drugs, and raped repeatedly until she was ready to turn tricks across the border. Lupe has forgotten her family, her hometown, and her birthdate.

"My aim is to end the commercial and sexual exploitation of children in Mexico." Ms. Orozco's melodious voice resonated throughout theater. She paused. The smattering of women in the room clapped and cheered, joined by some of the younger men.

Her smile tightened, but she continued. "Human trafficking is a crime with a complex social impact whose main characteristic is to turn people into commodities that are traded on national and international black markets, which work under the impunity given to them by the authorities."

She glared at "the authorities" populating the audience. I pictured them at their clubs, tequila shooters in one hand, stubby *puros* in the other, joking as they selected and rejected a parade of scantily dressed underaged girls with the face of Evie. I felt sick.

"It is important to fight the roots that lead to the phenomenon of trafficking in persons, for most children, women, young victims of trafficking come from backgrounds of poverty, resulting from the lack of educational and employment opportunities." Rosi Orozco paused and gazed at the audience.

Sounds of sniffling and nose blowing filled the silence. I could barely listen as anger and shame boiled up from someplace deep inside of me. I hated how humans could do this. Greed, that's how. And my adopted dad probably saved me from it.

As she spoke, I wondered how money and the power it buys could be more important than life. Is ruining someone's life worth making a few more *pesos*? Not that it was so different in the corporate world, but was I naive to hope that corporations acted lawfully as they screwed the world to get ahead? I was out of my depth. What made these *delictivos* tick?

The next story was Maria's. Kidnapped into the sex trade at age fifteen, she now lives in a women's shelter and is training to be a teacher. She was sexually abused by one of the immigration officers that rescued her.

I couldn't listen anymore. Was a life of abuse at the hands of sick men what Lily and Evie had to look forward to? Violence, drug addiction, AIDS, death? No! I vowed to find the girls and make someone pay. Would it be Aguirre? And which Aguirre?

The Summit talks ended and I didn't really want to join Senator Aguirre at the cocktail party. I never knew what to say at those things. For someone with a degree in investigative journalism, I sucked at small talk. I had enough trouble in English, how would I manage in Spanish? I headed for the ladies room.

But how would I answer the senator? I'd never even used my degree. Anyway, too many ideas crowded my mind. I'd have to consider his wishes later. What if this were yet another trick to...to what? Sell me into slavery? Wasn't I too old?

I used the facilities, washed my hands and the bathroom attendant offered me a linen towel. I noticed the tray of coins at her station. Yikes. Was this her job? To sit in a lavatory and sell hand towels for tips? I forced a smile as I said "*Gracias,*" and ducked out without paying. The Ugly American.

My next problem, how would I get home? I couldn't grab a cab unless I could convince the cabbie to wait at the door while I ran in for money. I was thinking it might work as I entered the lobby. Quint rose from an upholstered chair and handed me a Starbucks and a small bag. I stopped and looked at him.

"Coffee and a scone. I guessed you'd be hungry."

"Uh, thanks, Quint. White?"

"Yes. I hope 2% is okay. I didn't know what you like. You ready to go home?"

"You're driving me?"

"Unless you'd rather walk."

"No, I, uh...I owe you an apology, Quint. I'm sorry for

what I said. I-I...well, I didn't know my story or what happened to you, or my mother." I hung my head, focusing on opening the coffee. Quint gently held my arm and guided me to the door. I suddenly felt wrung-out like a shirt cranked through an old-fashioned clothes wringer.

"No worries. You deserve to be angry. I should have found you years ago, JadeAnne. I gave my word to stay out of your life, yet you deserve the truth," he said, holding the lobby door open for me and passing some bills to the doorman.

"Mom and Dad said my parents were dead." I leaned on Quint as I teetered over the driveway cobbles in my heels.

Again he helped me into the Mercedes and settled himself behind the wheel. "In Charley's eyes, I was dead." He sighed and pulled away from the curb. "I made some mistakes, JadeAnne. Your old man ain't any prince either, but at least Charley got you out of that God-forsaken country."

The city passed by our windows as the Mercedes glided toward the Condesa. In Mexico it was sometimes hard to tell if a building was under construction or demolition. I closed my eyes. So much was beautiful in Mexico, and so much was ugly. Dirty. Vile.

"What happened to my mother?"

"She died having you. Lan wouldn't stay in Saigon without me. Charley'd turned me in and I was in jail, awaiting my hearing. She went home to her family. It was a little village near Da Nang. The Viet Cong had broken the ceasefire and was sweeping down from the north. Da Nang fell. The army shelled, looted, and burned everything in its path. The village doctor fled and my Lan was left in the clinic to fend for herself. Your grandmother delivered you."

Quint braked, horn blasting. His arm shot out to protect me from flying forward. People don't die in collisions now that we have airbags. People don't die in lots of ways today.

Now people don't need to die in labor like my mother. People don't need to die for another to live.

Hot rivulets streamed down my cheeks. I snapped back when Quint handed me a thin brown napkin left over from the luncheon tacos.

I choked out, "S-sorry."

The car fell silent again. We turned past the good Condesa *taquieria*. Almost to Anibal's, almost to Pepper. I wished we were going to Varda Landing, to the Sarasvati where Pepper and I would be safe. Insulated from the evils of this world.

"What did you find out about the girls, Quint?"

"Consuelo lied."

"Are you surprised? Where are they?"

"Not at the embassy. No one there knows anything about two missing American girls. I've made a report. The senator is exerting his influence, but frankly, JadeAnne, I doubt anyone will do anything."

The light turned red. Four cars ran through causing a snarl in the intersection. Horns blared. Quint idled the Mercedes and skirted around the jam when the light turned green.

"Especially if Aguirre is behind the sex trafficking."

"Won't you try to believe me? He is not involved." Quint's voice sounded emphatic. He sucked in a breath and softened his tone. "Let's have dinner tonight. The senator doesn't need his car. Let me convince you that you're living in the viper's nest. And I'll tell you about your family." Quint winked as we pulled in front of the house, a grin on his face. Did he know that was the one thing I longed for?

I hesitated. I wanted to badly to know about my mother, her family, but I was scared. What if...?

"I don't know, Quint, I'm awfully tired," I said as I opened the door. Purple jacaranda petals pirouetted on the slight breeze. The neighborhood looked peaceful, quiet.

Welcoming.

I still questioned Anibal's possible involvement. He wasn't a bad guy, just a guy who hated his brother. I got that. My perfect sister was the loved child in my family. I knew what it felt like to be out of step, different.

Quint hustled from the car and caught me at the door. "I can't let you go in alone. You're not safe, JadeAnne. Please, get the dog and your things. I'll take you to a safehouse if you won't go to the senator's."

I slid my key into the lock and swung open the door. Pepper torpedoed out and danced around me barking with joy. Had he sat there all day? I squatted and hugged him, burying my face into his fur. He licked my hand and pulled away to sniff Quint.

I stepped into the hall then turned back to Quint. "I have a grandmother?"

He held the door for Pepper then followed me. "You had two. Lan's mother died in a re-education camp. My mom lives in a retirement community in Florida. She and Dad were snowbirds from New York until he died about three years ago and she stayed."

I dropped the empty coffee cup and the untouched scone onto a table and hauled open the metal elevator gate. "Come on. You can wait in the kitchen while I freshen up."

CHAPTER TWENTY

The Tide has Turned

The elevator clanked open on the first floor and Pepper made a beeline to the bag of dog food leaning in the corner and sat down, ears up, an expression of expectation playing across his face.

"It isn't hard to figure out what the dog wants, is it?"

"No, he's got me well trained. I'm late feeding him. Can I get you a beer?" I asked, while I dipped kibble from the bag into Pepper's bowl. Pepper grinned and jumped to attention, wagging madly as I set the bowl next to his water.

"Sure, whaddya have?"

Quint's grin widened. It was infectious. I smiled.

I gave Pepper a pat and spun toward the refrigerator. "Let's see. Um, Corona, Victoria, Bohemia. I'm having a Victoria."

"I'll join you."

I popped two bottles and clunked one onto the table in front of Quint. "Are you hungry? Peanuts? Chips and salsa?"

"No, go get yourself comfortable and hurry back. I want some real food. Think about where you want to go."

"You'll be okay here?"

"Why not?"

"Maybe you could walk Pepper down to the garden when he finishes?" I nodded to the stair door.

"I could do that."

"That's the key." I pointed to the hook that now contained door keys since our intrusion as Anibal had promised. "I'll be fifteen minutes."

"That'll be the day when a woman can freshen up in fifteen minutes," he joked.

Or I hoped he was joking. I laughed. "Quint, you don't know me. You'll see." I grabbed my beer and waved as I started up the stairs to my room. I heard Quint greet Pepper. Everything sounded friendly.

I slipped off my heels and trudged up to Anibal's landing. I didn't need fifteen minutes. Should I stop in and let him know I was home? Was he home? This might be a good opportunity to find out why I'd never been invited to visit his floor. With Quint and Pepper in the house, even if Ani was involved in something nefarious, I doubted I'd be in peril.

In fact, everyone was full of crap, I told myself as I reached for the knob. Ani was a sweetheart—except when it came to his family—other than Lura. I got that. I was a different person with my family too. It didn't make me a member of a drug gang. I turned the knob. The door swung silently on its hinges. I was surprised to discover that it was actually a metal fire door and opened into a foyer that resembled a waiting room. A short hall ran off the foyer and I saw a couple of closed doors, but a third stood open and I heard voices.

I recognized Anibal's tenor, but the deep one was unfamiliar, and I couldn't hear what they were saying. That little angel on my shoulder reminded me it was not polite to eavesdrop, but Celestine, the bad girl living in my head, shouted, "Go for it, girlfriend."

I crept down the hall, hoping the floor wouldn't squeak.

The stale smell of cigarettes and fresh cigar smoke assaulted my nostrils when I neared the door. Ani smoked? I had the impression he hated smoking. Well you learn something new every day. I stopped and craned to hear their words.

"Tito, *hombre*, I don't know. I don't think it's a good idea. Aguirre—"

"Forget *pinche* Aguirre. He's not a *pinche* player. It's the woman. We turn her, or we kill her. Either way, we take the *pinche* business." The gruff voice erupted into something that sounded like a fox bark, rasping bursts I took for laughter.

"You'd like that, wouldn't you?" I heard derision in Anibal's voice.

"I like what Z3 likes. He wants to tie up the trade in *La pinche Capital*. He wants what *pinche* Chapo has and we're going to give it to him. You and me, *hermano*. You're either in or you will find out why he's called *El Verdugo*."

Anibal's voice hardened. "You're threatening me, Cárdenas? You didn't like the little gift? Maybe I should remind you that you need the DEA backing."

"*Simón*, like they provided the *pinche* helo and weapons." The chair creaked as though the man had suddenly shifted forward. "*Dime*, what has the *pinche* DEA done for us lately? I don't see those *pinche* Sinaloans being popped. *Oye*, grab me another one of these." The sound of a bottle clinked onto a hard surface.

The helicopter had been loaned by a cartel?

"Sure, Tito. Calm down. This is a negotiation." A chair scraped across wood.

Uh-oh. Was Anibal coming out of the room? Heart pounding, I fled to the stairwell and silently pulled the door shut behind me. then sprinted up the stairs to the top floor.

I slumped against my locked bedroom door while my thundering pulse slowed. Then it hit me, a sledge hammer to the brain: if Ani suspected I heard his conversation, he'd kill me.

I'd really screwed up this time. Dex might not want to marry me, but he wouldn't kill me over it. That Tito sounded like he'd squash any cockroach crossing his path. Should I take Quint's advice and move to Polo's? Could I trust Quint? From the fire to the frying pan—or was it the other way around? I sank to the floor, my breath choppy with panic. Deep breath, deep breath, I chanted to myself as I inhaled Mexico City's rush hour pollution.

"Jade, are you there?" Anibal's voice scratched through the intercom.

My head jerked up. The realization settled over me like a heavy cloak: I was his prisoner. There was no way I could sneak out of the room. Shoot my way out? Ani had a bigger gun. I couldn't even count on Quint to know I was in trouble.

"Jade, answer. Quint and I are hungry. Get down here."

I dragged myself to my feet.

Ani with Quint? Well, that changed the scenario. "I'm almost ready. Give me five more minutes," I shouted through the intercom.

The men lounged at the kitchen table, a humidor containing cigars open at the center and condensation-beaded Coronas at their elbows. A Victoria waited for me. Where had Tito Cárdenas gone? Sra. Pérez bustled about the stove—where'd she come from?—flipping cheese dripping *quesadillas* on a *comal*. Pepper leaned into Quint's leg and gazed up at him with eyes usually reserved for me. He barely looked as I stepped into the room. Humph.

"I see you two have met," I said.

"Polo's muscle—" Anibal said, unsmiling, jutting his chin at my father.

"You look nice, JadeAnne." Quint winked and his grin widened.

I'd tossed on an aqua-colored ruffled tee shirt and form-fitting knit pants with wedge espadrilles. Quint had better make sure I didn't need to run for my life, or I was in big trouble.

Anibal bristled. "Yeah, you do, but we're only going for tacos."

"Thanks, guys. Actually, Ani, Quint and I are having dinner together tonight."

Anibal gave Quint a hard look. "You'll have to postpone, Jade. Some things have come up. We need to talk."

I eased into a chair at the end of the table and, not looking at Anibal, grabbed the Victoria and squeezed a quartered lime into it, splattering juice onto the table. I raised my eyes to his frown.

"Yes we do—talk, I mean." Like about who was Tito Cárdenas? What gift did Ani give him? And what woman needed to be dealt with? Consuelo, I supposed, because the business had to be the sex trade—that meant the girls. I couldn't bring myself to think what might have happened to them. All of them. Where did that helicopter go?

Anibal's lips stretched into a tight smile aimed at Quint. Like he was saying "See? She's with me."

Jeezus, men could be annoying. Quint continued to grin, relaxed.

I took a swig of the beer and yawned dramatically. "Ya know, guys, it's been a long day for me. I'm tired and don't know how much more energy I have for talk. It's been talk-talk-talk all day, Ani. I'll bet whatever you have to say can wait until tomorrow."

"No, Jade, I—"

My phone rang. I fished it out of my bag on the third ring and saw that it was Ani's contact from Gandhi. "Excuse me, I've got to take this." I pushed away from the table and skipped into the hall.

"*Bueno*?"

"*Bueno*, I am Fernando Torrens. Do you remember me?"

"Hi, Fernando. Of course I remember you." A clatter of footsteps approached in the hall.

Sra. Pérez. Spying? "Hold on a moment." I pressed the flip phone into my chest as the woman climbed into the elevator. "We on for sightseeing?" I asked, as soon as the door clanged shut.

"Yes, I would like that. Are you available on Monday afternoon?"

Rubber shoes tapped on the metal of the fire escape. The footsteps moved slowly. I held my breath and listened, craning through the window glass to see who was coming. A black-clad leg dropped into view, the toe of his Michael Jordans pointing at me. Then another shoe. Knees. An obscenely large silver belt buckle engraved TT and a handgun in its holster. I backed into the drapes and peered out. Ani's visitor was creeping down to the garden. Could Tito have been the man who'd been in the garden last night? If I could just see a bandage. I was sure Pepper had bitten him.

"Hallo? Hallo? Are you there?" Fernando's voice sounding far away brought me back to the room and I put the phone to my ear again. "I'm checking my agenda. Looks clear. Where do you want to meet?"

The tableau in the kitchen hadn't changed much. Only the plate of cheese-oozing quesadilla wedges sat next to the cigars and another round of Coronas.

"If no one is going to smoke those, why don't you put the cigars away, Ani? They stink," I said.

"Who was that?" Anibal's eyes bored into me.

"My office. I asked Qadir to look something up," I said, twisting a strand of my ponytail around my finger, hopefully with an air of nonchalance.

Quint narrowed his eyes. He couldn't tell I was lying, could he? No way. He didn't even know me. "Are you ready,

JadeAnne? Let's go."

I took a swig off my beer and sent Quint my best pleading expression. He got it, but too late.

"Yeah, let's go to Azul Condesa," Anibal agreed. "It's close, we can walk. Great food. Jade you'll love the duck with sweet mole, and you have to try the sangria. It's famous."

I shook my head almost imperceptivity. Quint smiled. "I don't know, Anibal. JadeAnne and I wanted to talk about the meetings today."

"You'd be bored, Ani. Anyway, I don't want to overstay my welcome. You need a break from me." I steeled myself and met his puppy-dog face. He looked so disappointed. Shit, I felt like a complete heel. Was I making a mistake? I wanted to scream. "Ani, I don't want to hurt your feelings."

"Then come to Azul with me. Bring him if you have to." He motioned toward Quint and Pepper so I wasn't sure who he meant.

"You buying?"

He started to laugh. "Sure. My treat."

I avoided eye contact with Quint, but I could feel his displeasure. So could Pepper whose hair rose to half-mast. That's odd. I whistled and Pepper turned to me. "I'm bringing them both, Anibal."

"*Nos vamos entonces*," he said, and swiveled out of his chair.

Pepper growled.

Quint caught his collar. "That's enough, *cabrón*."

But hadn't Pepper always liked Anibal?

"Ani, where are the American girls?" I asked, once we'd ordered.

I studied his face.

"At Consuelo's. Where we left them."

"I didn't leave them anywhere, Anibal Aguirre. You managed that by yourself. Now tell me the truth."

"Ouch. You're grouchy." His skin crinkled into laugh lines at the corners of his eyes. He was going to age gracefully, hot to the end. I reminded myself not to get sucked in. Anibal was a master of manipulation using his looks. And I'd bought it.

"Don't you try to evade my question. I've asked you where the girls are." I glared at him, then at Quint.

"Aguirre, JadeAnne and I paid a visit to Consuelo today. I'm betting you know the girls aren't there. Tell us where they are," Quint said in a tone that brooked no evasion.

Ani's skin paled, although his angelic smile stayed in place. "Ask Consuelo. I bet she took them to the Embassy." He fidgeted with a fork.

I glowered at him. "We did, Ani. She said you'd taken them to the Embassy."

"But you didn't, did you, Aguirre?"

The mean set to Quint's jaw scared me. I got that feeling again, he was a rattler ready to strike. Anibal's color bloomed.

"Consuelo is a drunk and a liar. You know that, Jade. Even Polo knows that. If the girls aren't there, she did something with them. I'll check the Embassy tomorrow."

"The Embassy hasn't heard of them." Quint held his tone low.

Anibal set his beer onto the table. I could see his hand shaking slightly. "You called?"

Quint's lips twisted. "I dropped by. Mr. Negroponte and I are old friends." He folded his hands onto the table, waiting.

"Why would you lie, Anibal?" I wished I could brief my father on the conversation I'd overheard. Maybe after dinner I'd get a chance.

"JadeAnne, you know me. I wouldn't lie to you. We'll

confront Consuelo tomorrow. I promise you we'll find Lily and Evie." Anibal illuminated the table with his halo.

I wanted to believe that adorable face with the almost quivering chin, but I felt my trust ebbing along with the high-tide attraction I'd had for him. Pepper had growled at him. That about summed it up. I always did better when I listened to my dog. And Aguirre? I didn't trust Polo Aguirre any more than before, even if Tito-the-thug didn't think he was a player. The Aguirre men made me wonder about Lura Laylor. Was she the woman Tito referred to? I didn't want to think ill of the dead, but the Aguirre clan had its secrets.

And Quint? Well, I didn't quite get his game. My long-lost father. What did he want from me thirty-two years later?

CHAPTER TWENTY-ONE

Quint Takes Charge

Sunday, August 12, 2007

For a rather tension-filled dinner, we sure took our time about it. Well, it takes time to drink a bottle of tequila. Ani put away more than half a liter. Quint didn't do too badly himself. I stuck to the sangria and agreed with Anibal: it was *muy rico*. Only Quint appeared to enjoy his food. Anibal picked at his, and I pushed my mole duck around the plate and ended up giving half of it to Pepper, to the horror of the waiter. I didn't know what Anibal's problem was, but I sure as hell didn't want to go back to his place. What was I going to do?

"Les get outta here. Th' senator wans th' car," Quint slurred. I hadn't realized he'd drunk so much.

"Quint, I forgot to get the photo of my mother. You need to see it," I said, as we walked onto the quiet sidewalk. It was almost midnight and not much was going on. We'd been the last diners to leave.

"Yeah, yeah. Mebbe tomorrow, kid."

Anibal tripped over an uneven brick and grabbed my arm. Great, now he'd attached himself to me.

"The muscle knows your mother?" Ani's slur sounded like a southern drawl with a Spanish accent. "*Espera*, you know this *cabrón*?"

"*Olvídalo*, Ani, forget it." I felt him tense.

He looped around to face me, almost pulling me over. "I thought your parents were *de la alta sociedad*. High class—"

Quint grabbed his free arm and righted him. "Long story, mate. I knew her birth mother." Quint had sobered up in a hurry.

Anibal stumbled again. "Thas a long time ago." We propelled him onward.

"You're right there, Aguirre. Come on, only another block. We'll get you tucked in."

Tucked in? Oh God! What if Anibal insisted on sleeping with me? I couldn't go there, but how was I going to get out of it? I'd experienced a drunk boyfriend before. Not a pretty sight, but Ani might be a homicidal drunk. Maybe he'd just pass out and Pepper and I could escape. But would Sra. Pérez prevent us? Quint made it clear he was leaving—to return the Mercedes.

The house came into sight. I'd left my light on. The room would be full of bugs. "Quint, can you help me get him in?" I shrugged out of Anibal's grip and fiddled with the key until the door popped open. Pepper pushed in past me and sat down in front of the elevator.

"Sure love, happy to do it." Quint deposited Anibal onto the settee.

Love? That was bold. I cleared my throat and opened the gate. Quint hoisted the now-snoring Anibal into a standing position and shoved him into the elevator.

"Where's his room?"

"I don't know. Try three." I punched 2 and 3. Pepper and I got off at the kitchen. He needed water and a pee. He hadn't lifted his leg on the way home.

I grabbed the key and the Maglite and trudged down the

stairs. A vision of Tito Cárdenas clouded my sight. My chest constricted. I gripped the banister and wished it were Lura's Glock, still tucked into my suitcase, instead. Pepper scratched at the door. My heart pounded and I squinted into the darkness through the window in the door. Was that a man hiding in the shrubbery?

I pointed the mag and flicked it on. A bush. No one hiding behind it, or any other bush I could illuminate with the high-powered flashlight. I would have to have to open the door and step outside to shine the light on the fire stairs and under the deck. I whistled "en guard" to my boy, fear clutching my chest, and flung the door open. Pepper sniffed the air, but stayed by my side as I did my best to shine the light into the dark corners. If anyone lurked, I'd see the intruder and jump back inside before he could shoot me. Well, that was the plan.

No one on the fire escape. No one hidden under the deck. No one in the foundation plantings. Pepper sighed, flung himself onto the lawn. He began to chew at a bone.

"Drop it!" I screamed. I swooped down and wrested it out of his mouth. Please God, don't let it be too late. Tito T might have tossed it to him soaked in sedative, or worse. Pepper put his head on the ground between his paws and rolled his eyes up toward me as I inspected the greasy lump and sniffed at it, it didn't seem tampered with, more than the job he'd already done on it. Obviously he'd been gnawing on it for some time, judging from the bite marks.

"Okay, boy, you can have it," I said, as I handed the knucklebone back to the dog. "But I'd rather you pee and come back inside." He groaned, but got to his feet, knuckle in mouth, and trotted off to a dark corner. Moments later, he returned, still holding the bone, and stood at the door.

"Oh, no you don't. That yucky bone stays outside." Pepper sighed again but dropped it onto the walkway in a spray of saliva.

"Good dog," I said, and opened the door.

Quint was back in the kitchen reading Anibal's afternoon newspaper. I'd locked and double locked the back door and the elevator. There was nothing I could do if anyone had a key or came over the garden walls. I couldn't stop him from coming in a window. I'd make sure the window opening onto the fire escape on my floor was locked.

I threw myself into the chair opposite Quint.

"Dog all right?" Quint asked, looking up from his article. Pepper grinned and dropped to the floor at his feet thumping his tail. "I'll take that as yeah," he said.

I laughed. "You've sure made a friend of my dog. He's usually dead-on about people's character." I hoped Pepper was right. If not, I was about to make a huge mistake.

"Yeah. Pepper is a great dog. Well trained. I had a dog growing up. Never got over it when he died." Quint shifted and pulled his wallet out of his pocket then extracted a tattered photo of a grey-muzzled Dobie and handed it to me. "Chester. Lived to fifteen. Dropped dead the same day I got my draft notice." Quint ran his hand over Pepper's head. "Worst day of my life. I'd graduated University, lost my 2S deferral *and* my dog."

He gazed across the room. I squirmed in my chair, touched by his emotion.

"I was only twenty-one and not ready to go back for an MBA. School wasn't relevant, or so I thought. I made a decent living selling pot and acid to my former classmates. After Chester died, I lost my motivation to do much of anything except party. I was going to kill myself or land in jail."

I felt my eyes tearing. "Well, you did land in jail. But you were so young."

"Yeah. Biggest mistake of my life."

"But that's past now. Quint, seriously, did you find Ani's room?"

He nodded.

"Third floor?"

"No, on the 2nd. He's got a sweet set-up on the third floor. He woke up and gave me a tour, if you can call it that. I hope he was blacked out, because he spilled some sensitive intel."

I glanced to the door and lowered my voice, "That he's a DEA agent facilitating some drug gang's takeover of some other drug gang?"

My father's eyebrows shot up. "You're a sharp girl. But I wouldn't expect anything less. How'd you find that out?"

"Eavesdropping."

"Ah, that's not polite. I bet Charlie's wife taught you good manners, the socialite. If anyone had a broom—"

"Quint, she's my mother."

"Sorry. Tell me what you heard. When was this?"

"Today on my way to change. I didn't need fifteen minutes. I told you. So I stopped off on the third floor to see if Anibal was home."

Quint frowned. "Not wise going over uninvited, girl."

I ignored his gentle reprimand. "He had a guest. A Tito Cárdenas wearing a dinner-plate sized belt-buckle that's engraved TT—"

"I thought you were eavesdropping."

"I was. Tito T left by the fire escape and I saw him out the window while I spoke to my—" I caught myself before I said friend. I was supposed to have talked to my office. "My researcher."

"Uh-huh. Did this man see you?"

"No. I think he was the one in the garden last night. Pepper bit him, but I didn't see a bandage."

"Why would he be in the garden?"

"I don't know. He threatened Anibal. He said the senator wasn't a player, it was 'the woman' and they'd either turn her or kill her. He said he wanted to please Z3, whatever that means, and get what '*pinche* Chapo' has. He said he and Anibal were going to take 'the business' in Mexico City. If Ani didn't do his part, he'd find out why somebody was named *El Verdugo*." Quint looked puzzled. "The executioner," I explained.

"Yeah. I know who he is, just didn't know what it meant. All them cartel people have crazy nicknames. What else did you hear?"

"The helo that picked up the kids at the safe house? Tito T made it sound like his people provided it. I guess it makes sense. I thought it was the CIA or something. Later, real gang types drove us around in a black SUV and stopped in Colonia Doctores to pick up a box that took two to carry. They did what Ani said, but I was scared. They were creepy. Hard. Sort of military types, but with tons of tattoos."

I watched Quint as I talked. He'd rocked back in his chair, and the more I said, the more he rocked up and down on the two back legs. He'd probably break the chair, fall and crack his head open. Just my luck.

After a moment Quint spoke. "I want you out of this house tonight. We're going up to your room now, packing your things—"

I opened my mouth.

"Don't bother to argue. You are not safe. You're leaving."

"But where will I go? Not to Aguirre. He's not going to protect me."

"Senator Aguirre is a good guy. How many times do I need to tell you this? You're a smart girl—"

"Woman!"

"Woman, and you're in a viper nest. That man you're calling Tito T? He's Tito Tormenta, otherwise known as Z2, the number two man in the Gulf Cartel's enforcement arm. They call themselves The Zetas and they're the most brutal killers on the planet. Your protector, Anibal Aguirre, won't live long enough to do right by you—if that's his plan, which I doubt." He paused to glare at me as he clamped his hand around my biceps. "If he's in a bid to take over the Mexico City plaza from the Sinaloa Organization, there's going to be trouble. His DEA ain't going to help him, especially if he's using his clout to screw them over. And mark my words, missy, young Aguirre won't live a day beyond his usefulness to Tito Tormenta. That animal enjoys his work."

By the time Quint had finished his speech, my mouth had gone dry and my breathing was so shallow I had to gasp for breath. What had I gotten myself into? Or was this some demented bullshit to scare me into changing camps where I'd be violated in some horrible way? Or killed—the ultimate violation. I wished my parents' Episcopal God would send me a road sign, but I supposed it was really too late to expect Him to help.

"Come on, let's get your stuff." Quint unholstered the gun he carried under his frumpy corduroy jacket. It looked like vintage 1975. Probably was. I got to my feet.

Quint cleared the closet and *buro,* neatly folding my few things into the suitcase like a pro. I guessed he was a pro. He'd traveled the world. It took me as long to pack my toiletries and sundries, mainly because I'd flung things all over the place in my constant state of perpetual motion. I sorted through the dirty clothes and towels in a heap behind the bathroom door and stuffed my things into a plaid woven shopping bag.

Pepper sat patiently at the door. Although sitting up, his ears drooped, matching his downcast expression.

"I know, boy. We're moving. It can't be helped," I said. He sighed and flicked his ears forward, but laid them back quickly. He knew what was up.

"Pepper is quite a dog, JadeAnne. Did you train him?" Quint sprawled in the arm chair, done with his packing, the suitcase closed and waiting at the door.

I stuffed a sweater and my journal into my backpack. "Not entirely. He was a gift from Dex. I got him when he was seven weeks old. Dex had him trained to protect me. I trained him to be a nice dog." I smiled at Pepper. "Yeah, look at my good doggie," I crooned. He rewarded me with a twitch of the tip of his tail. The bulletproof vest hung from the doorknob. I reached for it. "Can I fold this?"

"I wouldn't. What's it rated for?"

"Uzi."

"Yeah, city guns. How'd you get one of those?"

I opened the closet and pawed through Anahi's stuff, looking for anything Quint might have missed. "Pepper has one too. Anibal took us to Miguel Caballero."

"He paid?"

"Well, I sure don't have that kind of money. He said it was '*de rigueur*' in *La Capital*. I've got a smart-looking suede jacket too. You must have packed it. I don't see it," I said, pulling Pepper's vest from the pile of sewing stuff left over from Anahí's pathetic life.

"You never wondered how Aguirre has that kind of cash? He claims to be a government employee. Your vest must have cost upwards of a McKinley. The dog's must have been special ordered."

"McKinley?"

"A five hundred dollar bill. Don't you know your presidents?"

"I know more about sniffing out a story and writing it."

"Yeah, you've found a good one. I hope you've been making notes in that diary of yours." His eyes twinkled.

I spun into the room, holding a t-shirt and the missing left foot of my strappy sandals. "Quint! Did you open my journal?"

He winked. "Calm down, little girl. I didn't touch it. Your secrets are safe."

I slowly turned a circle, scanning the room. It looked like I'd packed everything. "One more pass through the bathroom and I'm ready."

"Did you get your toothbrush? Shampoo?" He sounded like a parent.

I didn't answer. Of course I hadn't. Or my razor either. I tucked them into the backpack and drew it closed. "Okay. Let's be gone."

"Put on the vest and your Glock." He handed me Lura's gun in its holster. "You can use it, right?"

"That was Lura's. Here's mine." I fished the Semmerling out of my purse.

"That ain't gonna do you much good unless you want your opponent to laugh to death. Carry the Glock."

"I've never had to pull it from the holster. Anyway, why all this worry? Where are we going?"

"Carry it in your hand or on the seat next to you."

"I don't want trouble, Quint. I'm tired." I zipped up the vest and gave the room a last look with a silent goodbye to Anahí's ghost. She'd been a victim of her rich patrón and her son now carried the resentments for her. I couldn't wait to be rid of the Aguirre clan.

Pepper bounded into the room as I turned to go. Quint waited with the case in one hand and held the stairs door open in the other. I carried the backpack, cosmetic case and the shopping bag. Pepper wore his vest. "Dog food and bowl."

Quint whispered, "Do you have your keys?"

"To my bus? In my pocket. I'll keep the house keys—just in case."

We started our escape.

CHAPTER TWENTY-TWO

"Y La Ciudad Ardió"

I stepped into the stairwell. Pepper pushed ahead and thundered down. So much for being quiet. Or did we need to be quiet? I started to descend the five flights, feeling like a thief in the night. Quint closed the hall door and descended behind me. Tap. Tap. Our shoes rang on the treads in unison. *Escalofrios*, shivers, ran up and down my spine.

We reached the third floor and the silence closed in. Pepper was already waiting at the second floor landing. No more clatter of dog. No more tapping of rubber on wood. The rest of the way was carpeted. My bag swished against my jeans. Quint bumped my case into the wall. We didn't speak. I pictured Freddie jumping out of the third floor landing door with his chainsaw. I held my breath. This egress was no *sua sua sua*.

Was that knocking? Footsteps? "Quint, did you hear that?" I whispered, over my shoulder. I was almost to the landing. My heart pounded.

"I heard it. Aguirre must be stumbling around. We're cool. You've got a gun."

The hard metal came alive in my palm. I had a gun. But could I shoot someone at close range? I heard scratching, like a key missing the lock. Okay, let him lock us out. I didn't want to go to Anibal. I couldn't shoot him. My gut said it all. I stopped steps from the landing. Petrified.

"Keep going. You can make it, JadeAnne. Pass the landing. We're almost there," Quint's voice was thick and sweet as honey.

I didn't budge. Quint stood on the step above me. I barely moved my lips, "He's there. He's behind the door."

Quint whispered back, "Don't be silly. He's drunk, passed out in his bed. Go on."

"I can't—"

"You will. A soldier just does it—"

"Shoot him," I finished.

Quint gave me a gentle shove, upsetting my balance enough that I was forced to move down one step. "You can. Keep going. I've got your back."

I leaped the last four stairs onto the landing and flew across. The door crashed against the wall.

"She's mine. Do you hear me, Quint? JadeAnne is mine! I'll kill you—"

Thunder rattled the house, a cannonball whizzing over my head, shattering the wall. I leaped into the stairwell, taking the stairs two at a time. Pepper barreled toward me. Gunfire exchanged behind me.

"Quint! Quint!" a voice screamed. Mine?

I leapt onto the landing and slumped into the kitchen door. Pepper barked and scratched at it. I fumbled for the knob. Shouting. My name. More thunder. A metallic clang.

The door gave way and we pounded into the kitchen. Where were my keys? What if…? I couldn't think that. Quint would blast into the room any second now. He would.

Sudden silence. I crept to the door and peered up the stairs. Smoke. The stairwell was on fire.

"QUINT!"

The light fizzed out. The smoke billowed down the

stairs. All I could see was the reflection of something flickering, ghostly on the opposite wall. Then a crash and thuds coming down. I squinted into the gloom. A black figure. Big. Square. Oh my God, Tito Tormenta? Carrying my plaid Mexican shopping bag and my suitcase? My knees buckled.

"Quint. You're alive." My voice croaked.

"Get out of the smoke, JadeAnne," he said.

I backed into the kitchen. "What happened? Is…is Ani okay?"

Quint spun around to face me. "How the hell did a smart woman like you ever get taken in by that crazy son of a bitch?"

"What do you mean," I said, my voice sounding prim, even to me.

"We still have to get out of here before the house burns down. Come on. Where are the stairs?"

I looked at him stupidly. My brain had disconnected from understanding. What was he talking about?

"Re-activate the elevator, or show me the stairs." he roared. "Now!"

My brain shifted gears. I grabbed my bag and the dog food then sprinted to the elevator. I reactivated the control and pressed the button. The door opened. We crowded in. The door clanked shut.

"Shouldn't we call 9-1-1?"

"I didn't shoot him, JadeAnne. He'll call if he's sober enough."

We jerked to a stop on the *planta baja* and raced out to the street. The wails and whip-whips of sirens came toward us.

"Hurry. Get in. We don't need to be standing here when the emergency crew arrives."

"I can't leave my *combi*, Quint." I ran to the garage, keys in hand.

"Bad idea, JadeAnne. Get in the Mercedes," he yelled after me.

"I can't leave it. It's not mine," I shouted back. "I'll follow you." The sirens were almost to the house. I wrenched open the driver door, Pepper jumped in and me after him. The good old VW engine roared to life and we jerked across the sidewalk onto the street.

Quint turned right onto Av. Oaxaca aimed for Insurgentes. Insurgentes? Why not drive through Chapultepec past Los Pinos? Wasn't he headed toward Polanco? He could cut up through Colonia Cuatemoc, I supposed. I wasn't so sure about that route, it involved an *eje* and I got lost every time I tried to use one of those thoroughfares. And I wasn't so sure about following Quint to Aguirre's anyway. But where else would I go?

I could get a hotel—and then what?

The looming traffic light turned yellow and the Mercedes slipped through. I downshifted the *combi* into second, rumbling to the intersection, and stopped. Now was my chance to make a run for it. Once lost in the maze of streets making up the Condesa, I'd be able to wend my way south to, well Jade, to where? I couldn't go back to Anibal.

Whatever I planned on doing, I'd better do it before I got to Insurgentes and the transit lines. You'd have to be an expert at driving in *La Capital* to navigate that mess near the transit hub.

"What'll it be, Pepper? Ditch Quint and find a hotel?"

He pricked up his ears, and I swear he shook his head.

"So you trust him?"

My dog smiled.

"But, Peppi, he could be anyone. How do we know what he's told me is true? He hasn't even said what agency he's with. Or is he with an agency? Pepper, how did a guy like

Quint get in with Aguirre?" That sinking feeling came over me. Once again, I felt like I was being played. *Dios,* I hated the suspense. The suspicion. The adrenalin making me clench my teeth and white knuckle the steering wheel.

The light changed and I accelerated to cruising speed. A dark-colored SUV stuck to my bumper like a dog after a bone. That couldn't be good. I stomped on the gas and roared around the next corner, but the bulldog kept up. Okay, this was personal then. I patted around my seat for the gun. The residential street was narrow and lined with parked cars. I couldn't go anywhere but forward, and the SUV couldn't pass me. I inched up my speed and the SUV slowed, falling back a couple car lengths. Why?

I looked ahead. A wall.

Suddenly a car spun into my path, coming fast. I yanked the Glock out of the holster, my eyes glued to the oncoming car. There must have been two cars and I didn't even notice. I thought I was so smart. Now I'd ditched the only protection — "Wait a minute boy, that's Quint!"

I took my foot off the gas and moved as close to the parked cars as I could get. The Mercedes stopped in the middle of the street in front of me. I braked and adjusted my mirrors to see behind the bus. The SUV had stopped down the block and two hulks scrambled into the street, guns glinting in the Mercedes' headlamps. A third figure bent down, hefted a weapon and turned toward me. In the brief illumination from the dome light I saw his face, covered with tattoos. Oh my God, it was Mr. America with the prison tats.

I clawed my way over the seat and shoved myself and Pepper out the door as fast as I could. The *combi* would shield me. I hoped—if the mounted gas cans didn't explode. If…

The sound of a little city gun brayed, and pings and thwumps of shot scattered. Was the Mercedes armored? I could see a mean-looking driver, Rambo, spraying the street with his Uzi. Where was the other guy? I scooted closer to the bumper and strained to see. My heart pounded so loudly I couldn't hear anything else. Rambo fell, his accusing eyes boring into mine. The other men retaliated with everything they had. The neighborhood morphed into a fulmination of blasts and the ground trembled. Quint needed me. If I could only get a clear shot, I'd slam that grotesque man and his creepy tattoos into Toluca.

"Stay, Pepper." I shot my hand out. He crouched and combat crawled under the bus. I rolled into the gutter and joined him. So much for my cute outfit. I was pissed now.

I slithered behind a wheel and sited along the Glock until I found the guy who rode shotgun. I squeezed the trigger. Once, twice, and heard a scream. The man fell, clutching his knee, and shouted, "Aguirre's bitch shot me! Under the *combi*."

Mr. America stepped out from behind the SUV with a rocket launcher, a grin plastered across his lips and ice in his eyes as he swung down and fixed my position. I froze.

A cannon thundered. Mr. America crumpled into a bloody pulp. My parent's Episcopal God answering my plea?

I puked.

Quint's outstretched hand appeared. "Come on, love. They're finished. You can come out."

"What?" I shook my head hoping to clear the ringing in my ears.

"It's okay. Just come!" he shouted.

Pepper nudged me as he crawled out from under the bus. I backed away from the wheel and the pool of regurgitated sangria and shimmied into the street. I was covered in filth. My new bulletproof vest dripped in vomit and automotive oil. My pants sported a rip at the right knee. What had just happened?

I surveyed the street. The SUV looked to be in pristine

condition but the Mercedes was a smoking hunk of twisted metal on wheels.

"What happened?"

"Rocket launcher. Let's get going before the police show up." Quint guided me toward the passenger door of my camper. "Pepper, let's go!"

We moved to the door, Pepper hugging my thigh. "Those were the men I told you about."

"Cárdenas's men—"

"What about the guy I shot?"

A gun popped, Quint and I spun around. The shotgun rider was hauling himself up against the SUV from the pile of gore that had been Mr. America. He opened his mouth to say something, struggling to aim a gun at us, but Quint fired, freezing his words on his tongue. He rejoined his pal in the street. I turned away, stomach heaving, but nothing came out.

"Get in, JadeAnne." Quint held the door while Pepper jumped in and I clambered after him.

"They'd been watching the house all evening. I saw the vehicle nearby several times."

I clutched the seatbelt as Quint jerked the *combi* over the sidewalk, around the corner and into traffic. "Not used to driving a VW, are you?"

"I had a bug in college," he said.

"Yeah, that was in another century." I sounded a little snarky.

"Yeah, it was, matter of fact."

"Well, I didn't see them. The thugs."

"Why would you? You weren't expecting the house to be under surveillance. I'm trained to notice."

"By whom?"

"Can't share that."

"Why not?"

"Top secret."

"So you want me to believe a guy who spent time in prison for drug smuggling has top secret clearance? Yeah, right, Quint. I'm tired of all this. Who the hell are you?"

"So Charlie told you."

"My father came clean over the phone today. I can understand why he didn't want to tell me." Why was I protecting my adopted dad? He'd lied for my whole life.

"Yeah. Did he mention that he was the one who turned me in?"

I shot up in my seat, straining toward Quint, to…to what? Shoot him? I took a breath and gritted my teeth. "You're lying. What's your game, Jackman Quint? Why have you stalked me to Mexico? What do you want?"

"Relax, JadeAnne. I haven't stalked you, but I'm sure as hell not going to let my naïve little girl get herself killed or worse by mixing herself up with a sick bastard like young Aguirre."

"Naïve! I've got a masters' degree from Stanford University. What do you have, jailbird?"

"Smart doesn't mean street savvy, girl. Your smarts are working in your favor, but you ain't a match to the Zetas."

"Get out of my bus. I don't need to put up with your insults." I felt my blood pressure rising and heard my ears ring. I opened my window and stuck my head out while I clung to Pepper. It was all true; why was I so angry? I sucked in a breath and held it for eight beats and let it out for eight more. "Why was the house watched?"

"Aguirre was negotiating with some tough customers. They were making sure he was on the level. You being there was a problem, I'm guessing."

"What do you mean?"

Quint shifted into fourth as we drifted onto the Periferico. It was too windy to keep the window open; anyway the city air smelled typically foul. "This is about the human trafficking trade. Young Aguirre turning up with a woman like you who's making inquiries into the business? They gonna think something, and it ain't gonna be pretty. Maybe one of the top guys wants you." Quint turned toward me and gave me a serious look. "JadeAnne, you are not safe."

Tears overflowed my eyelids. "Quint, you're scaring me. Why would you say things like this?"

"Because you would fetch a high price in the sex-slave trade."

"Anibal, sex trafficking? You're out of your mind." My voice squeaked as I added, "Ani rescued those kids."

"Aguirre stole the children from the Sinaloan safe house and called his Zeta pals to pick them up in the helicopter. Whaddya think the conversation was about?"

I shrank into the big leather seat as my birth father talked. It all made sense, but no, no, no! Ani couldn't sell children.

"They want all of them, you included," Quint added. "Pretty Americans fetch a high price."

CHAPTER TWENTY-THREE

The Irony of Aunt Lidia

I squinted out from puffy eyelids into a patch of sky smudged dusty blue between sand-colored cumulus clouds. It wasn't the cozy view through the dappled leaves of the Condesa. The fantasy of something real with Anibal had gone up in flames, literally. At least Pepper snored gently next to me and my *combi* was safely off the boulevard. But at what price? I'd been Senator Aguirre's prisoner once before and wasn't so sure he'd let bygones be bygones. After everything, I sensed he still blamed me for the death of his cousin, Lura. And now he would blame me for the death of the Mercedes. I wasn't sure this time I'd survive his wrath.

Oh, sure, Quint had no problem with it. He'd convinced me that the senator wouldn't give it another thought. In fact, he'd be grateful only the car had been harmed. Yeah, and pigs fly.

The light stabbed my brain as if I'd had a big night on the town. I needed a handful of aspirins. And I needed that Janis Joplin ear worm to shut up. Over and over, "Oh, Lord, won't you buy me a Mercedes Benz?" I buried my head in my pillow.

The dirty blue had warmed to rosy pinks and reds by the time I next awoke. Pepper was gone and a glass of water and a bottle of extra-strength Tylenol anchored a note to the bedside table. I downed four tablets and the water. The note read: JadeAnne. Gone to pick up some clothes for you. Took the liberty of checking labels for correct size. Have Pepper with me. He signed it, "Dad."

I smiled and for a nanosecond my heart warmed. I pictured my adopted dad handing me a check and waving me off with a twirl of his wrist when I attempted to model my new dress, or slacks, or shoes, in the sunroom at his cocktail hour. A tear trickled out of my eye, dampening the pillow.

Well, no wonder my eyes were so puffy. I'd sobbed in the *combi* for Anibal, the dead thugs, Lura, my suitcase annihilated in the Mercedes. But mostly for the loss of Dex, and how I never belonged anywhere or to anyone for very long. I felt the familiar sinking in my core, the sad wah-wah-wah that had played there since I was old enough to understand I wasn't anybody's real child. As usual, I needed to buck up. But my head still pounded and my entire body felt like it had been jackhammered. Hmmm, probably had: Jackman hammered.

"Oh, it only hurts when I laugh," I muttered to the bedding, as I threw it off and dragged myself out. My flip-flops, safely transported in my backpack, had been conveniently placed by the bed. Quint? I flapped into the bathroom. Who did that? A swell of heat rolled over me.

The senator hadn't outdone himself with this bathroom, but it was pretty and, more importantly, it was spotless. Decorated in a palette of cream, mint, and shell pink, it had gold fixtures and mounds of fluffy towels. He liked these gold fixtures, the same ones at the farm. Probably got a deal at Home Depot. Does a man with a Mercedes shop at Home Depot? Well, who used to have a Mercedes. "Oh Lord, won't you buy me…" I shoved my head under the hot blast of water and let the heat wash out the filth and aches and anxiety.

When I returned to my room to dress, I found Pepper and a shopping bag from El Palacio de Hierro, the nicest department store in Mexico City. The Tylenol and shower had done the trick and I allowed myself to remember the suitcase destroyed in Aguirre's car. "Oh, Lord..." I wondered if Janis would like what we'd find in the bag.

"Quint, thank you so much for getting me the clothes. That was so nice. What do I owe you?" I smiled and sank into the sofa in front of a plate of Goya's famous tiny tamales. My stomach rumbled. I unwrapped one and popped it into my mouth. *Chile verde* with chicken.

Aguirre entered the living room and made a stiff bow in my direction. "Good evening, Ms. Stone. I trust you are rested?"

Oh, Lord... "Yes, thank you Senator. I-I'm really sorry about your car. I feel—"

"Not another word about it." He raised his hand, his palm a stop sign. "You couldn't have anticipated any of this. I am well insured. The new model will be delivered next week."

"Wha'd I tell you?" Quint grinned.

Aguirre's twisted smile lacked Quint's warmth. "What is important is that both you and your father are safe."

"Yes, we're unharmed." I glared at Quint, the blabbermouth. "How long have you known that?" I asked Aguirre.

"Mr. Quint has always been forthcoming. His history is one of the reasons I have chosen to work with him."

"What do you mean? Why would you employ an ex-drug smuggler who abandoned his wife and baby to Ho Chi Minh's hoards?"

Quint spoke softly, "JadeAnne, that's Charley talking."

He took my hand and gazed at me. I squirmed, pulling my hand back. He continued, "I would never have left either of you. When I saw you at the senator's farm—"

I exploded. "I thought that was you at the farm. How would you have known what I look like? You were in prison when I was born. Never a birthday card. No 'Hi, how are you?' Nothing for nearly thirty-two years." My anger spilled out of me, tainting the purified air of Aguirre's pristine salon. I slumped into the couch. "My parents said you were dead."

Aguirre rose from his seat. "Perhaps I shall check on supper while you converse."

I waved him off, a gnat circling. I was too tired for this. I stuffed another tamale into my mouth.

"Charley sent me pictures and told me how you were doing. I've always known you. He said it was better that you not know about your past until you grew up; I agreed to keep my distance. Then you grew up and, yeah, he refused to tell you about me." He took my hand again. The city glittered outside the grand windows.

"I want a tequila."

Quint went to the cocktail cart someone had rolled into the room. "Silver or gold?"

"Añejo."

"Neat?"

"Yes. So why were you at Aguirre's farm?" Quint handed me a small glass, which I shot back, and handed him the glass. "Another."

He continued, "Yeah, I never stalked you. I was dumbfounded when you appeared in the Jeep with the senator. What were you doing in the clearing?" He handed me the shot.

"You were losing at dominos."

"Nah, someone else. I interrogated him."

"A bodyguard interrogates prisoners?"

"Jade, I'm not Aguirre's bodyguard."

I glowered at my father and snipped, "But it's top secret and you'd have to kill me if you tell me."

"Yeah, that's about it."

Chucho, the houseman, in his starched white dinner jacket, cleared his throat from the dining room door and tapped his tiny mallet over the dinner chimes, announcing the meal. Was this kid always on duty? After all Aguirre had pontificated regarding the evils of organized crime, could he be holding this boy as a house slave? No, that was absurd.

"Quint, what do you think about keeping servants?" I asked, as I took my father's proffered hand to help me up from the sofa.

He guided me across the plush expanse of oriental carpet, past the piano and into the dining room before he spoke. His face told me he was considering the implication. Maybe not so absurd. Maybe Aguirre didn't traffic, but he benefitted?

"Nah, you're off the mark, JadeAnne. He's putting Chucho through university. Smart kid too. He's studying computer science. For a kid from the streets of Mexico City, he's got a dream life."

"But he's always here on duty."

Quint held my chair and seated me to the left of the head of the table, presumably Aguirre's place. He sat at the far end in the chair Chucho held. I'd rather he sat across from me so I could look at him as we conversed, but two more places were set. More guests?

"*Gracias, Chucho.* Are you off to study now?"

"*Sí, Sr. Quint.* Just as soon as Señora Lidia arrives." On cue, the elevator bell dinged. "*Con permiso, señor... señorita.*" He nodded his head and left the room.

I heard voices in the hall. "Lidia is coming to dinner? With whom?"

"I dunno kiddo, but here's an opportunity to use those manners your mum taught you." He winked and stood up.

I sucked in a deep breath and fixed my most pleasant smile onto my face. Chucho held the doors open as Aguirre navigated his mother and a lovely woman about my age dressed in a sleek black sheath and an obscenely glittering diamond and ruby necklace.

"Mother, you remember Miss Stone and, of course, Mr. Quint? And allow me to present Señora Daisi Beltrán."

We all smiled and murmured greetings as Aguirre seated Lidia across from me and Daisi next to her.

"And I would like to introduce Señor Guillermo Lobo." Aguirre gestured toward us. "Mr. Quint from Washington and Miss Stone from California."

Lobo? The name sounded familiar. The man stepped around the table and shook hands with Quint, but I couldn't recognize him. He gave me the once over as though I were a horse at auction and didn't offer a hand although I stood up. Was there something wrong with my dress? Okay, I wouldn't have chosen it, but Quint liked it, and it fit, surprisingly. As did the underwear, jeans, and even a pair of sneakers from the fancy department store.

I sat back down and Lobo took his seat to the right of the senator.

"Miss Stone, it was very kind of you to come so far to pay your condolences for my niece," Aunt Lidia said, her smile cold.

I could see the words leaving her mouth as though they had a sour taste. I supposed they did. "It was nothing, Señora Aguirre. Lura—"

"Buendía."

"Oh, I'm sorry, Señora Buendía, I assumed…when you didn't correct me at the gathering for Lura…" I withered under her frosty stare. Why hadn't she corrected me at the funeral? This dinner was going to be torture.

Aguirre, his mother, and Quint kept the conversation afloat during the first course consisting of a ceviche made with freshwater bass, a delicacy of the mountainous region between Cuernavaca and Toluca. Aguirre wasn't well acquainted with the guests. The conversation probed and encouraged them to divulge their opinions and desires. Turned out Daisi Beltrán had been a beauty queen in the nineties. I'd never met a woman vapid enough to actually enter one of those contests.

No one seemed to take further interest in me beyond introductions. Why had I been invited? I felt ignored, uncomfortable, and on display like minor works by unknown artists at an impressionist gallery opening. I would have happily dined alone in my room. Instead, I concentrated on my fish and tostadas, paying little attention to the conversation. The ceviche melted on my tongue. The chef had used mint and lemon in place of lime and cilantro and I was sure the tiny black flecks were *huitlacoche*, the fungus that grows on corn. Although it could have been ground grasshopper for all I knew.

By the second course, I'd had enough wine to make me sleepy, but the conversation had begun to flow. Lidia described the fundraiser she spearheaded for a foundation both she and Daisi were affiliated with started by the last president. The former president's wife, Señora Fox, also sat on the board. Hard to get much higher in Mexican society. The mission was to raise funds for juried non-governmental organizations serving humanitarian needs. The event would be held in February.

"I'm so pleased Instituto Nacional Contra la Esclavitude has won the award," Daisi said. "They do such important work. Senator, do you know them?"

"Yes, Señora Beltrán, I am familiar with their work. A worthy organization. The INCE has had success where our governmental agencies have not. With the current criminal insurgencies, our law enforcement is stretched too thin to take on the rescue of trafficked children. Too, I have respect for the NGOs working to re-educate the victims and reunite them with their loved ones."

Ah, now I understood my invitation—fodder for the article. I focused. Lidia paid hawk-like attention to the exchange. I had the feeling that she disagreed with the choice of organizations, or maybe the need for them. Whatever, I sensed that she wasn't representing her true feelings. Daisi Beltrán, however, gushed over the importance of stopping sex trafficking and rescuing the poor enslaved kids.

"Ay, Dios, what is the world coming to? I think people who harm children should be shot on sight," she said, her doe eyes wide with sincerity.

"I don't think our constitution allows for that, señora, but it is a grave problem here in our country. One that we have ignored for too long." The senator smiled warmly at Daisi's cleavage.

"Leopoldo, Sr. Lobo has graciously agreed to help us with the fundraiser," Aunt Lidia said. "He'll supply the talent."

I shivered with the chills her smile sent down my spine. Why didn't I believe she was planning a humanitarian effort?

Daisi turned her beautiful smile on Lobo. "Yes, Guillermo is touted as 'the host of the decade.' He mounted that celebration for Salma Hayak in Plaza Constitución in 2002. Arturo and I went. Imagine, Guillermo made it possible for five-thousand people to learn about our heritage. Guillermo represents Gloria Trevi and Juan Gabriel too. I'm so fond of his music, aren't you Lidia?" She batted the doe eyes at Lobo.

The talent agent laughed and tipped his wineglass toward the simpering beauty queen. "Then I shall ask Juan Gabriel to sing for you. You're planning a *carnaval* for Fat Tuesday, I believe?"

"A party with all the pleasurable sins before we renew

our belief in our salvation through prayer, penance, repentance, atonement and most of all almsgiving," Lidia said, dryly. "Especially the almsgiving. We hope to raise fifty million pesos. How much will you pledge, Leopoldo?"

"Mother, I think our guests would rather not discuss pledges." Aguirre gave Lidia an inscrutable look. He turned to Lobo. "You must be relieved to be back in society, Señor Lobo."

Lobo stiffened; Quint grinned. I sensed something going on here.

The talent scout directed his reply toward Lidia. "A *pesadilla*, nightmare. I prayed for death, but *Santa Muerte* didn't come. To be accused like that. Locked up with violent criminals." He paused, sucking in a forkful of tenderloin and wax-scented air, expelling it like spent exhaust, and swallowing. "But my family and my business associates stood by me, knowing the charges were false. Luckily my friends in the government came to my rescue." He smiled, a caricature of a fat weasel, and bowed his head slightly. "I am grateful to you, Señora Lidia, for your belief in my capabilities."

I didn't believe a word of it. Nor did Aguirre. He fiddled with his wineglass, barely concealing sheer amusement— something I hadn't seen in him before. I didn't laugh. My role at the table was to play the debutante. Aguirre was introducing me to Mexico's *alta sociedad* and its wealthy, rotted core.

I caught his eye and winked. He almost spit his sip of wine across the table, but he caught up his laugh into a genteel cough into his monogrammed napkin. Why had Guillermo Lobo gone to jail? I couldn't wait for the nightcap with Quint and the senator. I'd wheedle all the juicy gossip out of them. But for now, I'd play the game. I was from California's high society. Why not?

"I attended the Summit on Organized Crime Saturday

and learned a great deal about human trafficking and slavery here in Mexico," I said, as the main course dishes were cleared by the white-jacketed server that had attended our meal.

"I had hoped to attend some of the sessions, but other responsibilities stole my attention," Aguirre said. "Have you had time to consider the problem and possible solutions, Miss Stone?"

"The sex industry is worldwide, lucrative and evil. But law enforcement does little to stop it. Often it's law enforcement that allows commerce in people. It's not only the sex industry: people are stolen, enticed, or sold by their families to traffickers and slaveholders for work. Children especially. Right here in Mexico City, traffickers sell street kids who've been promised food, shelter, and work to *los ricos* as domestic slaves. They aren't schooled or cared for. They work. Little kids—five-years-old." I took in the assembled guests.

Daisi's lipsticked mouth had fallen open and a tear slid down her cheek, washing away a streak of blush. Lidia shifted in her chair, her face stony. Quint nodded. I guessed he wanted to ask her about Nedda. Hopefully the child was in the air on her way home.

The server broke the silence in the dining room as he set out aperitif glasses and poured a tot of dessert wine into each. I'd already drunk enough, but the angel cake drizzled with diced *guayaba* and *mamey* fruits and mounds of whipped cream enticed me. I'm a sucker for *mamey*.

"Señora Buendía, has the senator told you about the children Anibal and I discovered in a home in Colonia Pedrigal earlier in the week?" I asked, watching Lidia with a polite smile on my face.

Lidia visibly flinched. Her expression told me she not only knew about the incident, but she had information I didn't. Now that was odd. I felt certain Lidia had something

220

to do with it. It couldn't be. Could she? That, I wouldn't ask Aguirre.

Quint played along. "And these children included the two American sisters left with Señora Consuelo? Senator, we were unable to locate them."

"I have had a call from the ambassador," he said. "Consuelo is an alcoholic and unreliable. I wouldn't believe anything she says, but we'll get to the bottom of this." He turned to Lidia. "Mother, you're acquainted with Consuelo. Please make inquiries."

Lidia's lips twitched into an enigmatic smile, a Mona Lisa look, but the fingers clenched around the monogrammed silver fork gave her away. Watching her eyes, I almost could read the thoughts swirling in her brain. Lidia not only knew about the children and Consuelo's whorehouse, but she was directly involved. And she looked pissed.

Lidia's voice sounded tight. "Of course, *mi hijo*. What happened to the children?"

"Anibal called someone, a helicopter showed up, and flew them away. That's all I know." I wasn't about to tell her about Tito Tormenta, and Quint's and my suspicions.

"Our work with the foundation couldn't come at a better time, don't you agree Guillermo?" Daisi said.

I smiled at Daisi. "Maybe I can help with your committee, señora. It's such a worthy cause. Those poor children held captive in a cave—filthy and nearly naked. Then flown away in a helicopter while the house was under attack. I was terrified. What must those babies have felt?" I paused and took a sip of wine, studying the guests.

Daisi dabbed away crocodile tears.

Lidia and Lobo steamed. What was his part in the trafficking ring?

"We'll raise millions for the children, Señorita Daisi," Lobo said turning his thousand-watt smile on her.

She blushed.

The living room smelled of the men's cigars, but that was okay with me. My adopted dad liked cigars and sometimes on the weekend he'd invite me out in the car with him when he smoked. Mother did not allow cigar smoking in the house, unless, of course it was a guest who wanted to smoke. She only entertained people of higher social standing. Lidia reminded me of her—a social climber.

Thank God the dinner guests were finally gone. I went around and turned up the lamps and changed the sappy mood music to something I found by the CD player. Not great, but mariachi music at least had some life. Aguirre and Quint joined me on the couch, The senator kicked off his shiny black shoes and put his feet onto the coffee table. Quint yawned.

"Time to kick back and chill, I see. Nice dinner, Senator. Thanks for including me."

"I appreciate your platitudes, Miss Stone, but don't give me that crap. It was an awful dinner."

I bolted up and gaped at Aguirre. "You're right. It was torture. But I didn't want to insult you or your mother. Who are those people, anyway?" I didn't want to tip my hand too early. Aguirre relaxed with me for the first time. I'd see what was on his mind before I let on what I thought his mother was up to.

"I can fill you in on some of it, JadeAnne." Quint's tone was serious. Or tired. "Daisi Beltrán is the wife of Arturo Beltrán, one of the kingpins in the Beltrán Leyva Organization. It's part of the Federation run by Joachin Guzman, El Chapo. Marcos and Daisi fancy themselves high society. She wants to be a star, so Marcos started Eventos y Artísticos de Estrellas with Lobo to promote her social climbing. They spend most of their time here in Mexico making connections and bribes on behalf of the BLO."

"Lobo may promote talent, but his real talent is money laundering for the organization," Aguirre added.

"Is that why he was in jail?" I asked.

We quieted as a meteor shower glittered on the horizon. The moon was dark. I bet the full moon rising outside Aguirre's living room window would be spectacular. I wondered if I'd still be here to see it.

"Trafficking cocaine," Quint said.

"Is it true?"

Aguirre snorted, "Caught red-handed."

"Then how did he get out of prison?" I asked.

"The Federation was protected by the Fox government. The AFI has been particularly helpful to the Federation. Lobo has friends in high places," Quint said.

Like Lidia?

"My committee is investigating him. Zocer was my AFI contact."

I struggled to keep my voice neutral. "Then I guess the real question is, what on earth is your mother doing with these people?"

Aguirre got up and paced in front of the window. "Mother is up to her armpits with these alligators. I don't know doing what exactly, but I suspect this fundraiser is a grand scheme to launder money." He turned to face us and I could see the pain in his face. Could Quint be right that Aguirre was an honest man?

"It sounds like a worthy cause."

"That's the irony, isn't it? Mother doesn't care about the cause."

I regarded Aguirre. He knew about his mother. "Because she's part of it."

He slumped into a chair. "She doesn't know I had her investigated. The company she keeps and her unnatural attachment to Consuelo. It's Mother's house. Consuelo works for her." He lowered his head into his hands.

The pain in his voice was a living thing. How awful for the man.

"So you look away and let her run her stable."

"I cannot do it anymore. She has become involved with the BLO and now the Zetas want some of the action. Mother is trafficking, not running a house of ill repute. I'm worried for her. She is making a deal with the devil."

"Tell JadeAnne about the Pedrigal house."

"Mother owns it."

"I believe it. She knew exactly what I was talking about. I could see it in her face."

"I don't know how to save her, Miss Stone."

CHAPTER TWENTY-FOUR

Must Make Amends

Monday, August 13, 2007

Aguirre's Polanco *cocina* made me want to chop onions or roll pastry dough. Utilitarian in cement and stainless steel, it held enough equipment and prep stations to serve his twenty-seat dining room five times over. I doubted the senator made much use of the kitchen, not even for a *cafecito* or a little bowl of late night cereal. Especially by the way the chef glared at me when Señora Arias de Barrera ordered an *omleta de queso y jamon, un cafe y un surtido de panes* for my breakfast. I further annoyed him by asking for a glass of orange juice, but when he rummaged around in a cabinet and pulled out a commercial juicer I understood his attitude. I'd find preparing my breakfast a disruption too.

I could have just drunk coffee, and if I ate eggs, I preferred *huevos rancheros*, but who was I to go against Aguirre's efficient assistant. She had everything in hand, including feeding Pepper, who was relegated to an enclosed service porch off the laundry. He hadn't looked happy, and I wished we could go back to La Condesa.

The chef slid a plate containing the perfectly prepared

225

omelet with a side of refried beans in front of me at a prep station stacked with well-seasoned *cazuelas* then brought me a stack of tortillas sweating in a towel, and a jam basket with three bowls of salsa: *mole rojo, pico de gallo* and *salsa verde.* I dumped the mole over the top of the eggs and took a bite. Heaven. The plate of *pan dulces* forgotten as I scraped up the last of the beans and mole from the plate and washed them down with the last of the juice. If I weren't in the clutches of what might be an organized crime family, I'd say this was the life.

On that thought, my phone sounded. My date. With Anibal out of the picture, I didn't feel a shred of guilt answering. *"Hola, Fernando, qué onda?"*

"Bien, bien. Qué pasa?"

Fernando's words tumbled one after the next and I had to pay attention to keep up. I turned toward the wall and cupped my hand around the phone at my ear. Chef was rattling pans.

"What would you like to do? We can visit the vortex at UNAM. Or would you like to see Diego Rivera's studio?" He laid out options for sightseeing.

I glanced toward the door. No one lurking, but I lowered my voice anyway. "Actually, I need to do some shopping. Why don't we hook up around one o'clock and explore Chapultepec Park? Or go to the Museo del Arte Moderno. I'd love to see the muralists again. And Las Dos Fridas. What do you think?"

"Okay, señorita. Anything you want to do, I'm your chauffeur."

"Yeah? What are you driving?"

"My Porsche. Why?"

My friends all drive Porsches. "Convertible?"

Chef crashed a stack of pans onto a metal clad table and I missed Fernando's reply. *"Espérame por favor."* I covered the phone and thanked the chef then scooted out of the kitchen. "*Entonces*, what did you say?" I asked Fernando from the quiet of the hallway.

"*Nada importante*. Where are you?"

"In a kitchen. Now I'm letting my dog off the service porch."

Poor Pepper sat in a patch of shade, ears down, looking forlorn.

"Where shall I pick you up?"

I opened the door and Pepper bounded into my arms, almost knocking me over. I dropped the phone.

"Hello? Hello? Pepper, you idiot." I hit redial. Busy.

Fernando didn't call me back for another thirty minutes. In the meantime, I wandered around the apartment, at least the parts Señora Arias de Barrera, who dogged my steps, would allow. I didn't see the senator or Quint and ended up in my room in front of my closet, contemplating the perfect outfit for visiting the modern art museum from my meager pickings. Flat shoes for sure.

Eso es mi vida como mambo de la luna. The chorus to Mambo de la Luna sounded on my phone. Lura would have loved it. "*¿Bueno?* Fernando?"

"*Si, señorita*. Where shall I pick you up? You can bring your dog."

"He's not much of an art aficionado."

"*Ni modo*, he can guard the car. Aguirre told me he is trained—"

"You called Anibal?" Alarm bells blared in my head.

"The other day, in Gandhi. So where shall I pick you up? Give me your address."

I had to hand it to him, he was persistent, but I didn't trust him to keep it to himself. I wasn't confirming anything. Fernando didn't need a reason to call Anibal, and Anibal needed to stop calling me. I'd had at least twenty calls today —all refused.

Something felt off about Fernando's response. Isn't

anything easy in this city? I pulled jeans and a peasant blouse out of the closet. I'd wear the Semmerling holstered under the loose blouse. And I'd leave a note for Quint.

"Meet me outside Pasaje Polanco at one. It's on Avenida Oscar Wilde at the corner of Presidente Masaryk. Think about where you'd like to go to lunch. My treat since you're taking me around. *Hasta la una.*" I hung up.

Fernando came across as friendly, polite and *muy, muy guapo*. Maybe a little too suave, but arm candy for the afternoon. A way to forget all the heaviness of the last few days with the Aguirre family and my new dad. From my boyfriend leaving me in the sights of drug thugs, to meeting a dad I thought was dead, and fleeing a psycho hooked up with the Zetas, and now a new abode where I wasn't welcome, and certainly in mega danger, I needed to chill. Now it turned out my sightseeing date was lying about— something. Why would he be talking to Anibal...about my dog? That was just weird.

I sat down on the bed and tugged on my running shoes. My jeans felt tight. I'd been eating too much rich food. I could stand a run and I bet Pepper would bless me if I took him out. I had time. I wriggled out of the new jeans Quint bought and stepped into my dirty running shorts. Would anyone mind if I did some laundry tonight?

"Come on, boy." Pepper crowded the door, ready to go. I grabbed the leash and patted my waist for the gun. I didn't trust this city anymore. And I sure as hell wasn't dragging Pepper along this afternoon. No sense jeopardizing him, even if he did have a bulletproof vest.

We made it into the elevator before the señora intercepted us. The jailer scurried behind us. *"Señorita? Señorita JadeAnne!"*

The door closed, cutting her off.

The fancy Polanco boutiques didn't interest me. I wouldn't be in the city long enough to need a city wardrobe. A couple more pairs of shorts and some tanks, and I'd be set to hit the resorts on my way up the coast to the border.

I'd made a decision. I was going home. I didn't need this intrigue anymore. Anibal was history and so was his vendetta against the senator, for all I cared. I'd seen enough death in three weeks to last a lifetime. I'd mourn Lura from Sausalito. I didn't need to avenge her. And even if Dex didn't want me anymore, I was still a partner in the firm. Mostly, though, the Sarasvati bobbed in the tide at her moorings, waiting for me. I missed my mellow houseboat. A breath of cool foggy air was what I needed.

A *pesera* chugged by, spewing exhaust into the gritty city air as I looked up Av. Oscar Wilde checking the traffic for a Porsche. *Nada*. Not a common car in Mexico City. Probably stolen in Del Mar and smuggled across the border. Anibal had said Fernando wasn't reliable. Maybe he wasn't exaggerating. I checked my watch. 1:22. Okay, I'd wait until 1:30 and *ya me voy*. Between the taxis and chauffeurs double parked awaiting their rich housewives, and the women, notoriously bad drivers, driving their own cars, the line of traffic hadn't budged in five minutes. Maybe he was stuck in the backup of honking cars?

I wandered a ways down the block past the Subway. They lined up out the door to lunch on what I'd only eat in a pinch. Whatever floats the *chilango* boat. Tacos were my kind of fast food.

The insistent beeping of a car jarred me out of my mental rant. Drivers in *La Capital* loved to honk. I turned toward the noise.

"Señorita, over here." Fernando waved.

I trotted to his cherry red sports car triple-parked in front of the Subway. He jumped out and held the passenger door, eyeing me up and down. Was I too casually dressed? No way. He had on a faded tie-dyed t-shirt and jeans with tassel loafers. Traffic honked. He stepped over the door and bounced into driving position like Frankie Avalon in one of those 1960s teen movies my mom loved.

"You weren't kidding. You do drive a Porsche." I grinned at him.

Fernando shifted into gear and the parade of cars started down the narrow Polanco street. "I restored it. 1965 Targa."

"If I could drive any car, it would be a '55 Speedster. They're impossibly expensive, even the kits. How'd you get your hands on this?"

He smiled at me like we shared a secret. "First, señorita, what do you want to do? Lunch or *museo*? I'm hungry."

We turned onto Horacio and sped up. Traffic thinned out. "Oh, by all means, let's eat. Where is good?"

"You're buying, you choose." He flashed an angelic smile.

Gorgeous blue eyes. How did I forget that? "But I don't really know anywhere."

"I know a little place that has the best *alambre* in *La Capital*. You like *alambre*?" We idled at the red light before a roundabout circling a fountain with a statue of a *campesino* and his two horses. Fernando waved off a man wanting to wash the windshield.

"I do. Hey, isn't it dangerous to drive around with the top off? I heard the *ladrones* have started cutting off fingers to get rings if you have an open window."

Fernando waved off a man selling bouquets of tired-looking roses then the helium balloon vendor. "I've heard the rumors, but I haven't had much trouble." He pressed a coin into the palm of an *india*, a tiny barefoot beggar with a baby slung on her back in a ragged blue rebozo.

The light changed. Fernando navigated the roundabout back into the direction we'd come. We caught the light again and this time he waved off a fire-eater. Now there was a profession that guaranteed a short life. "So what do you do, Fernando, I mean, when you're not spying for Anibal?"

A risky question, but Aguirre wanted me to write a story, put a face to organized crime—and I had to make amends for that car. I'd start here with Fernando Torrens. A DEA snitch. I tried to look innocent and interested.

We started rolling again. "I'm a dog trainer. I own a canine security business. Lots of people here want dogs to protect their homes. Speaking of dogs, where's yours? Aguirre says he's an amazing dog. Well trained." Again, the angelic smile.

"So you told Ani we were going to meet up?"

Fernando cranked up the radio. Tropical poured out of custom speakers and filled the car with bouncy music. I didn't know the artist, but I recognized it was the second time Fernando'd sidestepped answering me about his connection to Anibal. I turned the radio back down.

"Fernando—"

"Call me Fer."

"Like Maná?"

"Spelled differently."

"Okay, Fer, I'm guessing you talked to Anibal about seeing me. I'm not comfortable with that. Anibal is a friend, but it's none of his business who my other friends are. I hope you understand. Pepper went with my father for the day."

"Your father is traveling with you?"

It was my turn to dissemble. "You could say that. But enough about me. Tell me about your business."

I noticed the signs for Peri north as Fernando edged the car over. He was getting on the Periferico? "Hey, where are we going? Aren't we eating?"

"We are. Tacos Gil in Tlalnepantla. I'll show you my business as well."

"Is that far?"

The car picked up speed past the military school. I rolled

up my window to cut the noise of rushing air. I could see the Hippodromo in the distance; this was unfamiliar territory for me. Chills ran up my back, although the day was warm. I wanted to turn around. Maybe Fernando Torrens wasn't a DEA snitch. Maybe he was another kind of snitch. "Fernando, I don't want to go to Tlalnepantla. Let's stay in Polanco. Turn around." I had to shout.

He leaned toward me. "*Cálmate*. You'll love Gil's."

"But I have to be back where I'm staying at four. Turn around at the next exit."

"We won't have another chance to exit until Plaza Satelite, unless you want to take a tour of Naucalpan. We can drive over to a bad neighborhood and let you see the other side of the city." He bored the baby blues into mine and his innocent smile morphed into something scary.

Would I have to pull my gun on him? I watched as another exit slipped behind us and checked my watch. Almost two. "Seriously, Fernando. I'm expected back."

"*No te preocupes*. We'll have lunch and I'll take you back. We're almost there."

I was getting hoarse from trying to converse over the wind. "All right. You promise?"

"*Claro*. Maybe I can meet the dog when I take you back."

The Torres de Satelite loomed ahead on a small hill. I recognized them from another visit to Mexico City. I'd driven to Queretaro for the weekend. With Dex. The yearning I felt to see him, talk to him, feel his arms around me was physical. Fernando and I zoomed past the Torres and Plaza Satelite and soon exited into a baffling maze of streets that took us over a hill. I was lost.

"That's Gil's." Fernando pointed to a taco joint on the corner of a commercial street at the bottom of the hill. "Let's go," he said, and helped me out of the car. The aroma of cooked meats and tortillas made my mouth water. Maybe this wouldn't be so bad.

A corrugated door had been rolled up to expose the entire front of the restaurant to the street. Two *al pastor* cookers rotisseried hive-shaped cones of finely sliced pork stacked to make a massive hunk of meat. Tables scattered throughout the room, but people sat a long, low counter that faced a series of huge *comals* where the cooks tended all manner of meats, sausages, and some cuts I'd rather not identify.

On the other side of the restaurant, another low counter seated a couple of people watching a round, bald man flipping a mix of onion, bell pepper, meat, and cheese on a long metal griddle. I almost drooled. He flipped several tortillas, scooped them into a stack on a plate, and in one smooth move, divided the *alambre* onto two plates and served the diners.

Fernando guided me to a stool. "Gil! *Dos alambres, compa.*"

The cook looked up and his face broke into a jolly grin. "*Fernando. Bienvenido, güey.* Now I know why you haven't been in." The cook looked at me and winked. I felt my face heat up. "You better watch out for this one, señorita. He's a *cabrón.*"

CHAPTER TWENTY-FIVE

Betrayed

Fernando roared up to a wrought iron gate in an industrial area near Gil's and tapped a code into the electronic keypad.

The gate lumbered open, clanking against the spiked fencing surrounding the complex. We pulled through and parked in front of a low stucco warehouse with a corrugated tin roof identified as *Oficina*. He shut off the ignition and the car settled into silence.

"*Mi negocio*," he said, and swept his arm in an arc.

From a low building perpendicular to the *oficina* sounded a chorus of barking. Various barrels, fences, and jungle gyms scattered between the buildings. I raised my eyebrows, questioning.

"Training course. Let's go get a beer and I'll show you what I do." He helped me out of the car and led me toward the office door. His hand felt sweaty.

Inside, Fernando clicked on the lights and the air-conditioning, and invited me to take a seat on a sagging leather couch that had seen better days. Dog toys littered the floor. A cage sat near a metal reception desk suffocating under files, a computer, and a couple of landlines. I sat down. Photos of dogs covered the walls and a case of trophies and ribbons perched near the door. But was Fernando's business profitable enough to own that car?

"No receptionist on Monday?"

"Hold on, I'll go get a couple of beers," he said, as he disappeared through a door and clattered down the tiled hall. Staff lunchroom? He'd said he had employees.

I heard the sound of a refrigerator opening, closing. In a few moments he clacked back with two open Victoria *cuartitos* and a bowl of *cacahuates japones* on a tray.

I grabbed one of the little bottles and drained off almost half. "How come no one is working?"

"It's *comida*. We're closed between two and four. I've got a couple crews out on site. We raise and place watchdogs, and we train dogs for clients. On Sundays, we have group sessions for owners and their dogs. We also breed a line of *labradores* for show. Would you like to go visit the kennels?"

"I could use a bathroom."

"Here, use mine." He opened a door behind the reception desk and I realized it opened to his private office. I got up.

"Bring your beer. We can relax in my private office."

I grabbed it and the peanuts. We clinked bottles and drank as I passed into the inner sanctum. He pointed to the bathroom.

Fernando lived here. He had to. The bathroom was obviously used for showering, and a basket overflowed with dirty clothes. What could that mean? If he was some sort of snitch, he might have money to buy an expensive car, but from the way he talked, his business was everything to him. Why would he put an extra hundred grand into a car? I flushed the toilet and turned on the water then opened the medicine cabinet. Dental picks, analgesic, antiperspirant, cologne, first aid cream. Nothing unusual. I checked the drawers and under the sink. Fernando used hairspray.

I dried my hands on a dirty towel and took another swig off my beer. Vain maybe, but not threatening. I relaxed.

I opened the door and was struck by a stab of nausea. For a moment I couldn't remember where I was. Fernando floated toward me, smiling. A bed stretched behind him. Hadn't that been a couch before? I shook my head to clear my vision, but the movement made me dizzy. What was going on?

"*Reina*, finish your beer and we'll go see the dogs." Fernando had taken my Victoria from my hand and was tipping it up to my lips.

I pushed the bottle away. "No, I think the *alambre* upset my stomach. I need to sit down for a minute." I slumped into a chair and tried to smile at Fernando.

He came close, towering over me, wagging the near empty beer. "Are you okay, *Reina*?"

His voice sounded kind and I looked at him but he wasn't wearing his jeans, just those ridiculous tassel loafers. Calling me *Reina*—Queen? Something was wrong but I couldn't figure it out.

"Come, *mi reina*." He took my hands and pulled me from the chair, circled me with his arms, swaying to the music. Music? There hadn't been music. His hands soothed me and my stomach didn't hurt anymore. He danced holding me tight to him and his skin felt smooth and hot against mine. Everything fell away and everything became the flesh against flesh. Someone sang *El fuego de tu cuerpo, Todo todo todo todo*. I melded with the voice, with the flesh, into the *respira. Todo todo todo*. Everything disappeared. I soared. I grasped the bed so I wouldn't float away. I heard the slapping. I heard words, but the words didn't mean anything. *Sacerdote*—call and response: *Castígame. Te castigo*. The rhythm, the clapping, a bass drum keeping time. Thumping, the hot flesh slapping. Burning. Had we stopped dancing? He sank between my legs. The burning sword splitting me. *Electricidad. Todo, todo todo.*

I shivered, curled around a large dog on a stinking blanket. I ached all over, but the burning, stinging sensations in my nether regions frightened me most. What had he done to me? I unwound from the beast and bumped my head on the cage links as I lurched into a sitting position. Fernando had bound my hands with a tie wrap that cut into my flesh. The dog sniffed at the cuts and licked the blood. I pushed it away. That's when I realized I was naked. Then the dog licked the hot tears from my cheeks.

Hazy images of the afternoon flashed through my brain. We'd eaten *alambre* and come to his business to feed the dogs. We had a beer. Fernando scooping up clothes. My clothes? I patted the dirt around the blanket with my bound hands and, as my eyes adjusted to the dim light, I could make out my white blouse, my panties. I scooched to the panties and wriggled into them, covering myself in gritty dust. How would I put the blouse on?

I crawled farther from the blanket, feeling the ground. Shoe. Jeans. I smoothed the pants and felt something hard. My phone. How had Fernando missed that? My hands shaking, I flipped it open and dialed Quint. Voicemail. A misdial. Where was I? I tried to think. I hung up and tried again.

"No one is available to take your call. Please leave a message at the tone."

"Quint. I'm at trapped at ExpoCanina, north of *Satelite*. T-something. Panta? Hurry!"

I used the phone to light up the ground and found the other shoe and one sock. No sports bra. No Semmerling. The time said one o'clock. I'd been here for eleven hours. Quint must be worried. Or furious.

The dog leaned up against my side. I shifted to pet it,

wishing it were Pepper. It flopped over belly-up for a scratch and I shined the meager light from my phone onto a golden retriever who obviously had whelped pups recently. She stretched and flapped her tail half-heartedly, her sad eyes telling me she knew how I felt. I stroked her silky fur and cried.

"What did he do to me?" I asked her. She sighed and dropped her head into my lap. I shivered, my stomach churned and I felt a heavy weight pushing me down into a dark, dirty place.

The building erupted into barking, whining, crying. Dogs jumped on chain link cage walls and clanked into metal bowls. The lights blazed on. I pressed my eyes shut against the searing brightness and pulled the filthy blanket closer around me. The dog bounded up, barking. I shaded my eyes with my hands. Fernando bent down to the cage door and turned a lock with a key from a large ring. The dog's hackles went up and she growled. She was protecting me.

"Come here, Maya. I've got a cookie for you," he crooned.

"You bastard."

"*Señorita*, you're awake."

"You sick asshole. I know what you've done. Cut these ties off my wrists." I couldn't look at him.

He laughed. "You're a real wildcat, *mi reina*. Look at me."

He yanked the t-shirt over his head. His back was a mass of red welts and scratches. "Looks more like what you've done, bitch."

What happened to the 'my queen'? "Undo my hands."

"Can't risk it. They'll want to inspect the goods. Don't bother to get dressed."

Inspect the goods? My skin turned clammy and I gasped for breath. The bright overhead lights dimmed as I curled into the dog.

"Come, Maya." Fernando's voice sounded distant and hard. He reached into the cage to grab her, but she snapped at him, growling. He leapt back and slammed the cage shut. The cacophony of barking rose to a frantic pitch.

I shouted at him. "Let me out of here, Fernando. Anibal isn't going to let you get away with whatever you've planned, and he knows where I am."

"You're right about that. He hired me to keep you until he could finish the deal with Cárdenas. But Anibal Aguirre's a crazy *cabrón*. Showed up wanting to fight over your honor. *Pinche idiota*. Now I've got you both and it's my deal. They'll kill the fucking DEA snitch. But you and those *gabachitas* from the Consuelo's? You're worth plenty." He let loose with a high-pitched giggle.

My blood turned to ice. Lily and Evie—here? "You better not have touched those girls or I'll—"

"Shut up, *cabróna*. I have to think," he shouted, over the barking.

"Anibal warned me you're scum."

Fernando lunged toward the cage door swinging it open a second time. I shrank into the corner. Maya shot forward, teeth bared. Fernando scuttled back, slamming the cage door again. He moved across the center aisle and fiddled with a key. That cage was full height and he stepped in. I couldn't see what it was, but he bent to grasp it, straining to drag it out.

As he cleared the door, I saw a body. Fernando pulled it by the ankles past my cage and my stomach lurched. I could see blood matted in the man's hair. The way the hair curled over the man's collar, it reminded me of—Anibal. I crawled to the door, following their progress. Anibal had been bound and gagged, but he writhed, fighting back. Fernando punched him, and Ani stopped fighting. When they reached the end of the building, the lights went out, the door slammed and the dogs settled back down to sleep.

Maya came back and leaned against me. Her warmth radiated into my skin and my breathing came more easily as I calmed down. Fernando thought he was going to sell me to Tito Tormenta. He could have that traitor Anibal, but I'd kill myself before Tito Tormenta got his hands on me. I boiled in anger and shame. Quint had been right about Anibal, and Anibal had been right about Fernando. I'd escaped Anibal's house, but he'd betrayed me anyway.

I crawled to the cage door and rattled it. The hasp flapped and the door swung open, padlock banging against the chain links. Fernando had forgotten to put the lock back on? Amateur. First my phone and now the lock? My skin puckered. The night had turned chilly, or was it excitement? Fernando's errors were my salvation.

I crawled back to my jeans and dragged them on. My shoes were harder, but it didn't matter if I tied them. I intended to find something to cut the tie wraps on my wrists before I needed to run.

I tried Quint again. Voicemail. It was the middle of the night. Of course he was sleeping. Who wouldn't be? I'd just have to take care of this myself.

"Come on, Maya, let's go."

I rolled up my peasant blouse and stuffed it into the waistband of my jeans, wrestled the phone back into my pocket, and crawled for the door. Maya pushed past me and bounded out of the cage, yipping. The kennel erupted in barking again. Would Fernando hear it and come? I stood up and latched onto the cage wire as the blood rushed to my feet, leaving my head light. I sucked in a breath slowly to the count of eight, held it, and let it out to another eight beats. Maya nudged me with her nose, pushing me toward the door Fernando had dragged Anibal through.

"Okay girl, I'm good now." I felt the rush of adrenaline and anger fill my body with strength. No way some fucking low-life dog trainer would get away with what he'd done. He was going to learn the consequences—even if I had to tear him apart bare-handed. Anibal Aguirre too.

I hadn't always relied on myself, but things had changed. I was on my own and I planned on coming out on top.

CHAPTER TWENTY-SIX

A Deal with the Devil

Tuesday, August 14, 2007

Fernando could come back at any moment. I hoped Maya would hold him off, but better to find Lily and Evie and get as far away from here as we could.

I looked into each cage. The dogs yipped, some jumped up rattling the chain links, tails swinging, and all with noses busily taking my and Maya's measure. No teenaged girls. How could I use the dogs to escape? Maybe Maya would tell me. She'd bounded ahead, agitated and whined, scratching at the door Fernando had dragged Anibal through.

I caught up to her. "Okay, okay, girl. Calm down." I inched the door open. Would Anibal be behind it? I saw Ani, the loving cousin and sexy lover. Anibal, the insane monster in the stairwell.

My knees weakened and I reached to steady myself on the doorframe as I swung the door wide. The door wrenched out of my grasp and banged open. Maya barged past my legs and darted into the gloom, dispelling the images of the greedy betrayer and his thugs, Tito Tormenta and Fernando Torrens.

"Maya, Maya! Come back." My voice rose into a rasping shriek.

She barked. I closed the door and patted around the wall to find the light switch and flipped it to banish my visions of bogeymen into the hum of cheap florescent tubes. Instead of danger, I found Fernando's key ring on a hook by the light switch.

I scoped out a canine tack room. Leashes, cages, bins of dog food, a tool bench, towels, and dog beds crammed every inch of the space. Maya barked again, as if to say, *hurry up*.

"Let me cut my hands loose, girl."

On the wall above the workbench a pegboard held tools, various shears. I grabbed a sharp pair, cut the tie wraps and yelped as the blood surged back into my hands. Maya bounded over to lick me, dancing impatiently. It hurt like hell, but I flexed my fingers, made fists until my grasp felt strong then shimmied into my blouse.

Maya head butted me as I bent to tie my shoes. "What is it, dog?" Was Fernando coming? She nosed into my hands, knocking them from my laces. Whatever she wanted, I read her urgency and straightened up. I stuck the shears in my waistband and looked around for anything else I could use as a weapon. A heavy Maglite lay on the bench. I grabbed it and the keys and flicked off the light. If Fernando came in I'd hit him over the head with the flashlight. I felt my hands tighten around the shears.

The dog was not having any of this delay. She pushed me to the back wall and another door. I swung the Maglite in an arc and noticed a barrel of dog biscuits. She wanted biscuits? I offered her one. She politely took it and dropped it on the floor, intent on the door.

"You want to go through the door, Maya?"

She woofed and I opened it into a hallway with more doors on one side and kennels on the other. Maya bolted to a kennel, barking. A chorus of squeaks and peeps started up. I scurried behind her. Six tiny golden pups crowded the door. I inched it open and Maya flew to her babies, sniffing and licking until she was satisfied they were all accounted for and unharmed. I hoped the girls would be unharmed as well. I'd promised them safety and rescue. But what had I done? I needed to find them.

Maya settled into the puppy box and rolled over on her side. The babies crawled into place to feed and the kennel quieted down. I slipped back to the tack room and filled my pockets with biscuits. What was Fernando thinking separating the dogs? The pups couldn't be more than five weeks old. How could he call himself a dog expert?

I listened at the door before slipping back into the kennel to search the cages I'd missed. The dogs were quiet, some snoring. I tiptoed down the aisle and flashed the light into each cage. If a dog woke up, I fed it a biscuit. Soon the building filled with the crunch of Milk Bones. I made my way back to the tack room, tossing more biscuits to wagging dogs as I passed.

Maya wagged, but didn't get up. In the next cage, a Doberman with a cast on his hind end lifted his head. I tossed him a biscuit. The rest of the kennels were empty.

I started on the row of doors across the corridor from the kennels, stopping to listen now and then. The first two rooms were examination rooms. I smelled the antiseptics and cleaning solutions imbued into the walls. The third door opened into a large room equipped with several operating tables, gurneys, instruments, and cages of varying sizes stacked in an alcove. A chilly recovery room, its air tinged with dog breath and blood. Fernando wasn't a vet and hadn't mentioned being connected to one, but this had to be a veterinary hospital.

For a large dog-training business, it would make a great service to have a vet on site. But keeping it separate had its advantages as well. I came around one of the stainless operating tables and found Anibal chained to it. I gripped the flashlight tighter, but he appeared to be unconscious. I gave him a wide berth anyway.

The place echoed like a mausoleum. A chill ran up my spine. I might find the girls here, but would they…?

I aimed the flashlight into the alcove and saw movement in one of the cages. I squatted and peered in. A beautiful lab female sprawled on a pile of blankets, her belly sewn up. Spayed. She wagged and I slipped the cage open and gave her a biscuit. She grinned.

Two more dogs recovered in this area. Didn't this vet have overnight help? Pepper's vet had 24/7 supervision. I stood up and flashed the light into the next tier of cages.

Oh. My. God.

"Please. Help us," a voice whimpered from inside.

An abused street cur in stained panties, she curled in a fetal position, filling the width and depth of the cage. Her face was nearly unrecognizable from swelling and bruises, but I was certain I'd found Lily.

"Lily? Help me pull you out. Push with your feet." I grabbed her under her arms and she yelped in pain. But between us, she untangled her battered body and inched out of the cage. I could tell she needed a hospital. Most of her body had been battered. I gingerly held her, rocking until her tears stopped.

"What ha—"

"We have to get Evie."

"Where is she?" I asked.

Lily pointed up to a cage on the top tier. One that should hold a Pitbull, not an eleven-year-old girl. I peered in and the little girl curled tighter around herself and moaned.

I rummaged through a cabinet and found a scrub top to cover Evie's bare little body. Where had the panties gone? She clung to me like a terrified little monkey, the stench of fear and pee rising off her. At least she hadn't been beaten.

What had happened to her? What kind of animal would harm children? Hatred seared through my veins and my muscles tightened. For a moment the desire to kill consumed me, turning the room black. I gulped a breath and beat down the devil. I wouldn't be like them. I wasn't like Consuelo or Tito Cárdenas or even pitiful, sick Fernando. I had a job to do and I'd do it or die trying. We wouldn't be sold like cattle to be abused in unspeakable ways. I gripped the child.

"Girls, we've got to get out of here. Can you walk?"

Lily nodded, her hair a tangled nest. Evie clung tighter to my neck.

"Honey, you're going to choke me. I'll carry you until we have to run. Can you run?"

The little girl nodded into my shoulder and loosened her grip.

"Come on, let's go." I took Lily's hand and we started past Anibal toward the door.

He groaned. "Jade."

I flashed the light into his eyes. He threw his hands up to shade them, but was caught on the chain. He groaned again and squeezed his eyes shut. I steered Lily away from him.

"I know what Fernando is doing," he croaked out. "I can help you escape, Jade. Cut me loose. I'll get you and the girls out of here before Cárdenas comes."

"Shut up, traitor!" I lashed out with my foot, kicking his leg and pushed Lily on. Evie trembled.

"Jade, please. I came to rescue you. I didn't know about the girls, I swear."

"Liar!" Lily shrieked. "He brought us here. He made us do bad things. He did this to me. He did it!" Tears streaked down her face. She pulled toward Anibal.

I gripped her as hard as I could and shoved her toward the door. "Just go, Lily. Get past him—there's the door."

Her face twisted into a mask of hatred. "No! I want to kill him." She lunged at Anibal and snatched the shears from my waistband.

I wished I could let her do it. I felt it too. Anibal had betrayed all of us. I yanked her back. "No. Let the authorities punish him, Lily. They're coming," I lied.

The shears clattered to the floor. I navigated us into the hall past a reception counter and through the front doors.

The parking lot was empty but another locked gate confronted us. I let go of Lily and lumbered to the gate, fishing for the keys in my pocket with my free hand, gasping for oxygen in the filthy industrial air. With my other hand, I clasped Evie to my chest. She was heavy and slipping.

"I have to put you down, Evie. Lily, take her," I said, peeling the little girl off me.

"There's no lock."

I pointed the flashlight at the gate. She was right. No lock. Now what?

"We'll have to climb over." I surveyed the cyclone fence. My breath caught in my chest and my heart pounded. The fence rose ten feet and gleamed with razor wire along the top. The girls were barefoot.

The street beyond looked quiet and I noticed several promising hiding places in the next complex. I spun, taking in the layout of the building and enclosed lot. A narrow, weedy space planted with a couple of scraggly trees ran between the street side of the building and the fence. We could climb there, protected from view by the corner of the building and the trees, but not from the street.

"Come." I pointed to the corner. Lily nodded. A dumpster abutted the first tree and made a narrow hiding space against the building.

"Girls, hide here. I'm going back to get tape to wrap your feet. Get under the dumpster if you can." I guided Lily into the space. She deposited Evie onto the ground. Neither girl said anything, but I heard their fear: what if I didn't come back?

"If anything happens, stay hidden until daylight, then climb the fence and hide over there." I pointed toward crates stacked up in the next yard. "Get in a crate. Don't make a sound. Wait until Quint comes. He's my dad. He'll find you. I'm calling now," I said and pulled my phone out of my pocket. "Will you do this, Lily?"

Lily's tangled mop flopped around her chin as she looked up at me. Tears streaked her dirty face and she shook as she settled Evie under the dumpster and crawled in behind her.

I stole gauze and bandage tape, enough to make several pairs of shoes, and fled back to the dumpster. The sky was lightening. It would be dawn soon. We had to go now.

"Lily, Evie, slide your feet out." I squatted in the narrow space, laid out my supplies and slapped wrappings around the small feet. "Let's go."

They crawled out and we edged along the building until we were behind the trees.

I boosted Evie onto the fence and started up after her. Her strength waned and she sank, tears streaming down her cheeks. Lily wasn't much better. I pushed and pulled the children to the top. I hoped we would be invisible from the vet clinic.

In a low voice I said, "I'll hold up the razor wire. You climb under it and over the top of the fence. Hang on; don't fall."

Lily moved over the top and waited for Evie. I held her as one leg went over. Floodlights blinked on, bathing the compound in bright light and the fence vibrated as the gate rumbled open. We froze. Two black SUVs purred into the lot and parked.

CHAPTER TWENTY-SEVEN

Pinned and Wriggling

"They can't see us," I said in a breathy whisper. "Don't move a muscle."

Evie's little body stiffened as in game of Statues, but Lily continued to climb down.

"Lily, freeze. You're rattling the fence. They'll hear—"

"It's hurting my hands. I can't—"

I peered into the brightly lit compound through the trees. "You must," I said, my voice hard. "They've come for us."

I heard the soft thud as Lily dropped to the pavement in her bandage shoes. I tightened my grip on Evie. The razor wire vibrated slightly and I felt the warm seep of blood down my wrist. Lily shrank into the shadow at the edge of the fence. I released the razor wire and wiped my bloody hand on my pants, never taking my eyes off the SUVs.

The first one pulled next to a side door near the gate and parked while the second idled out of our view by the main entrance. Three black-clad men swung out of the SUV and took up positions in the parking lot. One loped toward us to take a position in the shadow of the dumpster. We held our breath. He turned his back to our perch and slung his weapon off his shoulder. Dex had taught me the distinctive shape of the Russian-made AK-47s. With a bayonet attached. I felt that raw, sinking feeling in my gut for my lost relationship, or was it a premonition of the way this was going to go down?

The gate guard spoke into a radio and the second SUV circled around to face the street. Quick getaway, I guessed. The driver sprang from behind the wheel and scurried to open the back door. Just as Fernando had said, Tito Cárdenas emerged with a briefcase. I tamped down a scream. How were we going to get away?

The other door opened and another man lumbered out. I couldn't see his face but the shape of his head and the way he moved—could it be? My gut flip-flopped. No, Zocer was dead. But hadn't Aguirre said something the other night? I didn't dare hope.

"Grijalves. Find that *naco* Torrens. I want Aguirre and the *putas*."

Zocer Grijalves? Now my heart fluttered erratically. But Zocer was AFI working against the cartels. Why would he help Tito Tormenta?

"Aguirre's yours. I'll deal with the women."

Cardenas's voice turned icy. "Fool." He held up the briefcase and grinned, his skin greenish looking in the artificial light. A living *Day of the Dead diablo*. "I bought them."

The driver waved his weapon at Zocer, a "get to it or else" move. I couldn't breathe.

"They're Americans. Unless you're looking for trouble, Cárdenas, why risk it? The Zetas are good, but not that good."

Cárdenas pointed his pistol at Zocer. "*¡Basta!*" He roared. "Get going, Grijalves, before I shoot you." For a moment the night went deathly still. Not a car moving or a cricket chirping.

The hospital door banged open. Fernando shoved

Anibal, still bound, onto the tarmac and jumped back into the building. I heard the door bolt screech into place and the lights went off. Anibal groaned. Zocer rushed to him, grabbed him under the arms and dragged him to Cardenas's SUV.

"Put him in the back," Cardenas said, then growled something I couldn't hear. The guard at the dumpster ran across the small lot to the bolted door and kicked. It splintered and gave way; both guards disappeared into the dark.

To the east an ashen horizon hung over the industrial park. Soon we'd be fully exposed. My arms burned with the weight of the little girl and with hugging myself to the chain link. Evie was crying, I could feel her chest heaving silently. We couldn't hang onto the fence much longer. Should I signal Zocer? Wasn't he on our side?

The thugs banged back into the parking lot, half-dragging Fernando, and dumped him in front of Cárdenas.

"The bitches are gone, *jefe*," one said.

"I think this piece of shit was trying to pull one over on you," the other said, and kicked Fernando in the kidneys.

Fernando screamed. *"Por favor señor. ¡Por favor¡"* he begged.

The guard whacked him with the butt of his gun.

Fernando shriveled into a ball, crying. "No *señor*, it's not true. *No estoy cupable.* I had them. It was Aguirre. He came and took them. *Te lo juro,* I swear it. That was his plan, to get the money and keep the girls." He openly wept.

"Tie this *pendejo* up and gag him. I can't listen to any more of his little girl sobbing."

The thug yanked a rag from his pocket and stuffed it in Fernando's mouth while the other cinched tie wraps around his wrists.

"Gracias a Dios. Now I can think." Cárdenas observed Fernando writhing in front of the veterinary door.

Evie's silent cries turned audible and I heard Lily grow restless below us. Silence was our only defense. "Be still. Please not a sound, girls. Just a little longer," I pleaded.

"No, I'm going to get help," Lily whispered and bolted into the dark street, her clopping footfalls sounding like ballet shoes on a wooden stage.

Evie opened her mouth in terror. I lunged to stop her scream, dropping the flashlight, which crashed onto the sidewalk, and setting off the clinks of chain links against metal supports. A dog barked.

Cárdenas swiveled. "What was that?" he asked staring straight at us.

"Dogs in the garbage, Tito. Calm down. The city is overrun with mangy street dogs. Look, there's the cur now." Zocer smiled and pointed to a mutt disappearing under the building across the street. "Relax. Everything is fine," he added, while his eyes locked into mine. "We'll take care of the problems."

"No, I don't like it. Javier, Flaco, check it out," he said, and jerked his head toward the gate. Before he vanished behind the SUV, he pulled out a pistol.

The men eased into the street, guns ready. They scanned the warehouse across the way warily, but any moment they'd look in our direction and see us stuck on the fence. I wanted to scream.

The taller man slowly turned. His quizzical gaze burned through the links until he realized what he saw. "*Jefe—*"

The muzzle flash of the gun lit up the parking lot as the blast knocked the man down. Confusion erupted. Zocer spun around and shot the two thugs hauling Fernando into the SUV. Cardenas poked his head out and fired at Zocer as the last guard rushed back to the gate.

"Let's go," I shouted at the child, hauling her under the razor wire. She screamed, but it didn't matter. The noise in the lot deafened us. I looked back, and saw Zocer duck into the building as Javier or Flaco sprayed bullets into the vehicles, the building, and, I hoped, Tito Tormenta.

Almost down. "Jump, Evie!" I yelled as I thumped to the ground. "I've got you. Let go."

Pow, braat, pop.

"Jump!"

"I've got the *putas*," a voice shouted. He turned and ran toward us.

"Evie, NOW!"

Pop pop pop.

The man flew backward to the ground, black blood flowing from his leg. He'd lost his gun, but he was alive. He lurched to his feet.

"Run, Evie." I yanked the little arm, pulling her off the fence and ran, dragging the girl behind me. "Run!"

Evie found her legs. We bolted across the street to the dog's hole. "Only a little farther," I said, between gasps.

Out of the shadows, a figure. A gun exploded.

Braaaat.

"Evie, run!" I turned but it was too late. The girl had fallen, a red stain blooming across her back.

"No. No no no!" I flung myself over the little body. I could revive her. I could. Hadn't I had CPR and advanced first aid training? Wasn't I certified? "Evie! Evie."

Suddenly I was washed in headlights as Cardenas's SUV peeled out of the lot and careened south away from the compound, plunging me into darkness again.

Then silence. It confused me. Was everyone dead but me? Lily? Did she make it? And Zocer. He didn't save us. I'd have to tell Aguirre—what would I tell him? His brother is dead. Everyone is dead.

I grasped the child, hugged her into my chest and sobbed as the sun slid over the horizon.

CHAPTER TWENTY-EIGHT

We're a Team

Arms tugged me away from the child. I let go, limp with fear, powerless to protect myself. It didn't matter. Friend or foe, I deserved whatever was coming. I'd failed. The arms grasped me, folding me into a vise-like embrace, smothering my tapering sobs.

Slowly the neighborhood sounds penetrated. The never-ending wave of traffic droning along the Periferico. Morning calls of birds. A roll-up door clanging open. The ubiquitous shouts of the gas and water vendors. I smelled hot tortillas on a draft and my stomach growled. Tacos at Gil's had been a long time ago. I had to face my captor at some point, and now seemed like as good a time as any. I opened my eyes and tried to push away from the man holding me.

"Let me go." My voice croaked and I coughed into his sweatshirt. I felt the arms loosen as I struggled away from him.

"Feeling better, daughter?"

I flinched yet my heart missed a beat and warmth spread through my rigid frame. Daughter. He'd come for me.

"The girls are dead. Anibal was kidnapped. It's all my f-fault." My voice rose and caught in more sobs.

"Where is Zocer?" he asked.

I shrugged. "He isn't dead? He shot Cárdenas's men before they saw us."

"He must have gone after Torrens. C'mon. Let's get you into the car."

I rounded on Quint, shouting. "What do you know? You came too late. I called. Where were you?"

With a rush my strength left me. I sank back to the pavement and held my head in my hands. I barely croaked out the question burning a hole in my heart. "Where's Pepper?"

"Both of us have been searching the city for you, JadeAnne. He's waiting for you in the car. Let's get going before the police arrive. Tell me what happened." He pulled me to my feet.

"The c-car?" I stammered. I shuffled toward the veterinary hospital. Evie's body had already been removed. Who did that? What would I say to the family? But it was the mother's damn fault, looking the other way as her boyfriend molested her children. Where was Lily?

Quint hooked his arm through mine and guided me over the curb.

My eyes burned and I squinted out through tear-swollen lids at the tarmac. My voice flattened. "Anibal's snitch kidnapped me. Gave me some sort of drug." Visions of Fernando dragging my clothes off me, flinging me to his bed —I sobbed, my voice lost in a wave of despair. "He r-raped me," I said, barely a whisper. I swiped the new tears off my cheeks as Quint steadied me over the next curb. My face burned. I'd been so stupid. "I thought we were having lunch together in Polanco."

Quint grunted and headed me into the clinic's parking lot. "Why would you have lunch with anyone connected to Anibal?"

I gulped at the air, held the breath and let it out. "Where

255

did you take the girl?" The resignation in my voice surprised me. No, I was supposed to fight for that girl, but there was nothing I could do now. I spun toward him. "Quint, have you found Lily?"

"Lily?" he asked, opening the door to an unfamiliar Mercedes.

"The older sister. These are the girls—don't you know what's going on here?" I planted my feet in the driveway and glared at him. "Fernando, or someone, raped them too, and stuffed them into cages." Now my voice sounded strong, knife-edged. Outraged. "He was going to sell us all to the Zetas."

"JadeAnne, I came as soon as I got your message. You didn't let anyone know where you were going, girl. What were you thinking?"

"I found the girls." Yeah, so much for finding them. One dead. One unaccounted for. I started to cry again as we approached the car. Pepper bounded to the window and yodeled.

"Don't cry. Just get in the car." Quint opened the door.

With a joyous bark Pepper launched himself toward me and almost knocked me over, sniffing and gurgling. I'd never been so happy to see anyone in my life, even the tail-wag beating he gave me. I flung myself around Pepper's neck and inhaled his doggie odor although Quint still talked.

"We'll find the girl. I promise you, JadeAnne."

He herded us into the backseat and slammed the door. Pepper leaned into me and I heard the chirrup of the alarm. Quint strode back through the clinic's entry.

I closed my eyes. All I could see was the little murdered girl. My blood froze as black hatred filled me. It scared me, this pure evil hate, but I couldn't sit here and do nothing. I had to—kill Fernando. How had I not known that before? What had happened to him, anyway? It didn't matter. Well, Pepper and I were going to find him. Right now. Then we'd find Lily and get away from here. Manic energy flooded through me. I pressed the lock release and shouldered the Mercedes's door open. "Come on Peppi. We've got a job to do."

I ran into the lobby, Pepper at my heels. "Quint? Quint!" No answer. My heart pounded. Had he made it to the kennels? I trotted into the hallway. The clop of my rubber soles on the linoleum echoed off the walls. The place felt cold.

The recovering dogs lifted their heads as I peeked in at them. At least they looked calm. Maya streaked into the hallway growling, a string of wobbling pups behind her. I signaled Pepper who sat. She yipped and the puppies cowered behind her.

"Maya saved me, Peppi. We can't leave her or her puppies here. Come Maya. Meet Pepper." The golden stiff-legged forward, hair raised. Pepper crouched, submissive. The six little yellow dogs tottered forward and pounced on him. Maya sighed, nuzzled my hand and wagged. "Go ahead, girl. Pepper won't hurt you."

Pepper gently rolled the pups off and got up. He and Maya circled and sniffed and circled and wagged.

"Okay, Pepper, we've got to find Fernando," I said. "Maya, you stay. I'll be back." She hung her head, but gathered her tribe and retreated to the kennel.

Where would Fernando go? He must know we'd be gunning for him—or somebody would. Those Zetas weren't people to disappoint.

I trembled as I pushed open the door to the tack room. Fernando could be hiding behind any of the mountains of crap stored there. Pepper pricked his ears and sniffed the air. I tensed and spun to see what alerted him, grabbing a heavy mallet from a table. Why hadn't I asked Quint for a gun?

Pepper whined then barked and bounded past me. I ducked under the table.

The kenneled dogs went ballistic. I stood up, clutching the mallet and the flashlight from the bench. Pepper had nosed open the unlatched door. He'd smelled the dogs, not Fernando. I hurried after him entering the hall of barred cages. Dogs barked, jumping against the chain links. As I passed, some growled at me and others cowered whining at the backs of their cages, but I didn't see Fernando or Quint. What would happen to the dogs, poor things? Would Fernando's work crew show up? Armed? I shivered. Quint would intercept them, wouldn't he? My imagination looped into a *what if?* But fantasies weren't my concern. Finding Fernando and letting Pepper tear him apart—that was my mission. I gritted my teeth and forced myself to tune the dogs out.

The outside door banged open and a man's silhouette filled the doorway. I threw my arm over my eyes to shelter from the blinding morning sunlight. Fear paralyzed me. "Quint?"

"Stop where you are, bitch. You've spoiled everything." Fernando's voice floated over the mad riot of barking.

Fernando! I didn't think he could see me. I held my breath, grabbed Pepper's collar, and shrank farther into the darkness just outside the circle of daylight flooding the door.

"Too bad you aren't armed. It might make a fairer fight." He cackled hysterically. "Pretty funny that I'm going to kill you with your own gun, JadeAnne."

Pepper slipped out of my grasp and leapt high, knocking Fernando thudding to the ground and pinning him by the neck with his teeth. Blood-tinged saliva beaded along Pepper's teeth and glowed under the harsh rays of sunlight. I sprinted after my dog, swinging the mallet.

"Pretty funny you didn't see my weapon, Fernando." I aimed a sharp kick into his ribs. His breath exploded through his mouth like a popping balloon.

He sucked in a lungful of dust. He sputtered, "Let me up, bitch," and wrenched his body off his arm. I saw the gun. I whistled. Pepper bit down on his neck. Fernando screamed. I dropped the mallet and pulled my gun from his hand.

Pleading now, he whined, "Please. Please. It was all Aguirre's doing. I never wanted..."

"Shut up or my dog is going to chew your face off!" I screamed.

Behind me a calm voice cut through the tension. "Call the dog off and hand me the gun, JadeAnne."

I started, almost squeezing the trigger. "Zocer? Is that..."

"Do what my *compa* says, JadeAnne. It's over for you." Zocer aimed a handgun at Pepper.

I whistled again and Pepper chomped down. Fernando squealed like a piglet. I spun around, swinging the gun into position.

"Drop it, Jade. The dog will be dead before you can squeeze the trigger."

The sun illuminated Zocer's face and I gasped. "I saw you in the church. But you were blown up on the pier!"

"Blown into the bay. The water saved me."

He didn't look like he should have been saved. "When did you go to the dark side, Zocer?"

The twisted mass of angry red wounds and blackened skin grimaced. "Same side as always. Drop the gun." He gestured toward the cement.

I eased the Semmerling to the ground. "Then how'd you show up with the Zetas? And why bother to save me?"

He shrugged. "Money is good in the slave business. *Oye*, I'm glad to get Lura's gun back. A memento. She and I'd have made a great team..." He sighed. "...but I couldn't get her away from her DEA cousin. Then you showed up. *Pinche gringuita* thinking she could play in the big time. Now it's too late to let you go home." He tossed me a pair of tie wraps and leered.

"Tie up that *pendejo* and call the dog off. I need to keep that *chingon* alive a little longer. He's going to buy me some points with Cárdenas's crew. You will fetch a pretty price. Enough for the surgeries." He grimaced again, or was that a smile?

My hands shook as I fumbled to pull the ties tight. The barking had quieted down but the tension in the hall ran high. My voice quavered, Pepper let go of Fernando's neck and positioned himself between Zocer and me. Zocer's lips twitched upward. No light shone in his eyes. How had I missed this? I'd danced with this monster.

"The dog will fetch a price too. All of them."

Fernando writhed, trying to loosen his bonds. "No, we had an agreement," he shouted. "They'll kill them. They'll butcher the dogs alive. You can't—"

Zocer swung down and I heard the sickening snap as Fernando's jaw broke. He screamed then groaned, tears glistening in his terror-filled eyes. The dogs howled and threw themselves against their cages as if they knew what Zocer planned.

My fingers closed around the mallet.

"That'll shut him up." Zocer pulled a leash off a peg by the door and tossed it to me. "Restrain your dog and put him in one of the cages. And no whistling tricks, JadeAnne. I'll kill him. And you." He pointed his gun at me again. "Get going. And shut these dogs up."

I stumbled back into the gloom, dragging the tool and a snarling Pepper with one hand and rattling cage doors with the other. Zocer kept the gun on me, but didn't leave the bright doorway. How had he not seen my mallet?

I had to do something. Warn Quint. Couldn't he hear the ruckus? But he thought Zocer was on our side, was partnering with him and Aguirre.

"I can't make them be quiet. The kennels are locked. I

260

need the keys," I shouted.

Zocer cocked that square head of his. He turned to the nearest cage and shot the lock off. A beautiful Doberman screamed and fell. He kicked the door open. "In there."

I edged along the cages, not sure if Zocer could see me in the dark interior. The dogs kept up their insane barking. If I could get to the tack room...

Gunfire erupted. I dragged Pepper to the floor with me and rolled into the tall cage as bullets whizzed and pinged over our heads. The noise escalated. I heard screams—human and canine. I covered my ears and clutched Pepper. The screams faded into distant sirens. Sweat streamed down my body. My muscles went weak and my mind drifted.

No! I had to stay alert.

I could feel it. Zocer was coming. Pepper growled low in his throat. I forced myself onto hands and knees and crawled to the back of the cage with Pepper. "Lie down and stay," I whispered to him. I scuttled back to the door. If Zocer carried a light, I'd die. But maybe he'd put his head into the cage to check on me and he'd die. I hefted the mallet and waited. My heart drummed, filling my ears, my skin prickling under his murderous intent. I felt a rattle in the cage, inhaled a steadying breath and readied myself. The stocky square-headed AFI agent toed open the door. How did he not see me? He saw Pepper, crouched down, and leaned into the cage. His gun came up. He looked right past me.

I saw my chance. The barking covered my steps as I twirled from the corner and swung the heavy iron in a perfect arc, smashing Zocer's skull. He dropped to the filthy cage floor halfway through the door, his blood forming a sticky lake around his head.

I vomited.

Visions of Mexican jails ran through my head. A siren wail pierced the hellish barking.

"Pepper, come!" I shouted over the discordant

symphony. And I ran.

I bolted the kennel door, hoping it would give me time to escape. We pounded through the clinic, not stopping for Maya and the puppies.

Please, let my dad be in the parking lot! Quint would be there, wouldn't he?

We skidded through the entrance. The Mercedes was gone.

A black SUV trolled the street.

"Run Pepper!" I wheezed and darted toward the neighboring business.

A volley of shots zinged around me as the sirens screamed. Pepper bolted under the building and I dove in after him. We'd never get away. They must have seen. But the shooting stopped and the SUV squealed around the corner ahead of the piercing sirens.

I collapsed in the dust, panting, and hunkered down to wait for something to happen. Pepper paced, a panther trapped, but he wasn't headed for the electric chair. Did they have capital punishment here? Why did my dad leave me? Again. I knew I spiraled into deadly territory, but my heart felt leaden. I should never have trusted him. Maybe this was what he wanted...

"Jade. JADE. Answer me, daughter."

I heard the panic in Quint's voice. The day had turned quiet. No dogs barking. No sirens. No static-y radios or men shouting. Only the crunching of shoes over broken glass and pebbles and tufts of dry weeds echoing through the foundations of the building where I huddled.

Here. Here I am. No sound came from my parched throat. Pepper nudged me and barked, wagging. I tried to sit up, but my body had stiffened and I felt a searing pain on my side. He nosed me again then whined and tried to lick the spot that hurt. I pushed him away. "Peppi," I whispered, "Get Quint."

He bolted for the entry hole. I curled into a ball to wait, clutching the pain, holding it in. I realized I was pressing a sticky cloth into a wound. I'd been hit by the gunfire from the black SUV. How long had I lain here bleeding? Was I going to die?

I woke up in a clean white room. My head floated lazily in the cosmos, a bird riding a sunbeam. Quint dozed in a chair by the bed and Pepper sprawled across my feet. Maybe I was in heaven. I scooched to a sitting position. Pain knifed through me. Not heaven. A hospital. Dogs are allowed? I patted my side swaddled in bandages and sagged back into the pillows.

Pepper woke up and pounced on me to smother me with doggie kisses. I groaned and stroked his fur.

Quint hovered over the bed, grinning, holding out a bouquet of fragrant yellow roses. "Hey, girl, save some love for your old man."

I smiled. My old man. My dad. "Thanks, Quint. Dad."

His smile widened and he leaned in to give me a bear hug.

"Ouch! Careful, there."

He let go. "I was frantic when you weren't in the Mercedes."

My lighthearted mood soured. "Yeah. Where were you? Why did you leave me?" I heard the whine in my voice.

Quint's mouth turned down and the shadow of pain crossed his brow. For a moment he seemed lost in time, but he asked, "You went after Torrens, didn't you?"

I paused before answering. "I wanted to kill him." Did I mean Fernando, or had I joined Quint and the phantoms of our linked past?

"Did you?"

"I found him," I turned to look directly in to Quint's eyes. A kind of blue haze formed around us.

"But did you kill him?"

The blue light faded to grey fog. "I killed Zocer." I squeezed my eyes tightly closed against the vision. "Then I ran. And you were gone. Where were you?"

Quint took a long breath before speaking. "Did Zocer shoot you? He was playing both sides."

Hot anger flared in my chest. "And you let him come to find me?"

"I was searching for the girl," Quint said. He continued, his voice soothing, " I'll never leave you again, daughter."

"It was them, in the black SUV."

The room clouded with emotions. I read regret on Quint's face. I was drowning in a cesspool of conflicting emotions. I took a deep breath and squeezed back the tears that threatened to overflow the rims of my eyes.

"Did you find Lily?"

"You don't know?"

"Know what?" I spoke more sharply than I meant.

"The girl risked everything. She stopped your bleeding and flagged me down when I looked for you. Then Pepper led me to you. She's here, talking with a doctor. She'll get counseling."

My heart did a flip. Lily alive! I hadn't completely failed the girl. I tried to smile as the tears gushed from my eyes. "So this really is a hospital."

Quint gathered me into his arms and patted my back. It felt awkward, and I realized that meeting me was just as hard on my dad as it was on me. Warmth filled my heart and spread through my limbs as I relaxed. Quint gently released me back to my pillow.

He pulled the chair up by my elbow and sat down. We sat in silence.

THE HYDRA EFFECT

"But what about Evie? And all the other girls?" I asked.

Quint's eyes shined as he took my hand. "Don't you worry, my darling daughter. It may seem impossible today, but together we'll see justice for your girls. We'll get the girls home. We're a team, JadeAnne."

This time I relaxed into the warmth of my father's embrace, inhaling his scent and allowing the protection of his love to close around me.

The End

ANA MANWARING

NOTHING COMES AFTER Z

CHAPTER ONE

A Home of Her Own

Wednesday, August 22, 2007

A hot sear creased my bandaged side as Senator Aguirre's new Mercedes jerked to the curb and stopped.

I clutched my side. "Can I open my eyes now?" I asked Quint, my driver and newly reunited progenitor.

"Wait a bit, girl. The surprise isn't quite ready." Quint slid out of the driver's seat, slamming the door behind him.

What if the Zeta thugs were following us? We had something they'd paid for—me. And from what I'd heard, that group would stop at nothing to get me back. No, Quint —Dad—wouldn't let them get near me, would he? How would I know what my sire would or would not do? I'd only met him eleven days before, but his concern for me while I was in the hospital had seemed genuine. I'd go with that.

I slumped down in my seat anyway, and again pain burned through my side. Shouldn't they have kept me in the hospital for a few more days? Or at least given me pain killers? Tylenol wasn't cutting it. The Zeta bullet had grazed my side, furrowing a trough deep enough to plant cabbages. I'd have a scar for sure. Either an interesting conversation hook or the end of bikinis for me.

Where had Quint gone? I didn't need to sit in a hot car with my eyes squeezed shut. I needed my dog and the elegant safety of my room at Senator Aguirre's high-rise condo in Polanco. I opened one eye.

"You're cheating. Slide out." Quint popped my door open and took my hand.

I squeezed my eyes closed again and slipped my sweaty palm into his calloused paw. All I'd seen in my brief scan was the ubiquitous bougainvillea-covered wall and the shadow of an iron gate. "Where are we, Quint?"

"You'll see."

"Not with my eyes closed."

I lurched against my father's wiry frame as I tripped over an uneven cobble. He snaked his hand around my back and steadied me. "Careful," he said to the squeaky whine of the gate opening. "All right then—on the count of three. One...two..."

From the trees I heard birds twittering. The air was filled with the smell of gardenias and fresh mown grass, overpowering the stench of smoggy Mexico City.

"Three!"

I opened my eyes. Behind my father rose a three-story pink stucco house roofed in red tile with rustic-looking wooden shutters flanking the windows, secured in black wrought iron grillwork. Ivy grew up one side, twining into the balconies, and geraniums trailed from window boxes in brilliant reds, oranges and pinks. Shrubs and flowers crowded around the foundations and the high wall surrounding the property. Purple jacaranda petals drifted onto the narrow lawn in the slight breeze. I gasped then sighed a long exhale in pleasure.

"Lovely. Where are we, Quint? This isn't Polanco, is it?"

"Calle Amores in Del Valle. Number 1060. I've rented it."

A chorus of barks and yips rang above a rhythmic percussion of paws on cement as my German shepherd Pepper beelined toward me from the open front door, a golden retriever on his heels and six golden puppies tumbling behind.

"Pepper!" I flung my arms open to hug Pepper as he jumped to his hind legs. His long tongue slathered my face with doggie kisses while Maya danced around my knees. I let Pepper go and dropped to the lawn to hug the dog who'd saved my life and tickle her wiggling brood.

"We're home, daughter. Come on, let me show you around," Quint said, as he dragged me back to my feet.

I scooped up two of the squirming pups and tucked them under my arms. "Home? I thought we were going back to the senator's condo. What happened?"

"After you were taken to the hospital, I went back to get the dogs—"

"The others? In the kennel? What about the ones in the vet hospital?"

"Slow down, Jade. One thing at a time. All the dogs are fine. I grabbed Maya and the pups and went back to Aguirre's. You know how he is about dogs. He barely tolerates Pepper. The puppies pushed him over the top. He threw us out. Lucky for us, his family owns this place and it was empty. He arranged it for us."

"Lidia. I don't trust that woman. She's got something to do with this mess."

"That's what we're going to find out, ain't it?"

"Oh, so you agree. Senator Aguirre's mother is connected to the Zetas." As I voiced my suspicion, it sounded ludicrous. She was a society matron. A grand dame with adult grandchildren.

"I didn't say that, but she does own one working brothel we know of," Quint said

We'd entered the house through the brightly tiled lobby

with stairs and an elevator leading to the living area above the street, reminding me of Anibal's house in Condesa. The polished door to the left must lead into the garage where, I supposed, my *combi* was housed. "Where's my bus?"

Quint pointed to the door. "She's got her own barn. Let's go up." He scooped the rest of the puppies into his arms and toed open the door, gesturing gallantly before him with an elbow.

I headed up, wincing with each step as my muscles pulled over my ribs under the bullet burn. Pepper and Maya followed, looking pretty chummy.

"I'm out of shape," I said to the dogs.

At the top of the stairs the dogs pushed the door open to reveal a smiling Señora Pérez. My heart stopped. Fear and rage exploded in my gut and I spun to flee, smacking into Quint. He steadied me.

"*Buenos días, señorita. Bienvenido. ¿Esta bien? Me asusté tu desaparacíon. Gracias a Dios ha llegado,*" the housekeeper prattled, ushering me into the kitchen.

"What's she doing here?" I hissed at Quint.

"Came with the house. After the fire, and Anibal's presumed death, she needed a job."

Señora Pérez busied herself at the stove preparing tiny *quesedillas* on a *comal*. "I think she speaks English," I said, watching her intently. No reaction. Doesn't understand? Or Lidia's accomplished spy?

"All right then. Let me show you to your room," Quint said.

"My things?"

"All upstairs. The vest too. You should have been wearing that."

"Don't nag me, Dad. I was having lunch in the Colonia with a gentleman. It was a date.

How was I supposed to know the guy planned to kidnap me and sell me into the sex trade?"

Quint snorted and his lips thinned in disgust, but he kept quiet.

The stairwell up to the second floor was narrower than that from the ground floor to the kitchen, and it exuded an odor of panting dog and dust. We were quite a parade of feet kicking it up out of the carpet. I sneezed. "Does Señora Pérez vacuum?"

"She just got here today. Give her a break," Quint replied and set the puppies onto the floor. I put mine down too and they clustered around Maya hungrily. Quint gestured to the second door at the end of the hallway. "That's your suite. I'm on the other side. That door is Lily's." He pointed to a door to the right of mine.

"Lily is here?" A wash of guilt engulfed me. "Isn't she under the embassy's protection?"

"Long story, JadeAnne. She's here under the senator's protection."

"A lot of protection that is," I muttered, as I surveyed the rose-colored room. "Very girlie. Whose bedroom was this?"

"A furnished rental, Jade. I thought you liked Louis *quatorze*." He laughed. "It's pretty awful, ain't it?"

"Maybe Lily would like it."

"Naw, she's got her own pink room and bath. You get a sitting room too. Look," he said, pushing through a silk-draped doorway into a den of red velvet accented with gilt trim. Everywhere. Antique oil lamps dotted the black lacquered writing desk and spindly occasional tables.

I aimed my finger down my throat and made gagging noises. "My own bordello."

"That's about the size of it. This was the madam's suite."

"You're kidding me, right?"

"The girls' cribs are smaller, but some have bathrooms. Lily gets one *en suite*."

"Doesn't this shout out something revealing about our landlady? Maybe her henchwoman, Madam Consuelo, did the decorating."

"The senator said he evicted the tenant when he found out what was going on."

"I assume he fumigated?"

I closed Maya and her pups into the bordello, shutting the door behind me, and lay down on the bed. Pepper jumped up with me and I wondered if whoever the frilly dotted swiss coverlet belonged to would mind if a shedding dog sprawled across it. I'd have to do something about the decor, but then, would I be here long enough to bother? Maybe now was a good time to go home, before I got shot again. That idea creeped me out. The shoulder wound was almost healed. They'd taken the stitches out in the hospital. I sat up, disturbing Pepper. He looked worried.

"It's okay, boy. I'm not leaving, just thinking."

He woofed softly and nuzzled into my hands. I stroked his head. He sighed and grinned.

"I'm happy to see you too. I missed you."

Pepper wagged.

"But what are we going to do? We can't turn our backs on Lily. It's my fault her little sister is dead," I said, tears stinging my eyes. "If I'd just let them go in the helicopter with the rest of the kids..." My mantra since that horrible day at the dog kennel.

The day that started it all flashed into my mind. The day Anibal Aguirre, the senator's half-brother, and I, discovered twenty-three filthy children aged six to fifteen cowering in an airless prison carved from the rock of Mount Ajusco in the Pedrigal district of southern Mexico City. We'd sprung them from their jail, and Anibal called his contact, presumably with the DEA, for a helicopter. But it wasn't the DEA. He boarded all but the two American girls, Lily and Evie, and the chopper lifted off to slavery as their original captors launched an attack on us from across the street. We'd escaped, and I'd received stitches for a gunshot wound. While I was out of commission, Anibal turned the girls over to Consuelo García—Madam Consuelo.

I slammed my fist into a pillow. "How could I be so stupid?" I'd believed Anibal was a DEA agent fighting against the drug cartels. He convinced me to stay in Mexico to help him avenge the death of his cousin Lura. Why hadn't I gone home after I found her? That was what I was paid for: to find the banker's missing wife in Ixtapa. Take a vacation. Go home.

The tears streamed down my cheeks. Lura hadn't deserved any of what happened. Angry energy exploded though me, and I sprang up from the bed. I hadn't deserved any of this either. "He tricked me, Peppi."

Yes, Anibal had meant from the start to sell me into the sex trade right along with the girls. I grabbed my belly and retched before flopping back onto the bed and curling around Pepper. "He was going to give you to Fernando, Pepper. If he weren't dead, I'd kill him myself."

Anibal was dead, wasn't he? All I'd seen was him trussed like a turkey and tossed into the back of the Zeta van. "Pepper, what if he isn't dead? What if he comes back?"

Pepper pricked up his ears and turned toward the door. My stomach clenched until I heard soft knocking and Quint's voice.

"Daughter, who are you talking to? You ready to get some lunch and have that talk?"

Pepper answered him by bounding off the bed to the door in two leaps. He woofed and Quint took that as a signal to come in.

"JadeAnne, are you ready?"

He scrutinized my face then told me to go wash it. This guy was falling into a parental role too easily. And I wasn't five years old.

273

After we corralled the puppies into a corner of the kitchen, we leashed the other two dogs and headed out on foot.

I took in my new neighborhood, eyes wide open. Our house, unlike most of our neighbors', was freestanding on what might be a double lot. Mature trees shaded our walls and the street. Two gates set into the iron fencing faced the street, a locked pedestrian portal and a buzzing electric vehicle entry. Mostly three-story buildings lined the narrow street, with compact cars and VW Bugs parked on both sides. All faced south. I'd need to remember it was a one-way street. We started walking, the dogs straining on the leashes, excited to be out for some fun.

"Have they been walked today?" I asked. I'd forgotten my doggie bag.

"Of course. I've kept dogs before."

"Yeah? When?"

"Growing up, we had dogs."

I looked up at my father and realized I knew nothing about him. He carried himself like a soldier, but exuded a squirrelly vibe that I mistrusted.

"Oh right. The one who died. Where'd you grow up?"

"I was born in San Francisco in 1950 and lived in North Beach until I was sixteen and I left home for college. I never went back."

"College at sixteen?"

Quint shrugged and looked down. "I was smart back then."

I laughed. "And now?"

He mumbled something that sounded like, "Not that you'd notice."

But never going back home? I'd barely left home by twenty-five. My parents weren't anything to crow about, but still, I'd grown up there. Could I never go back?

"How could you never go home? Don't you miss your family? Hey, what's my grandmother's name?"

"Slow down, Jade. I only crossed the bay to Berkeley. UC. Mum came to see me every month. The rest of them? I hated my drunk-ass father, and my three older brothers were just like him. Mean. Greedy. Violent. I was the youngest and learned to defend myself early. My studies were my escape. I graduated with degrees in math and business administration. Got my draft letter the day I graduated. Whoa Maya, that's a red light," Quint said.

Pepper patiently sat at the curb as the traffic crawled by. We'd left our quiet neighborhood and emerged into a commercial district. A breeze carried the tang of onions and chilies; I looked around for a market. The light changed and we crossed the street and continued toward the vegetables. "But you said my grandmother lives in Florida. Where? What's her name?"

"Audrey Quint. My father was Morris. He died three years ago in New York where they lived. He was a mean son-of-a-bitch to the end. Mum made me go see him in the hospital before he passed. She hoped we'd reconcile. I hadn't seen him in thirty-eight years. I never understood why she stayed with him."

"So, no sisters?"

"Yeah, two, but the oldest had already married and started having babies by the time I came along. Her escape. She was born in Sydney."

"Sydney, Australia? How's that?"

"Dad was a longshoreman. They say he killed a bloke in a tavern brawl and had to pack up the family in a hurry. It was just Mum and my sister Elizabeth then. Elizabeth died of cancer while I was in 'Nam. I don't know my cousins."

Horns honked and people streamed along the sidewalk. We'd come to the municipal market. "Have you been back to Sydney?"

"On assignment. I don't have people there. Mum's people came from Perth and they're all gone. Dad's? They were drunks and thieves." He sounded bitter.

The aroma of cooking meat set my stomach growling. The dogs tugged against their leashes and Quint picked up his pace. My side hurt.

"Here we are," he said, and held the door for me. It appeared Quint already knew this area.

I had no idea where we were. I looked at the sign: Don Capitán, and stepped into a typical Mexican joint with brightly painted wooden tables and chairs. A counter toward the back separated the diners from the grills and *el pastor* rotisseries. I salivated. So did the dogs.

"I can't believe they let dogs in here."

"This is Del Valle. Dogs go everywhere—like the Condesa. But unlike Condesa, Del Valle is home to mainly families. It's where the hip go to raise their kids. You'll find an organic market." Quint smiled at me, his look a little too hopeful.

Did he think I was going to cook and keep house for him? Señora Pérez would do that, though she'd probably poison us to avenge, the death of Anibal. Wasn't he her nephew or something?

I must have made a face because Quint gave me a puzzled look over the top of his menu.

"What?" I said.

He shrugged and went back to his menu.

"Don't you worry about having Señora Pérez in the house? What if she's loyal to Anibal?"

"I thought you were considering the organic market." My dad laughed. "Not taking over the cooking so we can get rid of her?"

Was this guy a mind reader? Could he divine how many fingers I held up?

The waiter arrived to take our orders. I asked for shrimp

al Diablo and a Victoria. Quint went for *pulpo en tinto*, octopus cooked in its ink, and a Coke. Yech.

When the waiter scurried off to get our drinks, I asked, "So, Quint, if this is a family district, how did someone operate a whorehouse on Calle Amores?"

ACKNOWLEDGEMENTS

I'm immensely grateful to everyone who has helped me turn the JadeAnne Stone Mexico Adventures from a heart-stopping encounter with narco thugs on a lonely Mexican highway to a published series of books.

First to Lisa Towles for hooking me up with her amazing, creative publishing support network: Editor Cindy Davis has brightened and tightened my writing, Tatiana Villa of Villa Designs has made the covers pop and Lisa Orban of Indies United Publishing House has taken a chance on me and JadeAnne. You've all brought a new level of professionalism and excellence to my books and I can't imagine doing this without you. Thank you.

A special shout-out to both my longstanding critique groups: *Wordweavers*—Kathy Rueve, Kerry Granshaw, Malena Eljumaily, and *JAM*—J.C. Miller and Mark Pavlichek, and my newest group: *Novelistas*—Jan M. Flynn, Crissi Langwell and Heather Chavez. Without your endless readings and total support, I would never have come so far.

To Alana Weaver—a trophy for beta reading, editing and critiquing in 24 hours! And huge thanks to all my Sisters in Crime siblings especially Lisa Towles, M.M. Chouinard, Thena MacArthur and Susan Alice Bickford, you've answered my questions, guided my process, and held my hand throughout COVID. You are the best! A Million thanks.

As always, my darling David has stood by me, encouraging me to get started, keep going and "hurry up and publish those books!" He's my greatest inspiration.

Finally to you, my readers—without you the story would never come to life. I hope you enjoy *The Hydra Effect,* book two of the JadeAnne Stone Mexico Adventures, and watch for books 3 and 4 coming out this year. If you have liked something in JadeAnne's adventure, please leave a review on Amazon, Goodreads and tell your friends.

Y, por fin, ¡Muchísimas gracias a todos!

About Ana Manwaring

Ana teaches creative writing and autobiographical writing through Napa Valley College in California's wine country. She is the founder of JAM Manuscript Consulting where she coaches writers, assists in developing projects, and copyedits.

When Ana isn't helping other writers, she posts book reviews, personal stories, and tips on writing craft and the business of writing at Building a Better Story. She's branded cattle in Hollister, lived on houseboats, consulted *brujos*, visited every California mission, worked for a PI, swum with dolphins, and outrun gun totin' maniacs on lonely Mexican highways—the inspiration for The JadeAnne Stone Mexico Adventures. Read about her transformative experiences living in Mexico at www.saintsandskeletons.com.

With a B.A. in English and Education and an M.A. in Linguistics, Ana is finally able to answer her mother's question, "What are you planning to do with that expensive education?" Be a paperback writer.

Learn more at www.anamanwaring.com

If you had as much fun reading this book as I had writing it, please consider going to Amazon, Nook, Kobo or wherever you purchased your copy, and leaving a positive review. Favorable reviews help authors continue to write books for your enjoyment.

To find out about new books and upcoming events, please take a moment to sign up for my newsletter, Writing on the Wall: http://www.anamanwaring.com.